Mys
HAY

AN
ARCHEO-FORENSIC
MYSTERY

MY LADY
OF
THE BOG

PETER HAYES

THE PERMANENT PRESS
Sag Harbor, NY 11963

For information, address:
    The Permanent Press
    4170 Noyac Road
    Sag Harbor, NY 11963
    www.thepermanentpress.com

Library of Congress Cataloging-in-Publication Data

Hayes, Peter—
    My lady of the bog / Peter Hayes.
        pages cm
    ISBN 978-1-57962-354-8
        1. Anthropologists—England—Fiction. 2. Cold cases (Criminal investigation)—England—Fiction. 3. Women—Crimes against—History—England—Fiction. 4. Civilization, Ancient—Fiction. 5. Bogs—England—Fiction. I. Title.

PS3608.A943M9 2014
813'.6—dc23   2013048493

Printed in the United States of America

To the supreme Lady,
Tara Artemisia Devi
and
for my grandmother,
"Nana"
Ellen Lamont Hayes,
who first sang me
Irish song and poetry,
watching over us all.

Acknowledgments

I wish to thank the many people who helped me in the writing of this novel: Laurence and Barbara Tarlo, who introduced me to the splendors of Dorset; Annie Grieg, who remembers the day I first conceived it there; Louise Krakower, who believed in it from the beginning; Marlene Adelstein, who helped me fix it; M. Z. Ribalow, my sorely missed, lifelong literary *consigliore*; Peter Holmes Dailey, my dear friend and counselor; John Collins, my divine Irish ne'er-do-well; my literary agent, Kenny Wapner, who sold it; Martin and Judith Shepard, who saw its worth; Barbara Anderson, who trained her eagle eye on it; Patrick Tierney, Michael Slater, Roop Sagar, Virendra Kumar Jain, Alex Denning and Avedan Raggio, all of whose subject matter expertise were key; my son, Siddhi, whose scientific brain and adventurous heart were—and are—an inspiration; and my wife, Uma, my biggest fan and severest critic, who read and reread it with intelligence, insight and a red pencil ever in hand.

And finally, to the people of the lands of Bhārat and Albion, who by sharing their love and wisdom with me taught me so much about myself.

PH
Accord, NY

*In the study of Antiquity
there is a sweet food of the mind
well befitting such
as are of honest and noble disposition.*

—William Camden
English Historian
1551–1623

Part I

ALBEMARLE

I met a Lady in the Meads
Full beautiful, a faery's child
Her hair was long, her foot was light,
And her eyes were wild—

—John Keats
La Belle Dame Sans Merci

Chapter 1

A peat digger found her, three-and-a-half feet deep in the bog, lying on her back, staring up at the heavens; though this was not revealed until the peat was later stripped from her body . . .

What the digger—an excitable lad named Sam—struck first was a shoe. It was a peculiar shoe, shaped like a kayak. Still, he had thought little of it. Items like it were forever turning up in Holders Fen, as if the bog were that place where all lost things—the key to the garden shed, the clip-on shades someone swiped from your room—eventually resurface, sooner or later. Except with this shoe, a *foot* was still in it!

Frightened, the boy pitched the spade and ran, screaming bloody "Murther!" Aroused by his cry, and misunderstanding, his father and brothers came careening around the hedgerows, sickles in their fists, ready to do battle with the murderers, if any. But there was only the splendid late April morning spread out upon the bog, in the middle of which lay the corpse—or, more precisely, the *foot*: a woman's shapely, well-turned member, which, though stained deep amber by the peat and water, looked almost as fresh as if it had tripped moments ago through the morning dew.

By the time I arrived, the village constable was there. A local girl had disappeared and it was feared at first it might be she. It was the constable who had directed the first partial disinterment—so that her face and the front of her body could be viewed. I gazed upon her. She was dressed in slippers, hide-side out. Otherwise, her corpse was nude. The red chevron of her pubic hair was visible, as were her rib cage and round, high breasts with surprisingly large areolas, the size and tint of old copper English pence.

But her face was the miracle: it was at once beautiful, wild and pained. A strip of cloth blinded her eyes, and her arms were drawn behind, as though bound. Her hair was rather stylishly done—braided to one side in a three-stranded plait— and over it was a delicate hairnet tied at the chin. Her clothes were neatly folded beside her. But the strangest part was the four forked sticks pinning her limbs.

The boy was right. This was not some girl who had lost her way and foundered in the fen. Someone had definitely buried her here. And whether dead or alive at the time of her planting, she was clearly meant never to get up again.

Because of the corpse's nudity, the blindfold and bonds, a sex crimes unit of the West Dorset CID (Criminal Investigation Department) had been summoned. It was they who had called me on their way to the site. Not that I'm with British law enforcement. I'm an anthropologist and American, to boot, a visiting fellow at nearby Exeter University, where I've worked for over eighteen months beneath these lovely, lonely British skies. Not that I'm complaining; England is an archeologist's heaven. Dotted with dolmens, barrows, henges and hoards, not a month goes by without some exceptional find.

By the time we arrived, the last day of April already was waning. Despite the nearness of the farm, the bog retained a certain primitive isolation. Still, it was an innocent wildness, and the only thing sinister, apart from the corpse, was the presence of some unruly rooks cawing in the trees that, unlike the spectators gathered below, looked on the body with a hunger that was more than lascivious curiosity.

"We're a-thinkin' she's one Mildred Carr," the constable averred.

Can you fall in love with a dead woman? For in that instant, with the evening light full on her, she looked like a goddess arisen from the earth.

"Mildred Carr?" I asked. "And when did Mildred disappear?"

"Sunday week."

"Then I doubt very much that this is she."

"And why's that, sir?" the constable asked. He squinted at the corpse. "Fresh as a daisy. Can't be more'n a fortnight dead."

"No, I'm afraid this body is considerably older."

"Is it now?" the constable asked in a voice that implied I was totally daft but that he was too well-bred to disagree. He peered at the body, stroking his chin.

"And her name isn't Mildred. I'll guarantee you that."

"Aye, sir? And how would you know that, sir?"

I looked at the corpse; its freshness was an illusion. "Because whoever she is and however she died, it was several thousand years ago."

Even before I'd laid eyes on the body I was almost certain it wasn't modern, for such archaic corpses—wondrously preserved—have been turning up in fens throughout the British Isles for years. The physics behind their preservation is simple: the peat bog's anaerobic waters inhibit bacteria, without which there is no decay.

Last fall I'd examined a similar cadaver. As it had a noose round its throat and a hammer of sorts embedded in its temple, there was relief bordering on jubilation when I pronounced it neolithic, and nothing the cops or anyone else need worry about that night. So it wasn't surprising I'd been called in again.

Still, I had never seen one in such immaculate condition. Bending over her now, I could make out the down on her upper lip and count the pores in her cheeks and brow. As I gazed, the unhappy expression of her face worked upon me, so that something inside of me yearned to untie the biting blinder that had sealed her eyes so long—a demand I resisted, not wishing to disturb the evidence.

For evidence it was. Despite the body's apparent antiquity, there is no statute of limitations on murder, and the case was thus a homicide first and only second, an archeological wonder.

However, my estimate of the body's age was overruled and my suggestion that we impose a grid upon the scene and, with trowels and brushes, extract the body carefully from the surrounding peat was disregarded, and the phone calls I made to my colleagues at Exeter and to several respected scholars in the field went straight to their voicemails. And so I did what I could to lend a hand while attempting to minimize the archeological damage.

But even a modern corpse, as the CID believed she was, could not be simply wrenched from the muck. Evidence had to be collected, something which their forensics team now attempted, while I used my camera and iPhone video to document the scene. At the same time, exposure to the elements would quickly rekindle the body's decomposition. So we had to work fast. I dug until I raised a blister, then donned some gloves and dug some more.

With the fall of night, we worked in the glare of flood lamps. While we labored, a blizzard of moths and other night-flying insects dazed themselves against the lights. The body was so entrenched that when the CID attempted to remove it, it threatened to come apart, forcing us to remove the surrounding peat. The corpse, in its raised platform of sod, now looked like a figure of inlaid gold. Finally, we took a crosscut saw and, with the blade pressed flat against the earth, cut through the peat, detaching the sod plateau.

We tried to move it. Impossible! Later, we found it weighed three-quarters of a ton, and it took another three hours, a large sheet of roofing tin driven beneath it, several thick chains, and the strength of a winch on the back of a lorry to lift it up . . . revealing in a hollow just below it . . . *treasure!*

For beneath the body was a cache of classical Celtic ornaments, curved and gleaming in the mackerel dawn, like so many gold and silver serpents.

At this point, I think, it did start to become clear that my estimate of the body's age wasn't wrong, as I have never heard of a modern murder victim buried atop an ancient treasure. No one on the crime team acknowledged this outright, though I did detect a shift in tone. When we were done, we left a bobby behind to guard the treasure, then drove the corpse to the local hospital, nine miles away. I sat in the back of the truck with the mummy, in the half light and open air. Dawn was a spreading gold stain in the east, yet in places the country road was so dark and overhung with branches that they threatened to sweep the both of us out.

In the hospital's imposing Victorian shadow, we winched the corpse onto a widened gurney jerry-rigged for the occasion, wheeled her inside, took her up in the elevator, and in a vacant room, off-loaded her peat-encased body onto three dissecting tables pushed together. I thanked the farmer's sons and the constable for their assistance, then breathed a sigh of relief and anticipation as they finally left me alone with my Lady, for that's how I thought of her: my Lady of the Bog.

The room was overheated and stank of mold. She should have had a cooler storage area, climate-controlled and antiseptic. But there was nothing I could do about that now. So I continued taking pictures of her. In all, I filled two 4GB memory cards with her portrait. When I was finished, it was only seven a.m. I went to the canteen and bought a milky coffee. Then I spent the next three hours lovingly scraping away at the peat. I bagged the specimens for pollen analysis. Seeds and spores in the matrix would reveal a picture of the climate and flora of the prehistoric valley in which my Lady had died.

I plucked an insect from her hair. It was a winged ant, tightly cocooned in a dark, reddish strand.

Just then, the coroner came in. He was a well-fed monster with a certain charming vitality. He resembled a Neanderthal beatnik, I thought: beetle brow, large splayed hands, thick, wet lips, granny glasses, and a thinning dome with grayish-yellow hair drawn into a ponytail. He had evidently just finished breakfast, as his mouth was making clicking noises and his tongue still worrying particles of food. He greeted me in a bogus brogue: "With all the damn murthers we're after a-havin', you'd think you'd be considerate enough not to be pilin' onto me workload one more ten-thousand-year-old man."

"*Girl*," I rejoined. "And I doubt she's anywhere so old as that. Probably more like two or three thousand."

"Fancy them a trifle younger myself. So why bring her here? To me?"

"A postmortem is in order, I believe."

"Oh, is it now? And why, pray tell, is that, old son?"

"'Treasure Trove.'"

He looked surprised, then most displeased.

"You haven't heard? A gold and silver treasure was recovered with the body. They're digging it up as we speak. And, according to a very old and peculiar law you people have upon your books . . . 'found objects of precious metals must be turned over to the local coroner, who will determine *why* the items were interred.'"

"I know the bloody law. What I want to know is *how* I'm supposed to tell *why* some bloody thing was buried? Especially in the year aught bloody two. And what's the point of a PM? There's no one to punish or apprehend. Whoever done the poor darlin' in has long since met his bloody end." He lifted his dripping hands from the sink. They were pale and white and slick and long like the bellies of somethings long ago drowned.

"Still," I said, "*if* she was murdered—and there's a good chance she was—you owe it to her to uncover how and why. You're the coroner. She died in your district, after all. Even if several millennia ago." I studied the insect pinched in my tweezers. "She died in the last week of July. Or, perhaps, the first week of August."

"And how the hell do you know that? You find a certificate of death?"

"No. I found an ant, winged."

He fixed his ironic gaze upon me. "And what did this wingéd insect say?"

"He said she died in late July."

"And how, pray tell, did he do that?"

"With his *wings*. Look, the males don't hatch until midsummer, then die within a week or two. If one was wrapped up in her hair . . ."

He studied me with something approaching admiration. "What a clever little *fuck* you are, Donne," he said, lathering both hostility and affection onto the ancient Anglo-Saxon word. He approached the corpse with an air of bother.

It was just an act. I knew he was as interested in her as I was. We were more than acquaintances, less than friends. "And what do you make of these?" he asked, pointing at the strange forked sticks pinning her elbows and her knees.

"What do *you* make of them?"

He shrugged. "Perhaps she wasn't dead when buried. I mean, why else pin her to the ground?"

"Could be," I agreed. "She may have been forcibly drowned. We'll see. Then again . . ."

"Then again . . . *what*?"

"Then again, maybe whoever buried her there didn't want her spirit walking again."

He looked at me with startled eyes. "You mean . . . ? She was . . ."

I thought for a moment. "I'm not sure exactly *what* I mean."

Chapter 2

So engrossed was I in the study of my Lady that I worked all day and straight into the evening. For such a find, combined with the treasure, was a rarity of the first order. Today, I knew, was a day of grace. Soon the mob would descend: reporters, scholars, officials, the public . . . all of whom would want a piece of my Lady—literally, if we'd allowed it. Also, the political wrangling would begin over who would conduct the investigation: scholars from all over would be vying for the honor. For this reason, I was intent on gathering all the data that I could before anyone knew enough to stop me. Having planted myself in the middle of the case, I was daring anyone to shoo me off it. Oh, afterward, I would be roundly scolded, told I had overstepped my bounds. That was for sure—but by then it would be too late, wouldn't it? By then, I hoped, I would have already discovered a great deal about her and made myself so indispensable to the investigation, I could not be all that readily dislodged. And so I continued my preliminary examination.

Her hair had originally been black or brown, the iron in the water having turned it red. The band of cloth that blinded her eyes was in a tablet weave and measured one-and-one-half inches wide. The forked sticks pinning her limbs appeared to have some writing on them, though given their age and waterlogged condition it was difficult to make it out. And it was then I had my first suspicion that she wasn't as old as I'd originally thought—for apart from some Egyptian

Old Kingdom hieroglyphics, writing isn't found in neolithic graves.

The hairnet's tie beneath her chin had prevented the horrid "mummy gape." Still, her lips were parted, as if she were about to speak—or *scream!* I introduced a flashlight. Her teeth were sound, save for a single shattered molar. Her fully erupted wisdom teeth suggested she was over eighteen. I made a note for the pathologist to check for primary arthritis which normally sets in around 40, as a way of bracketing her age at death.

I couldn't weigh her, encased as she was in peat, but I measured her. She was 5 feet 5⅝ inches tall.

I tunneled into the peat at her back. As I'd feared, her wrists were bound with leather thongs; her hands were ringless, one wrist encircled by a silken thread. They were hands of privilege, unmarked by labor, and the nails, though stained, were intact and long, their uniform striae showing no signs of malnutrition. Her body, in fact, was so magnificently preserved, I could trace the whorls on the tips of her fingers! I took her prints on the off chance that she *was* modern and her prints were on file, though this seemed to me unlikely, especially given the stakes.

Then again, staking bodies in England isn't only some quaint neolithic rite. As late as 1826, a suicide and suspected murderer named Griffith was publicly buried at the intersection of Eton Street, Grosvenor Place and the King's Road, London, with a stake through his heart. And if these were the ways of sophisticated Londoners, what might we expect from the good folk of country Dorset?

I recalled Tacitus's observation regarding the rites of the northern tribes:

> **. . . the shirker and disreputable are drowned in miry swamps, covered with wattled hurdles.**

So then was my Lady a murderess or adulteress?

It was eleven in the evening when I remembered the treasure. This may seem odd, but the golden trove did not overly excite me; what interested me most was what, if anything, it might tell us about *her.*

The country hospital was dreary at that hour. Light from bulbs of the weakest wattage coated the walls like a film of margarine—shine without illumination.

My colleague's door was almost hidden at the end of a long hall. A sign declared:

Wooland Strugnell
HM Coroner
By Appointment

under which some droll had scrawled:

or chance!

I knocked, then gently tried the knob, not expecting it to turn, and was surprised when it did. Strugnell, too, was up and working.

I asked him about the treasure and was apprised it had been brought here, to the hospital, earlier that evening, still encased in a block of peat. To have "excavated it properly," would have been "unworkable," he said, and would have required constant surveillance. And who was about to sit in a bog twenty-four hours a day? Not *he*! Plus, whomever he hired to guard the treasure—for thirty pounds *per diem*— would steal as much of it as they could carry. No, it was locked in the hospital cellar, and only *he* had the key. He said this in a grand and boastful way that was tinged, nonetheless, with self-deprecation, as if all he'd attained in his forty-odd years was a key to a cage in a hospital basement.

I asked him for it. He gave it up without demur. I took the elevator down. The treasure was behind a wire partition. Boxes of generic tissue, mop heads, and rolls of paper toweling had been pushed to one side. It was a woefully inadequate barrier to theft. Maybe toilet paper was safe behind it, but golden torcs?

I unlocked the cage and examined it more closely. It reeked of bog. A few of its pieces were finely worked ornaments: armlets, bracteates and pins; while others were smelted gobs of hack silver, electrum filings, and thumb-size gold bars, all nestled together and gleaming dully, like fish in a bucket.

It was then something stopped me cold. From out of the vat of worked and ceaselessly curving precious metals protruded one right angle, which, if I wasn't mistaken, was the corner of a *book*. It had not been visible when the hoard was uncovered; resettling, apparently, having brought it to light.

Every anthropologist in the world, I am sure, has had at one time a similar fantasy: to recover some amazing treasure rivaling the Rosetta Stone! In my mind, I had always seen it being lifted, dripping, from the pale waters of a desert lake!

Yet here in this musty English cellar, my fantasy was coming true—even if a book, or codex, as it is more properly called, was nothing one might expect to recover from an Iron Age or even Bronze Age grave.

I snapped several photos to record its provenance in the trove, then carefully withdrew it. Its damp leather cover was inset with a tree-of-life design of varicolored semiprecious stones, while its pages, made of skin or bark, were well-preserved by the bog's brackish waters.

"Pinching the Queen's treasures, are we? It's good I keep an eye on you." The coroner had come in without my knowledge, deceptively quiet for such a large-boned man.

"Look!" I said, holding out the book.

Strugnell studied it through his rimless specs. "Correct me if I'm wrong, but it appears to be a *book*. Come from there, did it?" He eyed the peat suspiciously. "Read it?"

"No. Should we open it and see?"

"Not really," he said dismissively. "You know as well as I we should have half a dozen scholars present, photographers, the BBC, a representative from the palace, and the grand rabbi of Jerusalem." He thought for a moment. "Then again, 'What the hell' is always a good reason. Sod it. Let's have a squint."

I opened it. It was the color of a partridge: all soft browns and grays.

Writing flowed across the page, though in the wretched light, I couldn't decipher the language it was written in. Then the characters I'd been trying to worry into *a*'s and *s*'s transformed themselves into something else. "The damn thing's *Indic!*"

This was remarkable in itself. For what was an Eastern document like this doing in an old English grave? The only explanation was that book and body were far less ancient than I had believed, dating no earlier than the thirteenth century—when Indian goods and artifacts began to flow into the Isles.

I'll admit I was disappointed. My Lady was growing younger with every revelation. And though it would still be interesting to know her, I was beginning to think she was a comparative youngster and not the grand old dam I had thought she was.

Chapter 3

It was well past midnight when my Range Rover's tires crushed the white gravel drive leading up to my home. A full moon flooded the matchless Dorset countryside: blunt, undulating hills and downs like the towering crests and sinking troughs of a restless ocean frozen in midswell.

The village I live in, Droopiddle Bryant, is one of Dorset's more ancient and quaint, consisting of half a dozen stony farms and thatched cottages. A ruined chapel, in the shadow of Bulbarrow, commands the valley as it once commanded the life of the town—until the mid-fourteenth century when plague had forced the villagers to shift to less polluted grounds, stranding the remaining huts and farms and leaving the chapel (which, after all, had *not* stopped the pestilence) marooned upon the heath.

For the New York-centric who haven't the foggiest where Dorset *is,* it's in southwest England. Its picture-perfect pastures are enclosed by hedgerows, with farms and hamlets scattered round; towns are few and tend to have been founded by the Romans. Along the coast, the fossils of extinct sea beasts are often recovered and Bronze Age hillforts claim the crests of hills. Dorset is the home of the novelist, Thomas Hardy; the grave of Jack Druitt (on everyone's shortlist for the Ripper); and the winding road where Lawrence of Arabia crashed his bike and broke his neck. Indeed, if one were to cast a circle with a radius of thirty miles and its center at my Lady's grave, it would pass through Stonehenge to the east;

through Glastonbury Tor, legendary seat of King Arthur, to the west; and to the south on the English Channel, through Lyme Regis's windswept quay, evoked so memorably in *The French Lieutenant's Woman*.

Nor is Droopiddle Bryant, queer as it is, a name unusual for these parts. The towns all around are like words in a rhyme by Lewis Carroll: Duntish, Ansty, Dewlish, Long Burton, Ryme Intrinseca and Sixpenny Hanley. And often on the night drive home, when my mind was befogged with lager and fatigue, it would make up ridiculous automatic phrases: "The duntish slut was feeling ansty." Or, "Donning his long burton, the captain looked positively *dewlish!*"

My cottage, per usual, was chilly and dark. I lit a fire, watching the kindling flare, then went to the kitchen and foraged in the refrigerator, returning with two cooked chops, a salt cellar and a stoppered bottle of the local ale. I threw a leg over the armchair's upholstered arm, shook salt on the meat and wolfed it down. I was hungry. I chugged the ale and belched extravagantly. There are compensations that come with living alone, though, admittedly, they're poor substitutes for company and affection.

Then I thought of my Lady and felt happy—like waking and remembering it was the last day of school. And I thought again of that night, as a child, I'd read a book on Peking Man. It described how a Canadian anatomy professor had gone to an herbalist's shop in Beijing and purchased a remedy made from "dragon bones"—except that these "dragon bones," to the professor's trained eye, were *hominid* and older than any he'd ever seen. Returning to the pharmacy, he'd rifled its drawers and come across the bones of a mammoth and an ancient horse. How many other priceless relics had been ground to dust in the apothecary's pestle? Then he'd bribed the druggist to show him where the bones were found. And there, washing out of a limestone hill, was the jawbone of an ancient man!

I can still recall looking up from the book that long ago New Jersey evening and feeling an inner acetylene flare. I was eight. To have found dragon bones in China that were really those of ancient men! Just thinking of it opened a dimension inside me I hadn't known 'til then was there—as if I were kissing the lips of something.

I read every book I could find on the subject. I read with a sort of religious exultation as if they'd reveal, on the very next page, some essential fact or missing link that would make me feel complete and whole. So budded my love affair with the bones and bodies of ancient persons.

To this day, I don't really know why the subject so compels me. An astrologer once told me I was born under Saturn, ruler of antiquities. She said it was also the ruler of nerds, a fate I like to think I escaped—if just. Still, I was a wonky kid, spending hours perusing scholarly papers and other scientific *esoterica*, and though I mixed socially, I enjoyed my own company as much, passing many a childhood Sunday digging holes alone in my backyard.

It was a vocation—or obsession—I brought with me to Phillips Academy, Andover, and then on to Columbia College and the study of anthropology. There, under the tutelage of the great Indic scholar, Dr. Jai Prasad, I had earned a master's and copublished several well-received papers.

Based upon them and Jai's strong recommendation, the University of Exeter had awarded me the prestigious Pitt Rivers Anthropological Fellowship, never given to an American before. And though my work had gone well enough, my career had gone nowhere. Radiographic analysis of Mesolithic skull fragments isn't something, I'm afraid, that stirs the world soul. In another six months, the fellowship was ending, and the few job offers I'd received thus far were unappealing: instructorships for little pay at undistinguished institutions.

Nonetheless, I knew an opportunity when I saw it, and one had just been dropped in my lap.

I threw the lamb bones on the fire, watching them char. Then I wiped my hands with care and took out the book. *What* book? Ah, you didn't know I'd taken it! Not surprising, since I didn't tell anyone—not even Strugnell, who, as he'd turned, had failed to see me slip it in my shirt.

Though admittedly covert, I certainly wasn't stealing it. I simply wanted the proper time and light in which to study it. I fully intended to return it in the morning and would have, surely, if events had not intervened. And though I should have asked the coroner's permission, frankly, I didn't want to risk being turned down. And so, with the book's damp cover pressing my chest, I'd relocked the cage and given him back the key—something he claims not to recall.

Now I looked the codex over. Fresh archeological items have what is termed a "stickiness": sensory clues, the smell of woodsmoke, for example, if a codex such as this had been read around campfires. But the book only smelled of the bowels of the bog. And when I was done, I knew little more about it than when I'd started—other than it seemed to be authentic, and with my limited knowledge of Indic, incomprehensible! I did think I saw the word *shah* repeated several times, which seemed to imply a Persian as well as Indic venue. Still, how old the damn thing was I couldn't say, though radiocarbon dating would. Then again, to be certain, we'd want to date the *ink,* as well as the parchment, as several recent forgeries have been done on sheets of ancient vellum.

Thinking these thoughts, I fell asleep on the couch.

At three fifteen, I came awake. I'd lived for a year and a half in the cottage but had never heard a sound like this. Some creature was hooting in a nearby shrub. I lay there alert, listening intently—for my cottage is remote, even for Dorset, and someone in the shrubbery at three in the morning would not have been a welcome presence. I listened to the strange *chew hoo, choo wit* and, though satisfied, at last, it wasn't human, got off the couch and went to the window.

The valley seemed preternaturally lit, the moon's candle-power far greater than I remembered it. Across the Black-moor Vale, Bulbarrow Hill rose in the distance—and on its peak stood a great wooden tower! By then, the bird, or what-ever it was, had ceased to call.

And that's when I heard another sound—the rising cries of a wailing woman. I couldn't imagine from where it was coming, as the nearest house is half a mile away. Which was when I saw her, suddenly, running through the open fields. She was dressed in white, her hands upraised in a gesture of horror. Transfixed, I watched her cross the downs, the sound of her wailing growing louder and shriller. I could not imagine who she was, or where in the name of God she was headed until, with a sudden influx of terror, I realized she was coming *here!*

No sooner did I have this thought than she passed through the unopened door of the cottage in a way that is unimagi-nable. Her white robes flared with a numinous splendor; a fluttering veil covered her face. Her screams had ceased and she stood before me in the cottage hall, holding open the codex before her, whose pages were riffled by a supernatural wind. And as I gaped upon her person, I saw she had the feet of a bird!

With a start and a shriek, I awoke. It was 3:27—almost the time it had been in my dream. I gazed out the window at Bulbarrow Hill. On its summit, there was no wooden tower.

When I woke again, it was half past nine. I got up, alarmed by the lateness of the hour, showered, dressed, then drove to the hospital, promising myself breakfast as soon as I'd replaced the book. But first I needed the key to the cage in the cellar. So I marched up the stairwell to the coroner's office, realizing halfway there it was Sunday and he was unlikely to be in.

And yet he was—and at his desk. There was, in fact, no evidence he'd ever left it. A stale, not unpleasant odor spiked the air: some blend of ink and Stilton crumbs, of half-smoked fags and of some deep, damp unevictable rot that riddled the building's bones. "And what's brings *you* here," he asked, looking up at me, "this lovely bloody Sunday?"

"I thought I'd have another go at my Lady."

He gazed at me oddly over his specs. "Really! Must you speak of her that way? You make her sound like a cross between your mistress and the Blessed Virgin." He fixed me with a look of pity. "I suppose it does get lonely living by yourself."

I ignored the remark. "What brings *you* here?"

"Death. Per usual."

"Anyone I know?" I inquired glibly, glancing round to see if the key was hanging, possibly, on the wall. (It wasn't.)

"Believe you do—or *did*. The Constable Rory Dahl."

I was taken aback. "But I was with him just . . . *yesterday*."

"Yes? Well, obviously, your company does not prolong life. Complained of chest pains soon after off-loading your Lady. There! Now you've got *me* saying it! Doctors thought he might have had a coronary and not known it. Gave him a bed, wanted to observe him."

"And?"

"They observed him, all right: have another—and *die*. Doubt he knew he had that one, either."

"Well," I said, sobered, "I'm sorry to hear that. It must have been the strain—of the excavation."

". . . yes." He frowned and rubbed his brow. "Had the most un*pleasant* dream."

"Really?" I said, remembering my own. "What was it?"

He looked up sharply. "Why would I be telling you?"

I shrugged. "Forget it, then."

He looked disappointed, then paused and conceded, "Well, no harm in it, I suppose . . ."

In his dream, the coroner had been standing at the top of a long and winding marble stairwell. In the air there was an uneasy feeling, like that low-pressure heaviness preceding a storm. That's when he'd heard a visitor enter and footsteps slowly ascending the stairs. And though he couldn't see her yet, he knew from the sound of her step it was a woman.

Then he was looking at the phone book from his village. His visitor's name was circled in ink and when he'd read it, he had found himself terrified beyond description!

"What *was* it?"

". . . *Alba Marla*. Or maybe, *Albemarle*. Odd . . . doesn't seem so frightening now."

"And who was the woman ascending the stairs? Did you see her?"

"No. All I saw was her bloody *name*. *Albemarle*." He frowned. "Now tell me why that should scare me witless?"

Chapter 4

I couldn't say. Only that the mystery surrounding my Lady seemed to have stirred something deep within us both. A moment later, we went our separate ways: I, to revisit my Lady, and Strugnell, to locate the key to the cage that housed the treasure.

I opened the door to the room where she lay. "Good morning," I told her, "I hope you slept well. Actually, you're looking bloody marvelous this morning." And she was. Before I'd left her for the night, I'd covered her with a sheet, tucking it in just beneath her chin so that she looked like a woman asleep beneath covers—though the stakes disfigured the drape of the cloth, and her blind eyes continued to disturb me.

I studied her face and, as I did, I had the most vivid sense of her presence. This was a *person*—even if dead.

But our silent communion was rudely interrupted by the coroner throwing open the door so hard it banged against the wall. "Sod it!" he said. "Can't find the key."

"What does it matter? You could open that cage with a screwdriver and a hammer. Look," I said, pointing at the stakes, "let's pull these, shall we? They're getting on my nerves."

The coroner shrugged and approached my Lady. I removed the sheet. He examined the stick forking her right knee. "Hello! There's some sort of writing on it." He squinted at the characters carved in the wood. "Well, it's not English."

"And how do you know that?"

"Just look at it, man!"

"I am. And, offhand, I don't see how you can tell it's not English."

He was getting bothered. "Because there are no bloody English letters, are there?"

I looked at him. "There are no such things as bloody 'English letters.' What you mean, I suppose, is they're not Roman—*a, b, c, d* . . . . But a language can be written in *any* alphabet. Look at *om*. Or *shalom*. You could write Churchill's speeches using Arabic characters. I don't mean *translating* them into Arabic—I mean writing Arabic in such a way that when it's pronounced it sounds like Churchillian English!"

He looked confounded.

"Now this," I continued, eyeing the markings, "could be *futhark*."

"What . . . ?"

"*Runes.* However, the *language* of the runes might be Middle English or Gothic, Norse or Norwegian. Who knows?"

"Who *does*?"

"Someone who can translate them. Not me. Ready?" We gripped the first stake. It came out with a sigh as the wet peat released. In a similar fashion, we removed the three others. I tagged each, indicating its position on the limb it had pinned. Then we tried to remove the blind. But I couldn't undo the knot (it was cruelly tight) and I didn't want to force it, fearing I would damage her face in the process, so I made do with moving it an inch above her eyes.

Unexpectedly, they were open; undeniably, they were blue; unbelievably, they were lifelike in the extreme—full of hurt and terror and some far-reaching ruined hope.

"My God," the coroner said, stepping back a pace. For with her blue eyes open and the stakes removed, it almost seemed at any moment she might revive and speak to us.

Her face was broad; her nose had a certain hawk-like flare. Her body was at once long-limbed, slender and broad-shouldered. Her ears (and her right nostril) were pierced—details that, for some reason, moved me.

We turned to her effects. A small feathered purse found with her clothing contained a horn comb, a double oyster shell serving as tweezers (several short hairs still adhered to an edge), and three round lidded boxes, no larger than silver dollars, containing what smelled like traces of unguents. There were no coins that might have dated her death.

"Why does it feel so creepy," he asked, "going through the dead's effects? You almost expect her to sit up, bat at your hand and say, 'Leave my bloody purse alone.' What are those?" he wondered, indicating the wooden dishes. "Medicine?"

"Makeup. Some sort of lip gloss, probably. And kohl for the eyes."

"They had makeup? Back *then*?"

"Where there were women . . ." I said, ". . . there was makeup."

We went downstairs. The morning was warm, the elevator overheated. No sooner had it reached the bottom and its doors reopened than I saw a ring lying on the floor. This was not a happy sign—and stepping out I saw at once the wire cage had been broken into and the treasure taken.

The coroner stopped, as though straight-armed by an invisible hand. "Pinched!" he screamed. "*Bastards!*"

I stared at the hill of moldering peat from which the hoard had been removed. "What bastards?"

He looked at me, almost suspiciously. "How the hell should *I* know?"

I won't dwell upon the sea of dreariness into which the morning descended: the police interviews, the coroner's alternately defensive and apologetic mien, or the appearance of the national press, for the discovery and theft of such a priceless treasure trove was news of the first order. The coroner was roundly criticized for his having left it in such a spot—though in his defense, the hoard was delivered on a Saturday evening when no museum or bank vault was open to receive it, and was partially embedded in a quarter ton of peat, from which he'd been cautioned it could not be removed. This had left him few options. He couldn't have kept it in his office—it wouldn't have fit—and the cage in the hospital basement had not seemed like a bad idea at the time.

In retrospect, it was ludicrous. You don't leave a treasure worth millions of pounds sterling overnight in a public building in a cage secured with a bicycle lock!

The police speculated that sometime after midnight, the thief had overridden the key that disabled the elevator's descent to the cellar, clipped the lock, and carried the treasure out through the loading bay to a waiting vehicle. The theft's childish ease moved one bobby to remark, "Whoever did this had to know *three* things: *one*, how to use a lift; *two*, how to clip a wire; and three, *how to drive a lorry*." He grinned. "*Cunning*."

Most worrisome was that the treasure wasn't inventoried, and our fear was that the hoard would be dispersed, for there's a booming market in looted antiquities.

Which was when I remembered the photos I'd taken. Though documenting only the topmost level, they would identify at least some of the pieces. I downloaded the pictures to Strugnell's computer, then copied them to a thumb drive which I gave the CID.

There wasn't anything more to do. Having squandered one archeological wonder, the police had concluded they must safeguard the body at all costs and were trying to devise some means. They were milling about; there was no way I could do any work or, more importantly, return the codex without answering a lot of difficult questions.

A couple of the younger officers were ogling my Lady. This annoyed me. "Excuse me," I said, and pulled the sheet up over her head. "*Plague*," I whispered, nodding sagely. They looked alarmed and backed off fast.

That afternoon I wrapped the ancient book in foam, insured it for a quarter of a million pounds sterling, and addressed it to my friend and mentor, Dr. Jai Prasad, Visiting Professor of Anthropology at Oxford University. I included a note asking Jai to examine it, posted the package, and drove back home.

Chapter 5

The Reader may have noticed a curious bit of avoidance here. For though eager to hear the coroner's nightmare, I wasn't as anxious to examine my own—for like us all, I would much rather face someone *else's* demons.

Mine had first surfaced at the age of fifteen when a girl I was dating broke up with me. It had been a totally childish affair. We'd roller-skate and, walking home, kiss beneath the violet night shadows of the trees. Once, she'd let me touch her breasts, bare beneath her Fair Isle sweater; this was the full extent of our intimacy. And yet, to lose her felt like being guillotined. I wasn't hurt so much as dead.

Unfortunately, in Asbury Park, New Jersey, in the year of our Lord nineteen hundred and ninety-seven, no one had diagnosed depression; no one even seemed to notice. Life went on, only now there were pins and shivs in things, and the most innocent memories hid eviscerating knives.

And so I dealt with it as best I could, though for several months after I felt like I was underwater, and it was a year before I was myself again.

For many years since, I had done quite nicely, until a prima ballerina with whom I was having a white-hot affair, ended it abruptly after just three months when she'd left me, New York and the City Ballet to be the next *étoile* in Paris. I found her sudden exit nearly unendurable. And though I'd left for England shortly thereafter, not a night had passed that some part of me hadn't ached for her. And to come across her name unexpectedly can, to this day, derail me—still.

Thus all attempts to match me up with one of the local lovelies had failed. It was as though my heart's RAM was full and no new name could be written there—no room. Couldn't, that is, until this evening. For the day was all but over with and I hadn't, I realized, thought of *her* once!

Now, I took a closer look at my dream. Clearly, it had to do with my Lady. Her veil, therefore, made perfect sense, as it kept me from knowing who she was. Ah, I thought, another unavailable woman, just the kind you love to love. The apparition's talons made me think of the Old European bird-footed death goddess with her V-shaped prints scratched in clay or stone. Given my Lady's probable murder, this mortal note made sense, as well . . . . Though I must say I fell asleep that evening dreaming of my Lady's wild, blue eyes . . .

Before I went to work in the morning, I spent some time on the telephone, checking and patching my political fences. It was agreed by my department chair and several other influential persons that, given the circumstances, I had handled matters well. The video and pics I had taken, now that the find had been "removed," were invaluable, and only underlined again the value of what we anthropologists do—when allowed to do it.

Thus, stopping at the hospital on my way to work, I was taken by surprise when Strugnell informed me that Sir August Rumple had been put in charge of my Lady. Strugnell seemed subdued: his face in the morning light was as gray and bleak as the Zuider Zee.

"What do you mean, 'put in charge'?"

"Sir August has been appointed head of a commission to investigate the find—by the Crown. There's a terrible row being made about the treasure." He looked baleful.

"I don't see why," I said, upset by this sudden turn. "It can't be worth more than several million pounds."

Sir A. E. Rumple, MPhil., PhD, Keeper-Elect of World Pre-History at the Cambridge Museum and author of *The Mystery of English Runes*, hadn't shaved. Or rather, let me amend that observation: he had shaved his cheeks and chin, but for some odd reason had failed to shave those other parts that required it as much or more, such as his *nose, temples, eyebrows, neck, chest,* and *ears*—all of which sprouted such a superabundance of grayish hairs that he looked like a spider plant in need of pruning.

I was surprised by my pettiness. Obviously, I was feeling insecure.

I introduced myself and outlined for him my role in the body's discovery and initial examination. I apologized for the lack of proper scientific protocol, but explained how I'd been overruled. I told him of the hundreds of pictures I'd taken and said I hoped to continue on as part of the royal investigative team.

"Sorry, old boy," he said, hardly bothering to look up, "can't use you, I'm afraid."

"Oh?" I asked. "And why is that?"

"You're . . . *uh* . . . underqualified."

I felt myself flush. "I'm a Pitt Rivers fellow at Exeter. And I worked on a similar cadaver last year. I have a master's from Columbia in physical anthropology. My tutor was Jai Prasad."

Jai's name brought Rumple's head up. "I've done field-work in Pakistan, at Dorchester and at Woodhenge. I'm published. And I have a paper coming out in *Antiquity* next month—on Lincoln Man." (All right, it had been *submitted* to *Antiquity* and I'd been favored with several editors' queries, though whether it would actually be *published* next month remained to be seen. Still, such posturing is an essential part of the profession.)

Rumple pretended to consider this, then made a gruff, dismissive noise.

"Sorry, Donne. But as I said, you really don't have the *bona fides*. No doctorate, I see. A bit of fieldwork. Some graduate studies, albeit with a famous scholar. I read *Antiquity* from cover to cover. I don't recall ever coming across your name."

I wanted to reply, "Of course you haven't! How could you read an article that won't be published until *next month*?" Instead, I said, "I helped to recover the body. I've already put in more than forty-six hours of study, collection, fieldwork and observation. I have 200 pics of the corpse *in situ* and another half dozen or so of the trove."

"And the commission will be indebted to you for sharing with it your notes and photos."

"I have no intention of turning over anything." I was, I'm afraid, beginning to panic. The prospect of losing my Lady unhinged me. "I practically *found* the damn body. I dug it up. And I did everything I could to keep it unspoiled. I think you owe it to me to keep me on the team."

"And I think not."

"All right then. I'll give you a good reason. If you won't, I'll go to Fleet Street with color photos of the mummy *and* the treasure and make a gigantic bloody stink and howl about the politics and incompetence that allowed the body to be removed in an improper manner and the hoard to be pinched in the first place, and how I, the one who *uncovered* the body, have been thrust aside by stampeding dons like August Rumple, bent upon quenching their thirst for public-ity and the furtherance of their academic careers . . ."

He looked up at me, seriously appalled. "You *wouldn't*."

"*You* wouldn't. *I would*—in a New York second."

He looked seriously concerned. "What do you want?"

I made a reasonable gesture. "Just to be part of the investigative team. Also, I should tell you now," I said, dangling a carrot in place of the stick, "I have in my possession an extraordinary document that was part of the trove."

"What, what, *what* document?" He looked professionally excited, personally dismayed. "Nobody said . . ."

"A book," I said. "It was with the treasure. I rescued it the night the hoard was stolen."

"*What? What book?*"

"I'm afraid I can't tell you its title, sir."

"*Book?*"

"Yes. I found a *book* with the *body.*"

"What *book?*"

"As I've said, I couldn't read it, sir, as I believe it is written in some form of Indic."

"Indic? *Wot?*" His eyes bugged out. "And where is this . . . this Indic . . . *book?*"

If he said "book" one more time . . . "I took the liberty of sending it to Dr. Prasad. I thought that he, if anyone, might be able to translate it."

"You did *what?*"

"Sent it off to Dr. Jai Prasad . . ."

"But that . . ." he was growing apoplectic . . . "is property of . . . !"

I knew what he was going to say and cut him off. "No, it isn't. The law of Treasure Trove clearly states the Crown is entitled to all forfeited treasure made of precious *metals.* The book is covered in leather and written in ink on some sort of parchment. In the meantime, I am continuing to assist the CID in a murder investigation. It seems likely the book could shed some light upon the crime. Once it is perused and studied, we will, of course, return it to its rightful owner, whoever that is determined to be—though I do hope, sir, before we do, that you may get a glimpse of it."

Rumple's face was a red balloon. It was the word *glimpse* that did it, I think.

"Right," I said. "I'll await your call." And I turned and left him sitting speechless. I stepped out into the hall.

"See the good doctor?" the coroner asked.

"Yes, indeed."

"Right. I was wondering if we could have a word."

"Wait half an hour and we'll have it over lunch."

"Uh, no," he said. "*Privately.* Some evening, perhaps." A crown of sweat marred his brow.

I opened my daybook, pretending to be looking for a free evening, when all my evenings were free as a bird from now until Armageddon. "Tonight all right?"

He nodded.

"Around eight?"

The confrontation with Rumple had left me shaken. This was *not* the way I normally do business. Sir August was a Knight of the Realm and my threat, I knew, would either win the day or plunge me into such hot water I'd never work in English anthropology again. Still, I'd had to do *something*. And it wasn't just to further my ambitions. For I'd panicked at the thought of losing my Lady! Some deep, unstated bond between us felt threatened in a way I didn't understand. There was nothing for it now but to hope that Rumple would react like the scandal-phobic don I believed he was—and to cool my heels.

Strugnell arrived a little after eight. As I've said, I knew him as a colleague only and not well enough to even tell you his wife's name.

So I was caught off guard when the first thing he said was that he had once killed a man, a maniac on the Brixton tram. The man he'd killed had stabbed two passengers, then slashed the driver before coming at Strugnell with death in his eyes. Everything, Strugnell said, had gone into slow motion as he deflected the lunge, wrested the blade and plunged it back into his assailant's chest. The hot snake of blood that leapt from the wound had announced he had hit the targeted heart.

By the time the police arrived, the passengers were dead. The driver had died in the hospital soon after. The maniac, a garish rose blooming on his shirt, was dead, as well. Only Strugnell—no action hero—was alive. And, as if I might doubt him, he drew from his coat a newspaper clipping, limp with age, that repeated the heroic story he'd told me with a photograph of Strugnell looking half his current age and size.

I must say, I wondered why he was telling me this. It was more than I really wished to know. In an awkward attempt to change the subject, I asked him how he liked his job, which seemed to me a difficult one, and he said he found the hospital morgue "agreeable" compared to his home and marriage.

For his wife was acutely unhappy, it seemed, and broadcast her unhappiness in palpable waves. Last night, he confessed, they'd had a terrible row. After a day of questioning by the police, bureaucratic reprimands, the disdain of the Palace, and the hostile inquiries of the press, he found he'd had to answer to *her*. She was belittling—sneering at his "stew-pidity"—until, afraid he might strike out and hit her, he'd left the house, walking to the village pub.

No sooner had he entered it than a young man approached . . .

"Wooland Strugnell, Esquire, innit?"

When he didn't respond, the boy went on, "Woo-land Strug-nell: bit difficult to pronounce. Doesn't roll trippingly off the tongue, now does it? *Woo-land. Strug-nell.* Sounds like

I used to feel as a kid when I got me arm entangled in me sweater."

Strugnell looked down at his torturer. He was a boy of eighteen or thereabouts, with a hoop in one ear and violet hair. Lodged in his eyebrow was something bizarre. Strugnell couldn't bear to look, the metallic gleam of what—a pin? *Ouch!* But no, he saw now it was a silver earring, or rather *brow*-ring, piercing the ridge of flesh and hair. It looked more like an accident than an ornament, as if the boy ought to be rushing off to a hospital rather than standing there, drink in hand. A spare, soft, black goatee completed the picture. Strugnell was not used to people who looked this way, much less their speaking to him, and he didn't know what to say.

"Hey, what's the matter, man?" the boy said, as if he hadn't a moment ago ridiculed his name. And then with a prescience that Strugnell loathed, "Have a row with the old lady?" Strugnell attempted to take refuge in his obvious superiority—of age, class, rank and education—but the boy didn't seem to notice it.

"Look," Strugnell said, abruptly. "What is it you want?"

"They's sayin' the body of a witch been recovered, 'long with some witchy treasure."

"Who is?"

The boy motioned with his head. "Lads." Strugnell looked up to see several weathered faces, shielded by the brims of their coarse woolen caps, turn back to their beers.

"That's ridiculous," he said. "A bog body was recovered. And yes, there were some artifacts."

"In no-man's land."

"No-man's . . . *what?*"

"That's why no one's claiming them, see? No one can figure out whose land it's on."

Strugnell groaned. Trouble coming. He could smell it. Not only did he have to discover *why* the bloody treasure was buried, but now, according to the boy, the spot was on some ancient join where three distinct landholdings met. There even seemed to be some question of *political* jurisdiction, as the find, he learned further, was on the seam between two parishes. Thus it was *truly* no-man's land. And Strugnell saw now in a hellish vision a mound of paper rising on his desk higher than the mythical Yggdrasil: illegible deeds and fraudulent and contradictory titles with everything in *hides, oxgangs, rods* and *perches* and other archaic means and measures. And on top of all this was a blizzard of writs and countersuits whose knotted skein of competing claims would never be untangled in Strugnell's lifetime. And, if he faltered, he was liable to judicial review.

". . . Holders Fen? I would assume some chap named Holder owns it."

"Ah, and so did I. But you know, guv, if we did, we'd both be wrong. 'Cording to a Mrs. Katy Lane, some sort of local historian hereabouts, the word was originally Huldres'. Though on an 1847 map, it's . . ." he paused a moment, referring to notes, ". . . H-o-l-d-r-e, some sort of intermediate spelling."

Strugnell was suddenly on the alert. "You're a reporter."

"Freelance journalist. Edwin Cummings." The boy offered his hand and Strugnell took it. It was disagreeably small, wriggly and hot, like holding a mouse.

Strugnell looked back down at the boy—from his crown of spiky blue-dyed hair down to his black, moldering high-top sneakers. This was a *reporter*? Then again, what did he think a reporter looked like? Some bloke in a trench coat with a fag parked in a corner of his mouth and a press pass in the satin band of his fedora? And Strugnell had the uneasy suspicion that the turning world had passed him by. For it seemed all wrong that a *real* reporter should be the age of his nephew, have skulls tattooed upon his knuckles and purple highlights in his hair. "Huldre, Holder, what does it matter how it's spelled?" he barked irritably, buying time.

"Because a holder is something what *holds*, innit? Whereas *huldre* is a *fairy*, see? Huldres' Fen, Fairies' Bog—witches, fairies, juicier story, innit?"

Strugnell supposed it was. He wasn't really listening. His mind was scanning like the automatic tuner on his car radio, dipping into different mental frequencies to decide which one he ought to hear. One message coming through loud and clear was that he really didn't have a handle on this thing. He didn't like the way the story of the find was already taking on a life of its own. Pretty soon he'd have the press camping on his doorstep and the division court breathing down his neck. Some might have welcomed this chance to display their talents and so advance their fortunes. But the coroner had no such ambitions. He had taken the position of West Dorset coroner precisely because it had seemed to him an especially unimportant one—one in which he would be left mostly alone. And the last thing he wanted was *anyone's* attention.

As he left the pub, two things surprised him: one, that he was drunk (his gums felt numb and the cobblestones beneath his feet seemed several inches higher than when he was sober); and two, that it was still so bright. A wondrous radiance pervaded the air. It had rained, wetting the grass.

He still didn't feel he could face the wife and so shouldered his way into the field behind the tavern, spray from the wet shrubbery striking him coldly. He was surprised when he saw the half-fallen circle of stones and realized where he'd come. He limped toward it—for though his wounds were emotional ones, he moved like a man who's physically hurt. He was aware that his shoes and socks were drenched. He was conscious, too, of the ancient dolmens, with their soft tracings of lichen and moss—and he also knew that he wanted from them something they could never give him, some cosmic form of amnesia and love. It reminded him of the two or three times he had sought out a church to relieve the guilty pressure inside him, but had always left feeling faintly cheated, the guilt still there, if somewhat allayed.

Beside the stones was a wishing well—not a manmade one, but a natural spring—that overflowed into a woodland pool above which swallows swept and damselflies hovered. Many old legends were attached to its waters. It was said the pool was without a bottom. It was also claimed St. Augustine had evicted the nymph inhabiting it, promising whosoever, while sipping its waters, asked a boon in the name of Christ would have his or her wish come true—though the waters' wish-fulfilling status was clearly some millennia older. Coins and ritually damaged swords from its depths had been dated to the Iron Age. The coroner looked down at his face in the wind-wrinkled water.

Perhaps some black star had dawned in his chart, some vile conjunction. How else to explain it? For the theft of the treasure for which he was responsible (to the *Queen*, no less!) had turned his world upside down. It would be a miracle if he managed to keep his job—and everything had happened so fast! He was like a man fallen from the top of a mountain: one moment he was standing on the summit, exultant; the next, he was broken on the road below. Staring at the pool, he had the miserable notion of drowning himself in it, loading his pockets with stones and walking into the bottomless lake, and he might have done it, he thought, if the result would not have been so demeaning. He saw his corpse like a clown's in dripping clothes, the rocks in his pockets, someone, the coroner (but that was *he!*) pouring water from his shoe as though it were a gravy boat.

And that was when he saw a slender hand break the water's surface, shining whitely in the twilight for an instant, then submerging, only to shoot up again. And this time a gleaming arm came with it and the dark, streaming hair of a woman or girl, each strand meticulously combed by the water. Strugnell glimpsed her white, wild face, violet eyes, and tender mouth, and even without his meaning to, braced himself for her cry of help, but the body sank back down again, without a sound, like a sword sliding back in its scabbard.

Strugnell leaped to the rescue at once. Kicking off his shoes and diving in, he shortly reached where the girl had been, but now he could not see her. He looked about, then dove and lo! she was just beneath the water's surface, open-eyed, her hair fanned discus-like in all directions. Clumsily, he embraced her, then kicked them upward. But oddly, the surface wasn't coming any closer. And though he swam and struggled the harder, he found instead they were sinking like stones.

And the coroner realized then this was the perfect finish to an absolutely *beastly* day: first the theft, then the row with the missus, then the boy in the pub, and now *this*—death by *drowning*! He shouldn't have been surprised, but he was . . . *immensely!*

Looking up, he glimpsed beyond the water's surface the silver twilight, and every cell in him ached for that airy world—even as the creature, her lips strangely smiling, carried him away . . . .

He paused to let me take this in.

"Well," I said. "You didn't drown."

"I awoke on the bank with the sun in my eyes. It was six in the morning. When I got back home, the lady wife was frantic. I'd never spent the night away—I mean, without calling her first."

"And the girl?"

"I thought I'd find her drowned among the reeds, but there was no one."

"Yet you saw her?"

"Saw her? She tried to *drown* me." He looked disappointed by my lack of alarm.

"Don't you see? First, I have that dreadful dream, then the treasure goes missing, and then I see someone who should never have been there and then *I* disappear—somewhere—for the better part of an evening. Tell me, please, I'm not going mad!"

So that was it. He needed someone to talk to. He needed a friend. Which, quite simply, is how I became one.

Chapter 6

When Strugnell had gone, I considered his tale, but couldn't make any sense of it. *Had* there been a drowning woman? Admittedly, he'd been drinking; had he mixed his liquor purposely or inadvertently with drugs?

For if a woman *had* drowned, her body would likely have surfaced by now. And if Strugnell had *saved* her, were we to believe she had wandered off into the night, leaving her rescuer unconscious on the bank?

Then again, as Strugnell had noted, local legend had long associated the pool with witches, nymphs and fairies. And against this mythic backdrop, the girl in the sylvan well was starting to look increasingly familiar. Her pale face, blue eyes, black hair and submarine home were all signatures of the Phantom Queen, whose avatars included Guinevere, Blanchefleur, the Lady of the Lake, and the myriad white mares and spectral white ladies who haunt so many English moors and castles.

If one pursued her pedigree further, down to the roots of her family tree, one came upon those Stiff White Ladies carved in stone and bone that guard so many neolithic tombs.

Stranger still, the coroner appeared to have tapped into one of the deeper levels of this mythic pool, where the oldest vestigial imagery dwells.

For while death is now "black," once it was white. In fact, death has been "black" a relatively short time. For tens of millennia before the conquests of the Indo-Europeans, death was the color of ghosts, of bone, of ash, of the winter snows, the waning moon, the pallor and hue of a three-day-old corpse. "White is the neolithic color of death," writes Gimbutas. How else were we to understand the identity and nature of Strugnell's lady?

Not that I believed Strugnell had encountered an actual Celtic goddess. Only that her archetype still flourished in the British imagination, along with a host of other dangerous and magical wraiths—mummies and nymphs—figures pivoting between love and death.

And here my analysis of the coroner's bizarre tale would have likely ended had there not occurred a revelation that completely upended my thinking about both the coroner's story, as well as my Lady's. For while dressing the next morning, I received a phone call from Sir August informing me that an autopsy of my Lady was scheduled for the following day and inviting me, as the newest member of the Royal Archeological Commission, to attend.

Overjoyed, I gratefully accepted. But that was only the first bit of good news: Rumple had translated the inscription on the stakes.

"And what do they say?"

"At first, I thought it might be *ogham*."

"I see."

"Celtic tree language."

"Yes, sir."

"But they're runes. Quite interesting, really."

"I can imagine. In what language?"

"M. E."

"Really! And what, sir, does the Middle English *say*?"

"Ah, yes, well . . . the inscription warns against removing the stakes and freeing the saga, Albemarle."

I was silent, then asked, "What the *fuck* did you say?"

He was taken aback, perhaps by my profanity. "A saga's a witch, a feminine sage; it's . . . archaic."

"Yes. I mean, no. The saga's *name*."

"Name? Well, apparently, it's . . . *Albemarle*."

I reject fantastic explanations, whether the result of other-worldly encounters or crackpot ideas like those of von Däniken, who sees in every Toltec ball court landing fields for UFOs.

Having said this, I must confess I was at a loss to explain this last revelation. For Strugnell, as you're well aware, had dreamt of "Albemarle" two nights before—a name unusual enough that the odds of his dreaming it up by chance seemed to me remote to none. As I rejected the inference that a supernatural entity had announced itself to him in this manner, I knew there *had* to be a *rational* explanation. The only problem was, for the life of me, I couldn't think of it.

I spent the morning at my office in Exeter, proofing a table of radiographic data, but I couldn't forget the bizarre development. It was like something stuck between your teeth that your tongue keeps working back and forth, and I kept pondering it, looking for some reasonable explanation.

I remembered a dream from some years before. While digging in Pakistan, I had, apparently, been exposed to tuberculosis. Fortunately, the disease wasn't active, and the doctor had assured me it was no big deal. I simply had to take a course of Isoniazid. That night, however, I had a terrifying dream in which an astronomer named Tycho Brahe was peering through a telescope at some ruinous new star.

When I awoke, I thought I had made the strange name up, for I had never heard of Tycho Brahe. Imagine my surprise when I learned he had been a real medieval, Danish astronomer! Still I couldn't imagine *why* in the world I had dreamt of *him*—until I paused to consider his initials. Obviously, news of my exposure had upset me more than I had thought. Equally odd was how I had imbibed Brahe's name with no conscious knowledge or recollection.

Something similar, I reasoned, must have happened with Strugnell. Perhaps he knew runes and had, subconsciously, read the name on the stakes. Or maybe as a boy he'd heard a now–lost local legend about the fairy, Albemarle, whose name his dream had disinterred. Or perhaps Sir August had botched the translation and the name on the stakes wasn't Albemarle at all!

I studied the inscription and its transliteration, a copy of which Rumple had faxed:

ᚻᚷᛗᛋᚾᚻᛈᛗᚻ

INGESUNAMEN

ᚱᛁᛈᛗᚻ ᚻᛈᛏ ᚦᚱᛋ ᚾᛈᛋᛃᚱᚾᚻᚠ

RIVEN NAT ÞAS HALYRUNA

ᚦᚾᛁᛁ ᛃᛒᛃᚻᛈᛗᚻ ᚬᛉ ᚾᛁᚱᛗ ᛒᛗᛞ

THAT YBONDEN ON HIRE BED

ᚦᚠ ᛁᛏᛗᛋᚠᚷᚾᛒᛗᛈᚱᚱᛁᛗ

ÞA ILESAGALBEMARLE

With the assistance of an online runic translator and a Middle English dictionary, I went over every rune and letter, but could find no fault with Rumple's work. In runic inscriptions, double letters are dropped, as if the effort of cutting the first discourages repetition. Thus, I could see in the final line how Rumple had gotten the reading: "illy saga Albemarle." He had added what he assumed to be a second missing *l* and *a*. Based on their style, he dated both the runes and the Middle English to the thirteenth century.

Now it was my turn to look for reassurances. I rang the coroner.

"Ever study runes?"

"Runes?"

"I'm trying to clear up a bit of a mystery."

"So are the police. Where is two hundred stone of missing treasure?"

"Look, there's something you ought to know. You'll be hearing it soon enough."

"I'm under arrest."

I ignored the remark. "Rumple translated the runes on the stakes. And . . . well, amazingly, our Lady's name seems to be . . . *Albemarle*."

Silence.

"I see . . ." he said guardedly. "And what precisely does it say?"

I read him a modern English rendition:

> **In Jesus' name**
> **Break not these holy runes**
> **That bind to her bed [or grave]**
> **The evil saga Albemarle**

There was a longish pause. Then he said, in a childish whine, "I suppose, we could always put them back."

"Put *what* back?"

"The stakes."

I barked a laugh. "It's a bit late for that."

Chapter 7

The revelation of my Lady's name I found at once disquieting and exciting; disquieting in that I still couldn't figure out *how* in the world Strugnell had known it, even if I was thrilled to know it now. I turned it over on my tongue. *Albemarle.* It only made me feel that much closer to her. *Albemarle, my lovely; Albemarle, my sweet.* It was a handsome name: antique and good. It was the name, in short, of a girl I could get involved with.

Now that we knew what my Lady was called, discovering her identity seemed somehow less daunting and, booting my computer, I began to try to track her down. Was she someone historical? Someone well-known? Had there been an infamous enchantress, Albemarle the Fey, of whom, in my ignorance, I was unaware? For once she had been greatly feared. Not only was she staked, but her burial on a welter of political borders only reinforced the supposition that her murderer had buried her there in order to confuse her spirit. It was the same logic that buries criminals at crossroads—as it reduces to one in four the odds their vengeful ghosts will follow you home.

I googled "Albemarle." But apart from the Honourable Rufus Keppel, the dashing, present Tenth Earl of, most of the British "Albemarles" were an odd assortment of dukes and countesses, the only "Lady Albemarle" of note being one Annie Lennox *(not* of the *Eurythmics*!) who'd died in 1789.

Nor was the normally instructive Oxford English Dictionary any more helpful. "Albemarle" was unlisted, and the closest I could come to it were *alb* and *marl*.

Alb was a Latin prefix meaning "white" as in *album*, a book of white or blank pages. (I considered, briefly, a Moorish derivation, as in *al-gebra* and *al-cohol*, but it seemed farfetched.)

Marl, according to the OED, was "an ancient word of unknown origin" denoting a type of lime-rich soil. A descriptor was often placed before it: as in *blue* marl or *plenus* marl, depending upon the soil's color and composition.

But while *marl* led nowhere, her name's initial syllable, *alb*, was intriguing. While *white* remains the color of the British Goddess, due to the effects of "linguistic drift," its original sense has been reversed and it has come to mean its polar opposite: "good," as in the terms, "white witch, white magic." And given my Lady's line of work, such a term might fit quite well, especially if Albemarle were not my Lady's name, but *title*.

For the grave goods accompanying her (*i.e.*, the golden hoard) would seem to indicate a person of the highest social status, not a hated, wicked witch. So that was a contradiction there.

But if Albemarle *were* her title, its linkage to the British peerage seemed to me remote. English countesses weren't condemned as witches and buried nude in unmarked graves.

"You've read his famous monograph, I'm sure: *Human Skulls from the River Thames: Their Dating and Significance.*"

"Uh, yes," I said, almost afraid to shake the hand that had written such a grisly title—though it did appear to be normal enough, attached as it was to the white-coated arm of the eminent paleopathologist, Dr. Harvey Phelps Morton.

A smaller coterie than I'd expected had gathered to witness my Lady's postmortem. In addition to myself and Morton, there were Rumple, Strugnell, a photographer and a police representative.

We began by removing the peat from the body. This was accomplished with hatchets and saws—the peat not in direct contact with the corpse being cut away and saved for further study.

The procedure's second phase was oddly intimate. We worked with wooden spatulas and trowels scraping away at the peat that remained, then using soft brushes and jets of cold water to remove the last vestiges clinging to her flesh. I had never bathed a naked woman, much less a dead one, and her skin was so soft and tender that I felt—you will laugh— like I was bathing a little child.

Autopsying mummies is controversial. The "preservationists" maintain that mummies are "people" and should not be dissected. But to my way of thinking, mummies are *corpses*: if they weren't, they wouldn't have been buried in the first place. And who's to decide that a knife is invasive but an endoscope is not?

Nonetheless, I found the autopsy difficult to watch. I undid the pins that were holding it and let fall her wet dark hair.

"Well, here's something," Morton observed, tweezing from her scalp a square piece of padding. "Probably from a horse's mane. She was using it to give her hair lift. Stylish bird, isn't she?"

This detail, like her pierced ears, moved me out of all proportion to its importance. I wondered, had she pinned up her hair knowing she was going off to die, to expose her skull and tender nape to the shock of the knife or rope? Or had she pinned it up thinking of her lover, never suspecting such a thing would accompany her to her grave and that a millennium later, men whom she would never know on an afternoon she would never see would be studying it intently in the subbasement of a British hospital morgue?

Morton unbound her hands, and as he did, I noticed again the thread on her wrist, whose meaning, I thought, would likely never be known.

Morton sliced the blind that had closed her eyes and examined her scalp: "Perimortem fractures of the posterior fossa, both left and right sides."

"In other words," I said, "she was hit on the head."

"And it didn't kill her. Though it likely knocked her out."

I hoped so. I didn't wish to think she had watched herself be murdered. As Morton moved from head to throat, he uncovered a rawhide noose cinched so tightly it had disappeared into her flesh. Just below it, the carotid was cut.

"Well, look at this!" Thin strips of flesh had been removed from her breasts, arousing the fear that unauthorized samples already had been harvested. But if so, Morton said, it wasn't by any modern researcher, as the wounds were contemporaneous with her death.

Morton continued his external examination. "She has several fresh insect bites on her buttocks, received, it appears, just prior to death."

He probed. "No bruising of the inner thighs. Vagina appears . . . normal. No tearing, no evidence of sexual assault. Though we'll take a swab and test for semen."

The external examination completed, I cringed at the sight of the first incision. She'd been preserved so well so long, it seemed like a desecration.

"Well, here's a surprise," Morton exclaimed. "No heart."

"You mean it's disintegrated?" Strugnell wondered.

"Removed. The aorta and vena cava are cut." He raised her arm, revealing below it the open lips of an incision. "So that's how it was done."

"How macabre," Sir August intoned.

"Well," Morton said, "she was long dead when it happened." This was a comfort.

He inspected her lungs. "The alveoli are charged with fluid."

Thus, it was no longer a question of finding the cause of her death, but determining which of three equally brutal means had killed her. For my Lady had suffered a triple death: she'd been strangled, drowned and bled, after first being clubbed.

"Seems like a case of 'overkill,'" Strugnell observed. "Why would anyone want to kill the poor Judy three ways to Sunday?"

I suggested: "Perhaps as a sacrifice to three different gods. Odin liked blood and hanging. Teutates liked his victims drowned. And Thor threw 'thunderbolts.' If you look at the blows to the back of her head, I'll wager they were made with a hammer. I would also bet she was struck three times."

There was a moment of suspense as the wounds to her head were reexamined in this light. Then Dr. Morton said, "I do believe Dr. Donne's correct."

"*Mr.* Donne." For I had no desire to claim degrees I didn't hold.

But Rumple had a major objection. (I'd have been disappointed if he hadn't. Objections are the coin of academics; they pull them out when they want to do business.)

"Interesting. Though there is one fact your theory overlooks. How could her executioners be pagans when the runes begin, 'In Jesus' name'?"

The heads, which had swung in Rumple's direction, now swung back in mine, like the audience at Wimbledon. My serve had been returned.

"Dr. Rumple," I said, using a technique I'd learned as an undergrad—always begin by quoting your opponent, for the human ego melts at the sound of its own words—"as you yourself wrote in *Language and Pre-History in Early Britain,* and I quote, '. . . there existed a hidden shamanistic culture that flourished in the English countryside, of which our many folk traditions are all that presently endure.'

"I'm sure these people were *nominally* Christian. We'll have to wait for the radiocarbon dating and for your own further analysis, Doctor, of the vocabulary and grammatical syntax of the runes. However, I have all but abandoned my initial opinion that our Lady is neolithic. I think it's safe to say this is a *medieval* burial. Still, I would assert that the marks of a classic Celtic ritual death are so apparent in her execution, that if you hadn't written that sentence, Doctor, I would have had to."

There was an uneasy silence. The arrhythmic precipitousness with which my thought ended, combined with the obscurity of what I had said, made a rejoinder nearly impossible. It was like one of those returns with so much backspin and "English" on them, they twirl and hover on the edge of the net, mesmerizing one's opponent and appearing not about to make it over—until they do, plopping in for the point.

Rumple subtly bowed.

My Lady's stomach was examined next. "She ate some hours before her death."

"Can you tell us *what*?" the coroner wondered.

"Yes . . . from the looks of it . . . seems like . . . *a Big Mac!*" Morton grinned. "Kidding!" He probed with his scalpel. "Gruel." He removed her stomach for further study. "Well," he said, opening her uterus, "she may have been a sacrifice, but she wasn't a virgin. She'd borne a child."

He returned to her head: "Full eruption of the third molars." Her groin: "The iliac crest of her pelvis is fused . . . ."

Her back: ". . . while fusion in the vertebral spine of the sacral bodies is still somewhat incomplete."

"Meaning?" the coroner asked.

"In her mid- or late-twenties to early thirties."

Meanwhile, the coroner had turned to my Lady's clothing, and in the folds of her shift, found a small skin bladder with a primitive zipper: a bronze pin that could be inserted into a row of eyelets. He hefted it and something jingled inside.

With much anticipation, we removed the pin, spilling the bladder's contents on the gurney: flint flakes, several dried berries and shriveled fungi, a desiccated snake's tail, a long curved claw, bronze tweezers, charcoal, and a small flint blade wound with gut.

The coroner pushed at the claw with a surprisingly grimy nail.

"Well," Rumple said, "at least we know she wasn't libeled."

"How's that?"

"As a sorceress. If this isn't a witch's bag of tricks, I don't know what is."

And in truth, it did appear to be "*eye of newt and toe of frog . . .*" Unless one viewed it as the medicine pouch of a country healer: a claw to probe wounds and puncture abscesses, tweezers to remove thorns, flint and charcoal to kindle a fire, a knife for small surgeries, the gut for sutures, the withered sloe, rich in vitamin C, and the birch fungi for its bactericidal powers.

When the autopsy was over, the coroner announced what was apparent to all: there was ample evidence to suggest that Albemarle's death was "violent and unnatural," because of which, it required an inquest.

As it was past five and Strugnell was already late in picking up his children, he asked that I communicate the PM's findings to the hospital's secretarial pool. That way, he explained, he would be able to file his report with the Registrar of Deaths first thing in the morning.

While Morton and Rumple conferred, I dialed the extension and got a young woman who put me through a litany of questions. "Victim's name?"

"Albemarle."

"Is that the first or last name, sir?"

"It's both. You know, like Sting or Diana."

"Gender?"

"Female."

"Age?"

"Oh . . . twenty-eight."

"Race?"

"Caucasian. She has beautiful blue eyes."

"Religion?"

"She was probably a worshipper of Thor—or Odin."

"Thor?"

"Put, 'Pagan.'"

"Home address?"

"Unknown."

"Date of death?"

"End of July. Thirteenth century." There was no sound of any input device. "Circa July 31, 1250."

"*Time* of death?"

"Evening. The mosquitoes were out."

As I spoke, a videotape of her execution began playing inside me. Naked, led by a thong, she walks beneath the pearlescent sky while rooks shriek in the trees and grasses, ancestors perhaps of those very same birds we had seen the other evening. She feels the bath of evening sun, and the caress of the south wind's boneless hand seems to her sweeter than the touch of her lover. A mosquito bites her inner thigh. She doesn't feel it in her terror. Does she struggle, scream and beg for mercy? Doubtful. Not *this* lady. Her slippered feet strike the beaten earth as though driven by her destiny. Three priestesses accompany her. She is no victim of an angry mob. Hers is a sacrifice, a ritual killing, and apart from the gods and her executioners, the only witnesses are the gliding sky-larks and hungry rooks who, through some sixth, carnivorous sense, know when blood is about to flow.

Is she a willing victim? Maybe. It's Lammas Eve. The crops are fair, the housewives pregnant, the wheat as thick and blonde as hair. The gods must be thanked—and appeased.

Resigned, perhaps, if not wholly willing.

At the peat cutting, she falls to her knees and bends over, her hands tied behind her back. For a moment it almost seems like a sexual position—that the bound woman will be taken from behind. Instead, three blows from a hammer fall as the thong is cinched around her throat.

Senseless, she topples forward, even as her head is lifted up (loose strands of her hair stream down into the cutting) and her throat is stabbed. Blood geysers in the twilight and is caught in cups, spraying her killers and staining the bog. At once, her head is thrust beneath the water as her blood infuses the rank brown soup. Crimson bubbles blister the surface, when suddenly the body convulses and sits up, scaring the *bejesus* out of her killers, who quickly pin it down with stakes. Now all that can be seen above the bloody surface are her kneecaps and the tip of her nose. Forked sticks are pounded down upon her limbs. Then peat is laid over her and a boulder finally rolled on top.

"Cause of death?"

"Stabbed, strangled, beaten, drowned."

"Culpable party or parties, sir?"

"As of now, 'Unknown.'"

Chapter 8

I left the postmortem feeling drained and depleted, like a father who's just viewed his daughter's remains. It was odd. I'd examined any number of ancient bodies and never felt what I felt now. This one seemed so personal. What was my bond to this unknown woman, dead for nearly a thousand years? And why did I feel the need to defend her—and *avenge* her?

The telephone rang. "Donne?"

I lifted my head from the pillow. It was four fifteen a.m.

"She just came again."

"Who?" I was still only half-awake.

"You *know* who."

I sighed; I did.

"In the dream," (he was whispering; I imagined his wife asleep beside him) "I was lying beside her . . . in her *grave!* I knew what it was like being tortured like that, pinned to the bog for *centuries. Imagine!* Lying there, under the wet cold peat, while kingdoms rise and kingdoms fall! While the armada goes down, and the Roundheads and Jacobins fight over your head, and the wheel of the seasons turns . . . dead—*but somehow still alive!*"

"Wooland . . ."

"I felt her fury—and her *rage!* To be enchanted like that, held down by the stakes!

"Then she was dancing in utter abandon, naked, around the circle of stones. Oh, she's so happy to be released, to see the stars again, to taste the lovely English wind. She won't go back. She wants to *live*. Then, just before I woke, she said, 'If you won't have me, I'll go to Xan.'"

"*Xan*?" I repeated, nonplussed. Finally, I asked him: "And what do you think she meant by that?"

"Haven't the foggiest. Thought, perhaps, it was a city somewhere. You know, Fez, Balt, Xan—don't know. Listen, sorry to wake you. Jesus!" he added, by way of apology. "Look outside! How's a body supposed to sleep when the sun comes up from the bleedin' hills at four o' bloody clock in the morning?"

He rang off and I sat for some moments on the edge of my bed. So this, then, is how your madness begins: with a fact you neither can accept nor deny. Maybe it's your rape in the childhood dark by a man you thought was your kindhearted Uncle Charlie, and the threat of your death if you breathe a word—or the sudden, sickening intuition that your beautiful and beloved Mummy, with her pills, her lipstick and her pearls, doesn't give a shit about you, never has, never will.

For Xan is not a foreign city, but a diminutive of Alexander and the pet name I was called as a boy. The only person to call me it since was Jai. So how then had this creature known it? But listen to me: this *creature*. There *was* no creature! And I watched my paranoia spread like a spider web of cracks in the ice of reality—the hard ice on which we stand.

Eventually, I fell back to sleep and I, too, dreamt of Albemarle. She was seated beside me on a smooth wooden bench in the hospital basement. She was extremely quiet, simple and still, and we sat there, unmoving, reveling in each other's company. The light that fell through the clerestory windows was the soft, worn gray of old, Indian Head nickels. Our knees were touching and between us was the sweetest sense of easy union. In my dream, she was just a girl—no witch, nymph or claw-footed harpy—just a sweet, young, innocent girl, who was counting on me to solve her murder.

Chapter 9

The inquest into my Lady's death—at which I briefly testified—returned the verdict "unlawful killing." There was no attempt to ascribe motive or guilt. That was up to the Royal Commission. As its junior member, I was assigned the task of coordinating the different parts and parties to the investigation, a chore I readily embraced. For there were any number of ways to study my Lady: through linguistic analysis of the codex and inscription; or from a cultural-textile direction, by examining the weave and fiber of her clothing; or genetically, through her DNA. There was paleobotany, entomology, and the results of the postmortem.

The main thing was to accommodate the different specialties and not let any one discipline throw the study out of focus.

As for the treasure—which might have told us so much— it was not recovered. It seemed to have dematerialized into thin air—or returned, as the locals claimed, to the elfin realms from whence it came.

And so, my biggest hope for learning my Lady's history remained the Indic book. Yet, eight weeks had passed since I'd mailed it to Jai without a reply. My half-dozen calls had been answered by a recorded greeting, informing me Jai was "out of station." Though there was a record of the book's delivery, I chided myself for not calling him first and I worried constantly, imagining the irreplaceable manuscript on the floor of the Oxford University mailroom, lost beneath a welter of mail-order catalogues.

It wasn't until mid-July that an e-mail from Jai informed me he had been in India where he had gotten married. Through his marriage, which had been arranged, Jai had acquired a wealthy young bride "of royal blood and heart-pounding beauty" who brought with her a rich dowry, while she had obtained "an old prof with a pot belly."

Apart from his obvious joy in the matter and the fact that Jai, despite an Oxford education, truly believed in the values of his culture—I found the idea of an arranged marriage *trying*, at best, even when augmented by modern technology, as theirs had been.

I clicked on a multimedia attachment as my study filled with a whining *shenai* playing some extravagant oriental melody, while the monitor flashed with stills of the wedding. Jai wore a turban, looking every inch the *mahārāja*. The pictures of his bride were less clear. In most, her eyes were lowered as befits a dutiful Hindu wife, while in several others she was actually walking several paces behind her new husband in the most subservient and traditional manner—one that would make a feminist scream. Only in the last, poised atop an elephant, was she gazing at the camera, and the look in her eyes was riveting, wild. A postscript added:

> *By the way, received the book half an hour before I left. Took it with me to Mumbai and on honeymoon. Interesting. Why not celebrate our good fortune, meet the Missus and pick it up? Usual place. July 28; 8 p.m. RSVP. Om Shāntī.*
>
> > *Your,*
> > **Jai**

I found it maddening he didn't say more. What, if anything, had the book revealed about my Lady? And what was so damned "interesting"? The book or honeymoon? The whole thing was infuriating. But that's how Jai was. There was nothing for it but to go to London.

Before leaving, I met with the Royal Commission and we agreed not to speak about my Lady to the press until we had finished our preliminary study. For we all wished to avoid a repeat of the circus that often accompanies these extraordinary finds, such as the one surrounding Ötzi, the 5,000-year-old Tyrolean iceman who, upon his discovery, was identified as a shepherd boy dead from exposure in an autumn storm—only later to have his handlers concede he was a forty-five-year-old neolithic warrior who'd died in the spring from an arrow in his back, the head of which was still embedded in his shoulder! No, we agreed, such precipitous pronouncements gave forensic anthropology a bad name.

Afterward, in his office, I met with Strugnell to coordinate our efforts and access to materials while I was away. We also spent a few minutes looking at some snapshots of the treasure. Several pieces appeared unique—the most prominent being a large bracteate, or gold medallion, with a nick in its rim. Several small torcs were also visible, one made of three entwined gold strands, while the other two were likely formed of silver cylinders. Finally, though shadowed, the hilt of a sword was visible in profile, cast in the form of some fabulous, stylized beast. "Any progress with the investigation?"

But Strugnell indicated there was none. As I rose, he called me back to confide that he'd been to a hypnotist, a local woman, to relive his encounter with the drowning girl and to try to circumvent his amnesia. He asked me if I'd care to listen and before I could answer, tapped a button on his mobile phone, activating an audio file on which a woman's soothing voice was saying: "Sit back now and close your eyes. I'm going to ask a few questions. Don't edit. Just say the first thing that comes to mind. Ready? So, you try to save the drowning girl. She puts her arms around your neck and starts to pull you under. What happens?"

There's a long, searching silence. Then Strugnell's voice says, "She's pointing at the bottom. I can . . . see a light. Way . . . far away . . . . I'm having no trouble breathing."

"And the girl?"

"Her arm's around me . . . . She's . . . guiding me down."

"Down where?"

"Well, it takes a while, doesn't it? The water's getting colder, darker. I turn and look back up at the surface; it's the size of a bleedin' . . . postage stamp! Then . . . we're at her house. It's charming. The light is good. She . . . offers me something . . . I think it's wild honey."

"You eat it?"

"Oh, no. Fairy food, innit?"

"And then . . . ?"

"She shows me her bed. She wants me to . . . lie down with her."

"And?"

"I'm . . . *afraid*."

"Afraid of what?"

"Of her . . . of who . . . and what she is."

"And who is that?"

"Someone who . . . she *knows* things . . . about the crops, the beasts and stars."

"What happens then?"

"She's hurt and angered by my refusal. She begins to cry. Just like any woman. And then . . . she *curses me!*" he says, surprised.

"Curses you? How?"

"I . . . don't know. She's . . . angry! Super*naturally* angry!"

A full fifteen-second silence follows, at the end of which he sighs and says, "Returning now. Breaking the surface. Ah, but the air is sweet! Blinking. Sun's in me eyes." He taps the phone, as the audio stops.

"And who *was* this creature?" I ask him now.

"You know who. Your Lady Albemarle."

"And why did *you* see her? Was it by chance?"

"Oh, no. She called me. The way she's calling you."

"*Me*? I see. And why is that? Why *us*, I mean?"

"Don't be an idiot! You know damn well!" He looks at once furious and frightened. "We gave her her freedom. When we removed the bloody stakes!"

Part II

JAI

In traditional Hindu medicine
a fairy tale giving form to his particular problem
was offered to a psychically disoriented person,
for his meditation. It was expected that
through contemplating the story
the disturbed person would be led to realizing
both the nature of the impasse
and the possibility of resolution.

—**Bruno Bettelheim**
The Uses of Enchantment

Chapter 10

Jai Prasad was one of the world's foremost authorities on ancient Indic life and culture. His early work had transformed the course of Vedic scholarship, even if his rivals could credibly claim that Jai's success was due more to his predecessor's incompetence than to his own native wit. For all Jai had done was to translate the ancient verses *correctly*, pointing out along the way, in wry asides disguised as footnotes, the numerous errors made by the eminent Wilbur Liebecker, Stanhope Professor of Dead Languages at Ball State, in his translations of the admittedly difficult texts. Liebecker's sin, Prasad had shown, was that he had no understanding of the spiritual system from which the verses sprung—without which his exceedingly literal translations were as cryptic, naïve, ungrammatical and bizarre as those instructions in English accompanying Chinese radios.

> *Strive, break, O spotted, Tvāsthar!*
> *As to me, Bull, with the Moon*
> *He pours upon the six conjoined,*
> *Him increasing in his home,*
> *Brilliant like the sun,*
> *Serpents entwined in everlasting!*

Identifying this translation from the *Rig Veda* as typical of much of Liebecker's work, Jai had pronounced it (and the many more like it) *unintelligible*, as anyone could plainly read (but no one had had the nerve to say before), claiming, further, that only an unconscious contempt for the ancient peoples of the East would make one think their greatest bards and mystic seers had written such appalling *barf*, memorized it, and taught it to succeeding generations for the next three thousand years. "Him increasing in his home," *indeed!*

Then Jai had posed a provocative question: Would such a translation of *Western* religious literature be seriously offered? It was, he asserted, tantamount to translating the opening lines of the Bible's Gospel of John as:

> **Word was at start, Deity is,**
> **Was Word, and with Word Deity was**
> **Not cognizant of**
> **Envelope of darkness,**
> **Which was eating, not knowing . . .**

and then remarking, drily, upon the primitive obscurity of early Christianity.

Of course, if Jai was controversial, this was only to be expected in one whose career was a lifelong effort to pry prehistory from the Western-centric grip of American and European scholars—the nearsighted vision that relegates anywhere south of Crete and east of Baghdad as the rim of the universe, and credits the East (and the Chinese, at that) with a mere *two* of the planet's billion inventions: gunpowder. And *noodles!*

London was . . . well, *Loondun*, full of, among other things, many beautiful and stylish women. Just as all Gaul, according to Caesar, is divided into three parts, so womankind, to my way of thinking, is divided into two: those you would go to bed with and those you would not. I have always prided myself on the extreme restraint that allows the vast majority of human females to pass into the latter column. Though as I've grown older, I've watched my sense of discernment erode—either that or the girls are getting better looking—for the number in the first category increases yearly.

In fact, if viewed with a certain eye and distance, London is a continuous feast. There are so many delicious foods to taste, splendid and handsome clothes to buy, books for sale, people to meet, historic and elegant places to see, and comely women to make love to. Why then couldn't I walk through its streets continually tasting the best of everything, continually filling my senses with bliss?

I don't know—but I couldn't.

I checked into a boutique hotel in Chiswick. It wasn't a place one stayed for long on a research fellow's earnings, but then again, I didn't intend on remaining there, or a research fellow, long. I showered, changed into a summer tuxedo, the nicest suit of clothes I owned, and walked through the old-rose-gold and platinum twilight to Jai's flat. Once, I thought I was being followed, but chalked it up to a gibbous moon playing peek-a-boo between the buildings, rather like a pink balloon being drawn on a long, invisible string.

Jai's bride greeted me at the door. "It's Xan, isn't it? My husband asked that I fetch you the *instant* you arrived." She paused, then added with a shy, disarming smile, "I'm Vidya," and offered me a golden hand at the end of an arm as thin, bare and graceful as a tendril. She had bangles on her wrists, rings on her toes, and hands and feet inscribed with elaborate temporary henna tattoos, traditional for a Hindu bride: fronds, fruits and burgeoning leaves—symbols of fertility.

All in all, she was unbelievably lovely: sinuously sexy yet obviously refined. Her black hair, a dozen strands of it oddly braided with twisted strips of colored twine, swarmed around her brown shoulders like bees, and her eyes were the color blue that certain works ascribe to paradise. A yellowish diamond, small, but flawless, studded her nostril, while a thumbnail-sized emerald, green as Eire, sparked at her throat. It was a formal dinner and the new Mrs. Prasad was dressed for the occasion in a magnificent gold-embroidered *Kanjeevaram* sari worn in the most daring high fashion without the underlying *choli*, the fitted brassiere. The sari hid the front of her breasts, to be sure, but left bare their sides, exposing one almond shoulder and the delicate fluting of her ribs—so that while the other young beauties were equally uncovered, flaunting low-cut gowns with deep cleavages, it was Vidya's tan and tender sides that drew the men's stares and the women's daggers.

"What a bizarre fashion," a dowager whispered as Vidya and I passed by.

The new bride, who might easily have ignored the dig, flashed at the woman a smile of such wattage that the old lady froze like a deer in the headlights. "Oh, not at all," Vidya laughed, "it's *traditional*, really. It was the missionaries who made us wear *cholis*, so as not offend their Victorian tastes. Before that we were quite content with jewels (*jew-ells*) in a few strategic places."

Having defended both her dress and her countrywomen with an argument of such boldness and impeccable political correctness it could not be touched, she bowed graciously, threw me a grin, and, confident I was right behind her, headed off toward the den where Jai was holding court.

A vigorous, handsome, white-toothed man of extraordinary personal charm and charisma, Jai Prasad stood out in the world of academia like a movie star. At the conferences we attended several times a year, his entrance made the coeds' pulses quicken and sent shivers of excitement running through the hall. His lectures were always SRO—for if, as a scholar, he was controversial, as a teacher he was mesmerizing. Later, you would ask yourself what the hell it mattered if you now knew that *hag* had meant originally *holy* (as in *hag*iography, the life of a saint) and was applied to a woman at menopause when her "wise blood" was no longer lost, and that it was only much later—with the church's efforts to break the power of these "witches"—that it took on its current derogatory spin. Still, listening to Jai, it seemed to matter *vitally*, as if you were on the cusp of uncovering some secret set of correspondences that would connect all the dots and explain *everything*. Later, in the rheumy blue eyes of the crone who sold the evening paper, you saw someone staring back at you you'd never seen before.

The dean of students was speaking with Jai as Vidya smoothly inserted me into the conversation, saying, "Xander, I hear, is Jai's star pupil."

"He's more than that," Jai corrected her evenly. He gave me a warm and affectionate hug. "I'm grooming him to be my spiritual heir, and yet . . ."

"And yet?" the dean queried.

"Obviously, we're still in process. The training for that is still going on."

I was surprised by Jai's answer. Something was up, though now was not the time to pursue it.

Sensing the awkwardness, Vidya slipped her arm through mine, declaring there were a dozen guests to whom she *had* to introduce me, and whisked me off, employing for her purpose that excessively cheery neo-British manner we Americans so deplore.

And yet I found myself enchanted by her, and more than willing to stay by her side. She spoke a lovely, lilting colonial English, with a cadence less clipped and musically richer than London speech. Nor was she strictly *Indian*. Her family, I learned, were ex-patriots in Kenya, a part of the Asian community there. They were, I gathered, part of one of those clans who appear on the surface more British than the raj itself—with splendid, impeccable nineteenth-century manners and a father who is managing director of a firm that manufactures motor cars; and whose home in Mombasa is tastefully done in rattan and *vrai* bamboo with zebra throws and wildebeest heads, and pictures of an adorable, adolescent Vidya and the twin boys standing on a reviewing stand beside Lady Mountbatten in the African sun. Yet, if one ventured deeper into the house, one came across a grand *amma* sitting on the floor, chanting in Hindi before a *pūja* displaying the family deity, Kali, who brandished a sword while dancing on the body of her dead husband, Shiva, amid a welter of *kumkum*, smashed coconuts, burning camphor and sacred leaves.

At one point I followed Vidya out onto the balcony. The sunset over the River Thames, the soaring steeple of Christ Church and the unexpected lowness of the railing—or maybe it was the odor of Vidya's perfume, my manic mood or the three big whiskeys I'd just gulped down—made me nearly pitch into the street before steadying myself and ducking inside.

"Arranged marriages," someone clucked over dinner. (It was the crone who'd disparaged Vidya's outfit.) "I didn't know such things were permitted nowadays."

Vidya stiffened, as if a rod were lengthening in her spine. "Actually, it's quite civilized. Much more civilized than basing it solely on passion, don't you think? Look what happens.

~ 75 ~

The passion fades, the marriage founders. And then it's the children who suffer."

Everyone nodded over their mulligatawny. For how could one not, without seeming to favor the suffering of children? Jai, who had spent a lifetime defending his culture, nodded proudly.

Mrs. Vidya Prasad, I remember thinking, was going to make one hell of a faculty wife.

Most of the Indians I had known before Jai were physicians, newsstand owners, or computer engineers who had turned their backs on "superstition." What was different about Jai is that while he was a thoroughly modern fellow who dressed like a preppie in Gap work shirts, chinos, and kelties by Cole Haan—or, this evening, in a white silk Bijan tux that had cost *some*body three or four grand—he truly believed in the wisdom of the culture that had raised him.

Which was why he'd submitted to the apparent lunacy of an arranged marriage, I suppose; though I was beginning to think, gazing at Vidya, that his submission had the lunacy of genius.

Several times over dinner, I tried to get him to talk about the book. He wouldn't. In this way he was your typical East-ern trader. You couldn't just pay him and walk off with the goods; that would have been too simple and insulting. Instead, you had to sip endless cups of steaming *chai*, chatting about everything under the sun but the one thing you were inter-ested in before you could begin to get down to business.

When I pressed him on it, Jai demurred. "You don't really want to talk shop tonight, do you, Xan?"

"Shop? We're speaking about what could be one of the more significant archeological discoveries to come out of England in years."

"Oh, it's that, all right!"

I looked at him, at once heartened and maddened. "Can't you at least give me a hint?"

But Jai was as indifferent to my desire as the Lord Buddha was to his own. He only smiled graciously and shook his head.

"When?"

"Later. Now I have guests." And he returned to his soup and Beaujolais.

With the appearance of the duckling, brilliantly spiced with ginger and soy, the discussion moved to other ancient traditions such as the *svayamvara,* in which suitors vie for the princess bride's hand. Everyone agreed it was "gender-empowering."

"And then there's human sacrifice," I said, unable to resist lobbing a verbal grenade.

"Well," Vidya said, "and what's wrong with that?"

There was a dumbfounded silence, in the midst of which I raised my eyes. "You can't be serious, Miss Vidya," I said.

"Oh," she laughed, "*Americans.* You think if everyone has *enough to eat* and *a decent education,* they'll behave like good little boys and girls. Well, rot! Human beings, as you may have noticed, have an insatiable need for violence and gore. They *love* blood, love to see it spill and run. The Germans were fairly well-educated chaps, as were the Romans, Moguls and Brits. Didn't stop any of them from trying to conquer the whole bloody world and killing anyone who stood in their way. At least public human sacrifice channeled that need so that it didn't come out in less acceptable ways. After all, what would you rather (*rah-tha*)? A handful of criminals sacrificed to the gods, or several hundred innocent children shot to death in Brooklyn?"

There was another longish pause, during which Vidya challenged me with her eyes.

"Well, then," I said, raising my glass. "to arranged marriages. And to human sacrifice. All those in favor, say 'aye.'"

"Here, here . . ."

I turned to Vidya to make sure she was not offended. Her glass was raised like all the others, and she was looking straight at me with a cool blue gleam of pure amusement—or was it interest?—in her eyes.

Chapter 11

It was midnight. We were alone in Jai's study with snifters of brandy, sans the cigars. Jai was seated. I was standing. On the wall beside him was a wooden rack displaying half a dozen antique swords.

"So?" I asked.

Jai looked up but still said nothing.

"The *codex*, Jai. What is it?"

"Language? Old Gujerati with some Chagtai, Persian and even a smidgeon of Middle English."

"Ah! And what's it about?"

"Memoirs. Of an Indian prince."

"I see," I said, feeling somewhat deflated, for my hope had been it was about my Lady.

"Yes, you will see. I've translated it." He nodded. "It's practically all I've done for the past six weeks."

Again my interest flared, for I still hoped between the book and the body there must be *some* connection.

"Actually, Xan, I know a bit more about all this business than you suppose. Sir August rung me. Claims you lifted the book from a royal find, disturbing the sequence and context of the remains." He frowned. "Did you? And why would you do a thing like that?"

"Like *what*?" I bristled. "Anyway," I said, "the entire treasure was filched that night. In actual fact, I *saved* the damn thing."

Jai sat back and thought for a moment. "I also hear you blackmailed your way on to the Royal Commission. Threatened Rumple with a god-awful stink."

"Well?" I said. "I had to do *something*. He didn't seem to know who the hell I was."

Jai only smiled and in the silence that followed, I wished I could have taken my last remark back. His face darkened. "Listen to me, Xan: Until now, you've had it easy. Everything you've wanted has come your way: position, recognition, opportunity, acclaim. And it isn't that you don't deserve it. But there's a downside, too, to that kind of good fortune. You begin to think life owes you it. You've never had to face— or wait out—adversity." He held up a hand. "Don't interrupt. Then there are your chronic complaints about being single. But you've given precious little that I've ever seen to any woman who's wanted to change that. You forget I *know* you, Xan. I've seen you disappear into some trench in Crete whenever a woman has tried to claim you. Or are you still pining over that prima donna? Christ, Xan, that was *years* ago!

"Anyway, that's *your* business. But now, with this last bit, you've crossed a line. You claim to '*love*' anthropology, but don't submit to its most basic laws. Bloody Christ, you know it's about *context*: not *what* you find, but *where* you find it; what it's next to, above, below.

"And your sense of entitlement! Unreal! The police call you in to view a dead body and from that moment on, you, apparently, believe that the body now belongs to *you*. How dare the bloody *Queen of England* appoint a commission to study it that doesn't include *you*—and you've no hesitation in applying whatever measures are needed to get your way."

"It's called hardball, Jai—as opposed to cricket."

"Yes? Well, don't be fooled by Sir August's manner. He didn't become a Knight of the Realm by being a wuss." Jai pressed on. "Then there's the matter of a fourteenth-century manuscript that you so blithely dropped into the post—without anyone's prior knowledge or consent. You're a bleedin' *Yank*, Xan! What makes you think you can dispose of England's archeological treasures as you deem fit? Did you know it took me the whole of two mornings, a barrister's counsel, and all my powers of eloquence and persuasion to prevent the Yard's antiquities squad from clapping you in jail?"

I hadn't. No. Jai held up a hand.

"Happy to do it. After all, you're *my son*. I *love* you, Xan. And that's my point. When you love someone, you don't count the cost. You do for them whatever you have to do." He paused to let his words sink in. "Love is *sacrifice*, Xan. That's the whole of the Vedas—and the Bible to boot."

I rolled my eyes, but Jai only pushed back coldly and said, "Of course, that's something you don't understand because you've never sacrificed anything for anyone, have you? And you know why? I'll tell you why. Because you lack greatness, kingship, *largesse*. And if you stay that way, it's going to be your ruin!"

I looked up. I had no idea what to say. Jai had never, ever spoken to me this way before.

"I thought you were . . . compassionate, Jai."

"This *is* my compassion," Jai hissed back, ramming the volley back down my throat.

I was too stunned to even feel hurt. I thought for a moment. "What can I do?"

Jai sat back and smiled for the first time. "Well," he said, "you can change."

Chapter 12

I won't pretend that what Jai said that evening hadn't been said to me before. I *will* say *this* time I could not so readily dismiss it. For Jai was one of the few people I loved. In fact, when I was younger, I'd worshipped him. It was not just his brilliance, but his personal style—a zest and an elegance that had set him apart. Even in his poorest days as an instructor, he had managed to drive a Mercedes coupe, and he'd some-times worn an ascot (or "foulard" as he called it, the only man I'd ever seen on whom it didn't look asinine). And as marvelous as Jai was with people, equally marvelous was the way he handled *things*.

Once, he went shopping and returned with a single, forty-dollar silver teaspoon. It was all he could afford, but it was beautiful, lustrous and heavy as a trowel. He would take it from his pocket, wrapped in a handkerchief, and use it to eat his institutional meal. When he was done, he would dip it in his water glass, wipe it dry and replace it in his pocket. Jai claimed that next he would buy a fork, and then a knife, until he had acquired the entire eighty-piece set.

His superb library was ordered—not anal-compulsively, but in a most natural, logical way—and he didn't, therefore, spend hours, like me, looking for lost and misplaced texts. Though we were equally poor, Jai wore clothes of the finest fabric, and they were always clean and always mended, even if they were old.

He neglected nothing. Once when I remarked on this, he said, "I was taught that if something's yours, it's your duty to preserve it." And he went back to whatever it was he was doing, something I would never do in a million years: oiling the toaster or polishing a bowl.

Later he told me, "My family worships Vishnu. Vishnu is the preserver of the universe. He's not its creator or destroyer, but its sustainer. There's something wonderful about taking care of things, don't you think?"

"You mean *maintenance*?" I cried, in disbelief. "You mean getting your shoes shined, cleaning the refrigerator and washing the goddamn eighth-story windows? Are you *mad*?"

He smiled at me kindly. "I mean . . . *conservation*."

It got to the point where I loved to watch Jai handle *things*, almost anything. Just to see the way he picked it up and laid it down made you want to do the same (although when you did, it was nothing special, just a scarf of gray Irish wool, nice and all, but hardly the sensual treasure it had seemed to be between Jai's fingers).

Then there were Jai's ideas, which weren't like anyone else's. He'd once defined government as "the science of punishment," referring to the ancient secrets of statecraft by which a rajah rules his kingdom—and prevails.

And his most recent declaration, "Love is sacrifice." It wasn't a remark I myself could have made—springing, as it did, from a worldview as alien to me as it was venerable and old, one that harkened to the caves of Lascaux, Father Abraham, burnt offerings and flaming oblations of *ghee* and gold. Nor was Jai's wisdom book knowledge only. Born in Mumbai, schooled in London, he had traveled widely with a father in the Indian diplomatic corps. Young men tend to define themselves by what they've experienced, and I was envious of his many exotic (and erotic) adventures. Jai had not only sampled the girls of a Turkish brothel (one whore, Jai claimed, had slipped a pillow beneath her buttocks, something which at the time had seemed to us the nadir of depravity), but had spent a night in meditation in a Maharashtrian cremation ground.

"Someday, when my work is done, I'll retire to the forest," Jai once told me.

"What forest, Jai? Muir Woods?"

He laughed. "Hardly. I doubt the National Park Service would permit me to wander around it skyclad."

"You mean *nude*?"

"I mean clothed only in the wind and ether," he'd said, spoofing himself.

Despite his tone, I sometimes wondered if he wasn't serious. I imagined the distinguished professor emeritus wandering the woods bare-ass naked, living on roots and tubers. It was certainly a different model of retirement than that advanced by the Marin County Chamber of Commerce.

Now, for the first time, I considered what I'd done. It's true I'd disturbed the integrity of the trove—but the manuscript had flared before me in the dark, an archeological wonder I could have for the taking. I didn't think of myself as "entitled" and "indulgent," only "special" and "lucky," which were just other words for the same damn thing. Somewhere along the way I'd lost my humility, focus and perspective. Jai was daring me to get it back.

Then there was Vidya, whose face and form had haunted me since the party—though here, at least, I was fully aware of my pattern of attraction to unavailable women. The girls who'd loved me—and there'd been a few—never seemed to evoke in me that same wave of cosmic connection that the ones who hadn't did, and do. And I saw now it was an emotional trick to keep me from becoming involved with a real, live, flesh and blood woman instead of her romantic imago. I thought, now, too, how that was a part of my Lady's attraction: she was real, and she wasn't—and her demands were few. High class, low maintenance. Just the kind of girl I adored.

Part III

VIDYA

A similar experience befell Menippus,
a disciple of Demetrius the Cynic.
For as he was going from Corinth to Cenchreae,
he met one in the form of a beautiful foreign girl,
apparently very rich,
who said that she was smitten with love for him,
and in a friendly manner invited him to go home with her.
He in his turn was taken with love for her
and lay with her often and even began to think about marriage,
for she had a house decorated in a royal fashion.
But after Apollonius had examined everything in that house,
he exclaimed that she was a Lamia
who would quickly devour the young man entirely,
or afflict him with some notable injury.

—Nicolas Remy
Demonolatry

Chapter 13

In the early morning hours of July thirtieth, I was awakened by a phone call from Vidya Prasad, informing me that Jai was dead. She gave no details, only asking that I come to their apartment "straight away."

Ordinarily, I would have been skittish about walking the streets of London alone at that ungodly hour, but the spirit of death that had slithered through the wires accompanied me, its rod and its staff keeping lesser anxieties at bay.

I'd expected to see an ambulance or police, but the street before their mews was empty. Vidya answered their apartment door. She was stunningly dressed in a sheer white, gold-embroidered sari. There was blood on her hands. To my look of astonishment, she lowered her eyes. A bloodstain on her shoulder was in the shape of the state of Florida. The hall inside was overbright.

I followed her inside to Jai's study. What greeted us were flies. They orbited the room like a miniature, gleaming belt of asteroids. On the floor lay Jai, wounded beyond description. *Cut down*, I remember thinking. *Slain!* For the violence done unto him cried out somehow for archaic language to describe it.

I didn't check his vital signs. It would have served no end. Death was proclaimed by the stillness of his corpse. It looked bereft, its spirit fled. Jai's eyes were half-open, their blind whites half-showing beneath their lids like in portraits of *yogis* in *samādhi*. A pool of blood on his chest had dried at its edges, congealing like gravy. Everywhere was splatter: on the walls, rug, desk, ceiling. Hundreds of flies were clustered on Jai's face, drinking from his nose and eyes, so that it seemed as if his face were moving. I remember for an instant clinging to the notion that he had died naturally—fallen, perhaps, and cut himself on broken glass—and then in the next instant, admitting he'd been slaughtered.

"Would you care for some coffee?"

I looked at Vidya. She wasn't staring at the body but at some meaningless juncture of the floor and wall.

"Coffee?" And only then did I realize she was in shock. Her eyes were glazed, and as she turned and passed into the living room, she performed a series of meaningless rituals: fluffing pillows, straightening chairs, brushing nonexistent dust from the arm of the couch.

I turned back to Jai's corpse. He lay atop a shattered lamp, surrounded by the wooden splinters and spindles of the chair in which he'd apparently been sitting. A *shatoosh* shawl was wound around his throat.

The ancient book lay open on the rug before him. I recognized its vellum cover inset with semiprecious stones. Two drops of Jai's blood were drying on its leather, as though hardening into jewels themselves. Reflexively, I picked it up. I called to Vidya, "Did you phone the police?"

"Police?" she repeated, in a tone that clearly said she hadn't.

And so, I dialed 999. While it rang, I stared at the body of my mentor and dear, dear friend, and waited for something, a thud in my heart—but there was as yet only a smoke-filled vacuum.

"How may I help you?" an operator answered.

"Send the police. There's been a murder." I hung up. The 999 system logs the caller's address and I wasn't about to stay on the line to answer questions. I looked down once more at Jai, then backed out and shut the study door. For dying—like sleep, like making love—is something one does behind closed doors.

Vidya was in the kitchen, watching a coffee filter drip. I looked into her face—so beautiful and exotic—though marred now by a flicker of something like static electricity around her eyes.

Discovering I had the book in my hands, I placed it on the table. Vidya looked at it, but said nothing. "What happened?"

She shivered. "I . . . just found him . . . like that . . . when I came home."

"When?"

"Oh," she said fretfully. "Three thirty, four."

"In the *morning*?"

She looked about her, and I followed her eyes. The kitchen was extremely neat, except for a pile of torn circulars and magazines on the counter.

I looked at the clock. It was just after six. "And what have you been doing since?"

"Oh," she said stupidly. "Straightening up."

Jai's death had clearly pushed her over the edge.

Perhaps it had pushed me over it, too, for as our eyes next met, I was shocked to discover a palpable sexual tension between us.

I stood motionless. The material of her sari shivered. I don't suppose it was composed of anything so western as crinoline, and yet it made a noise like it as she shifted her thin and elegant limbs.

She looked at me. Then she sighed and surrendered herself, inviting me to her then and there. I cannot describe how she did this, other than to say she lifted and exposed her throat, tossing back her thick jet hair with a noise that is not in any syllabary, East or West, but is, indubitably, the syllable of desire. I don't recall approaching; I do remember crushing her to me, the sound her sari made in protest, and the sudden hot *wuhhhh* of her breath in my ear as it rushed from the delicate cage of her ribs. I opened her lips; her tongue was wet silk, so soft and indescribably thrilling that the fleshy petals of some exotic flower blossoomed in my belly and a suffocating intoxication made me nearly ill.

"This is . . . *mad*," I said and pushed her back. We looked at each other in disbelief, both amazed, I think, by the outrageous act. Our embrace so violated both our standards that it was, in the end, freeing. It had all the hallmarks of possession: the sense of being seized by some greater power that laughs in the face of all one's scruples, resolutions, ethics, plans.

"You have blood on you," I said at last, rather thickly.

"Oh," she said, holding up her hands. She looked at my shirt. "You do, too."

The doorbell rang and both of us started. Then I remembered I had called the police.

Chapter 14

Two plainclothes cops were standing in the hallway. I swear, they grow them for the job. Either that or promotion to homicide dick excites a gland that emits a hormone that turns your face into an Easter ham. "Someone here reported a murder."

"*I* did," I said, stepping back from the door.

"Lootenant Mick Houlihan," the first one pronounced in flawless Brooklynese. "And this here's Detective Sergeant Lee Raposo."

"You're *American*," I told Houlihan.

He looked at me mirthlessly. "So're you."

They entered. Houlihan had a presence about him: a looming, raw-boned menace to his movements that made one instinctively back out of his way. His one saving grace was a pair of crystalline eyes, pale as rain on the Irish Sea. They were at once outraged and wistful-looking, as if they'd seen more mayhem than any living soul has the right to endure but still hoped, against all hope, for a vision of the Virgin.

The one from the Yard was slim and dim. He had almond eyes and elephant ears from which depended long, Buddhistic lobes, like those mournful heads that lean from the sand on Easter Island. He was probably Italian. So why did the word Samoan come to mind?

Big as they were, filling the small foyer, they had a wonderful air of detachment about them, as if they were in the apartment, yes, but not of it; investigating a murder, yea, but not besmirched by it in any way.

I closed the door and led them down the hall to the study. I had expected them to be inured, but at the sight of Jai's body, Raposo sucked a breath as though slapped. The flies, aroused, boiled up from the corpse and began careening around the room, like numberless tiny black bats out of Hell. "Jesus, Mary and Joseph," Raposo said.

For his part, the New York Celt just stared at Jai for the longest time, then plucked and squished a fly from his cheek, adding, almost mournfully, "Better call the M.E."

"Who was he?"

"Dr. Jai Prasad."

Houlihan drew a notepad from his pocket. "What kinda name is that?" he wondered.

"Indian," I said. And so there'd be no confusion: "From India."

"You the wife?" the one from the Yard—Raposo—asked. Vidya nodded.

He continued: "Two of you *gank* him?"

I didn't understand him. Neither, apparently, did Vidya, for she said, "I don't know. I just found him like that. When I came home."

"From where?" Houlihan interrupted.

". . . the theater."

"When was that?" Raposo wondered.

"Oh, around . . . four."

"In the *morning*? That what time the theater quits?"

"No. I stopped off . . . for a drink."

"Uh huh. And where was this?"

"At an 'after hours' . . . I don't know which . . ."

"There's hundreds . . ." I added.

"You were with her?" Raposo asked.

"No."

Then shut the fuck up, he told me with his eyes.

"You alone? Friends?" Houlihan wondered.

"Alone," Vidya said.

"How long?"

"What? Oh, was I there? . . . some hours."

"Yeah?" Houlihan nodded. "And then what?"

"I came home. Found Jai . . . lying there. I called . . . Xan."

"Why him, not us?" Raposo asked, sounding almost hurt.

"I don't know," she said, quietly, in a way that would have melted any decent person's heart. "I . . . needed help."

The four eyes shifted in my direction.

"And you are . . . ?"

"Xander Donne."

"Relation to deceased?"

"Former student. Friend."

"Hey, you do this one together?" Raposo wondered, just like that.

"This one *what*?" I asked.

"Lee," the lieutenant begged, "go easy."

Lee just shrugged.

"Excuse me," I told Houlihan. "I'd like to have a word with you." And I stepped into the hall. The flies, disturbed, poured from the study and began to circulate the rooms.

Sighing with the effort, Houlihan got up from the arm of the couch, and followed me out.

I turned on him. "What in hell's the NYPD doing here?"

He gave me that flat, blank, gunmetal glare that cops reserve for just such questions: "Leeayzing."

"Great," I said. "Liaise all you want. But don't tell me you think that . . . that *girl* in there had something to do . . . with *this*." I waved in the direction of Jai's body.

Houlihan appeared transcendentally unmoved. "Lemme ask ya. You wouldn't be screwing Mrs. Vidya?"

"Mrs. Prasad," I corrected him. "And no, I wouldn't."

"'Cause you got her lipstick on your chin. You aware of that?" Instinctively, I reached in my pocket for a tissue. "Hankie, too," he said, eyeing it shrewdly.

"Look," I said, wiping my face, "the lady was . . . bereft. I . . . we embraced. It was . . . solace."

"She's about your age. And gentleman in the study, he's a good deal older than the two a you."

"What the hell does that mean? I don't know how old Vidya—Mrs. Prasad—is."

". . . twenty-six, -seven, maybe. And a very sexy twenty-seven, too. I mean, look it, I wouldn't blame you. By the way, what's that dot on her forehead mean?"

"That . . . she's married."

"Well," he sighed, "guess she's gonna have to redo her makeup." He sighed once more. "This Prasad. Now what kind of doctor of what was he anyway?"

"A doctor of linguistic and religious anthropology," I said, aware I had lost control of the conversation.

"Yeah? And who'd wanna kill a guy like that? Doctor Religious Anthology and all."

"I don't know," I said, pointedly. "That's what you're here to figure out. Remember?" I looked around. "Maybe it was a robbery."

He looked around, too. "Anything taken?"

"Maybe the murder weapon." I pointed to the rack of swords on the wall of the study. "Two nights ago, there were four swords there. Now there's three."

"Anything else?"

"I wouldn't know. You'd have to ask his wife."

"Doesn't look like a robbery, less they knew what they wanted."

"Look," I said, disturbed by the general tenor of the conversation. "You're not suggesting . . . ?"

Houlihan shrugged. "Don't really know *who* did it. Do we?" he asked, pleasantly enough. "It's just . . . the energy." He seized on the word. "Daughter, Celeste, she's always saying things to me like, 'Daddy, I don't like his energy,' or 'There's something bad with the energy there.' *Energy*, for cryin' out loud." He chuckled to himself. "When I was a kid, energy was friggin' *coal*, know what I mean? Now . . . anyway, that's the problem, least ways I see it. Something's funny with the *energy*. I mean, guy's dead, cut to ribbons, and you and the wife are sitting around like youse just swallowed the fucking canary."

"Maybe we're both in a state of shock."

He appraised me coolly for a moment or two. "Yeah," he nodded, "could be that."

Some years back, in my student years, when "liberation" groups were proliferating daily, some wags got together one night on drugs and founded one called Dead Liberation. "Treated like dirt," their manifesto read: "Can't work, can't vote, the most downtrodden folk on the face of the earth."

Now, watching a small army of forensic technicians invade the apartment, I saw that what they'd said was true; at least it was for murder victims. Having been deprived of your life, you forfeited all your other rights, too: your drawers were searched, your mail opened, your wife questioned, your pockets turned inside out, your bank statements analyzed, the dirt beneath your fingernails culled and your hands sealed in Ziploc bags—even your genitals swabbed for emissions— while at the autopsy to follow, your liver and lights would be weighed in the balance, like some *bardo* procedure in *The Book of the Dead*.

I went to the kitchen and sat down beside Vidya. She squeezed my hand, and instantly, I felt better. For wretched as everything was at that moment, there was this other thing in the air between us. Whatever it was, it cast a glory light and weird, sweet beauty upon the sorry business all around us: the technicians dusting for prints, the ringing phone, the constant traffic.

Houlihan returned, requesting that we come down to the station and make a statement.

"Mrs. Prasad's solicitor will be joining us."

"Hey, whaddaya, whaddaya need a lawyer for?" he complained. "We just wanna axe ya couple of more questions."

"You already did. And maybe if you and your friend from the Yard hadn't framed them as accusations, we might be feeling differently. But you did, so we don't. You want anything else from us, talk to our attorney."

For their harassment was outrageous. Jai had been butchered in a frenzy by some maniac wielding a sword or machete. One of his hands was almost severed at the wrist. A great red medallion of blood, like molten metal, was pooled on the floor, hardening along its edges. I had no intention of being bullied or of allowing Jai's widow to be victimized by New Scotland Yard and New York's Finest, even as his body rotted in the study.

For Vidya was a stranger in a strange country; it was my duty to protect her. Jai would have wanted me to. And there arose in me a wondrous energy: masculine, mustachioed and patriarchal.

And anyway, I was in love with her by then.

Chapter 15

The Chiswick stationhouse was not what I'd expected, which was something more circus-like and Runyonesque: arguing prostitutes posed in doorways, telephones ringing, bearded men in inexplicable pink pinafores, weeping. It wasn't like that. It was one of those modern amalgams of brick, glass and metal so abhorred by the Prince of Wales that manage to look too new for the neighborhood and rundown at the same time.

Vidya was, incredibly, still wearing her bloodstained sari. She reminded me of Jacqueline Kennedy, following her husband's assassination, in that pink suit with black piping. The difference was that Jackie had a nation's sympathy while Vidya, apparently, had none but mine.

My statement wasn't long. I wrote down exactly what had happened with two key omissions: our passionate encounter and the bloodstained book. After that, I waited a very long time.

Finally, Houlihan appeared. He looked pissed off. "Girlfriend's gonna be a couple more hours."

"Not my girlfriend."

"Yeah, you told me. Why don't I believe you?"

"The real question is: how you can think she had anything to do with that? Christ, man, you know splatter. You cut someone up like that, you end up looking like a Jackson Pollack. But except for some transfer, her clothes are clean."

Houlihan remained profoundly unmoved. "Coulda changed them." He leaned in so close I could smell his cologne. "Knew this lady once, 'porter for the *Post*? Did a story on this maniac what chopped up a waitress and afore you know it, she's trumpetin' his cause. I said, 'Fuck is this, Margaret, you think this guy's *innocent*? They found him, right? He's walkin' down a country highway, waving *body parts* at passing cars. Where he get Susan Radford's *arm*, he didn't do it?' Know what she says? '*I know his heart better than you ever will and he never could have done such a thing.*' And that was that. Evidence don't matter. And this was *not* a stupid lady. So you see? *Denial*. Hell of a thing."

Jai's solicitor arrived around noon. I left the station and took a cab to the hotel. I wanted to bathe, not my flesh so much as my mind and memory, to delete from it the sight and smell of Jai's body. Then I'd return for Vidya.

But once in my room, the emotional force of the morning's events finally hit me, and I wept like I hadn't wept in years. It didn't feel like grief so much as pure emotion, as though Jai's death and Vidya's kiss had unstoppered my heart and the precious oils of *all* my feelings—feelings of love, feelings of horror, feelings I hadn't known were there—were spilling out.

They scared me. They were overwhelming. I really couldn't handle all of them now. Even my sudden love for Vidya, while intoxicating, felt frightening. If I let it in, where would it take me? Where would it lead, if I let myself go? And yet I also felt an animal alertness. For someone close had just been murdered and Houlihan's vibe had a dangerous edge.

I showered, shaved and was getting dressed when Vidya rang. Her questioning was over with and, for now at least, she was free to go.

I returned to the stationhouse. A policewoman accompanied us to the apartment, where Vidya was allowed to remove her sari (which was impounded) and to pack her toiletries, along with several changes of clothing and, from the safe, her jewels, which she refused to leave. As the flat was a crime scene, she could not remain, and I insisted she return to my hotel, at least until we could sort things out.

We hailed a cab. No sooner had we entered my room and the door shut behind us than Vidya reached into the folds of her *salwar kameez*—a loose-fitting tunic emblazoned with miniscule mirrors over drawstring pants—and brought out the ancient book.

Her presence of mind to snatch it from beneath the noses of the cops was impressive. And I found myself moved that, in the midst of all her hurt and horror, she'd extended herself for me this way.

"So . . ." I said, "they give you a hard time?" It was the first chance we'd had to speak privately.

"*Rah-tha.*"

"What did you say?"

"The same thing I'd said before. Not that they believed me. The *leftenant*," she added, "claimed that you had 'spilled your guts.' And that if I didn't 'come clean,' I was 'going down.' I wasn't certain what any of that meant, but it *did* sound disagreeable. Jai's solicitor advised me not to answer. He accused them of trying to coerce a confession. But I didn't mind. I told them there was nothing to which *eye-tha* of us would confess, as there was nothing criminal *eye-tha* of us had done."

I nodded. "Thank you for your vote of confidence. So, if we didn't do it, who do you think did?"

She shook her head.

"Because it doesn't look like a robbery, Vidya. And I find it hard to believe it was some kind of fluke. I mean, could it be . . . *political?*"

"Such as . . . ?"

"I don't know. Was Jai . . . a *spy* or something?"

This was not so far-fetched as it sounds. For years, anthropology was practically a subsection of the national intelligence agencies, for who better than an anthropologist has a reason to wander about the remote parts of a foreign land? And if on the way to your site, you happen to pass a military convoy or snap a wonderful desert view (with an atomic facility in the background), well, of course, you're going to share it with your government, especially since it's helping finance the dig.

"I met Jai seven weeks ago. You were his friend for many years. You would know far better than I. Jai was an intensely private man. Even on holiday, he spent many hours alone on some project. He could have been colluding with double ought seven, for all I know."

He certainly could have. Though more likely it would turn out to be not that way at all, but one of those tragedies that make life look like a crapshoot, with snake eyes rolled in the form of the super's son on leave from the bin who just happens to be visiting his dad that evening, bringing with him all his homicidal urges.

Yet even this scenario was preferable to another. For what if Jai weren't the intended target? What if, because of her past, her beauty, or something about her that I didn't yet know, it was *Vidya*—and Jai had simply been in the way?

I laughed, nervously. "You're not a spy yourself, are you?"

"For whom? *Kenya?*"

Put that way, it did seem doubtful.

"I'm sorry," she said. "I know you mean well. I'm just—knackered. Let me make some calls, and I'll be out of your hair."

"Vidya," I said. "You're not leaving. There's plenty of room here. I'll sleep on the couch."

"You're kind, but I won't intrude. Anyway, this is the last thing you need. These scandals have a way of . . ."

"I'm not concerned about scandal. I'm concerned about you. The last thing you need right now is to start schlepping yourself all over London, looking for a place to stay."

"Look," she said, and took a breath, dropping into a deeper gear. "I've thought about this thing . . . with *us*, I mean. I don't know why that happened as it did. But whatever the reason, now is not the proper time . . . what with . . . *everything* else that's going on."

"Thank God, " I said. "Someone, at least, has their wits about them. I couldn't agree with you more. Our timing was so . . . disrespectful. I'm sorry . . . I . . ."

She waved me silent, while coming closer and clutching my open shirt with her hand. "It was both of us. And the shock. But no one would understand that. Everyone else is bound to see it as the purest perversity—or some sort of desecration."

"Well, of course, they would. And who could blame them?"

I took her hand and removed its clutching fingers. They made me tense—though I failed to let them go.

Vidya cocked her head and looked at me then with such an appealing sweetness that I shivered. "Well," I said. "I'm glad that's settled. I feel better already."

"Yes," she agreed, "and so do I." And she gave a pained, unhappy sigh.

What happened next, I'm tempted to pass over. For our bodies suddenly snapped together, as though compelled by a *force majeure*. I covered her face and throat with kisses. I found her mouth and unlocked the vault of her throat with my tongue.

There was nothing cool or regal about her. She made sounds out of Africa and left bite marks on my shoulder.

And in the midst of it all, it began to storm. Lightning flared. Thunder rattled. The rain came down in wind-whipped sheets. Afterward, lying on the rug beside her, listening to the violent wind and weather, I felt content—and, despite Jai's murder, happy—for the first time in my life.

While Vidya dozed, I opened my laptop. A new e-mail from Jai gave me a shock, until I saw it was sent the previous evening. There was no message. Yet it contained Jai's parting gift to me: his translation of the ancient codex. And so I opened up the attachment and read:

Sikandar Shah Nama

Or

The Adventures of Sikandar Shah

Oddly or not, Sikandar's name was the eastern edition of my own.

Glory be to You
Who raised me up,
Whose greatness knows no limitations.
The loveliness of the girls in all the worlds,
including those in Heaven's harem,
are rose petals
scattered in the dust of the road
that leads to the Garden of Your Infinite Beauty.
The paths of Scholarship & Religion
are vanishing goat-tracks
in the desert of Your Being;
Poetry, one impoverished village
in the infinite country of Thy Name.

This is the story of Sikandar ibn Musa Khilji al-Hind,
Prince of Hindustan.
It is the report of a Caravan
from the Palace of Splendor
To the Tavern of Ruin
Made by the Caravan Master's slave,
(God bless him!)
Who cries:
*"I would give up
the thrones of
Samarkand and Rome
for the black mole
on my Beloved's thigh!"*

I invite you, Reader, to drink of this cup.
It will cost you nothing.
The grapes & I have already paid for it
with our lives.

I found this invocation rich and inviting. Yet before proceeding further, I checked on Vidya. She was sleeping deeply. Happy to see that, I returned to my computer and crawled through the monitor and into the tale, though had I known what I know now, I would have thought two or three times, surely, before slipping in that digital door.

It was daybreak in Rajasthan when, leaving my companions swaddled in sleep and the smoky shawls of cooking fires, I rode out with 'Abd al-Wali Mirza to reconnoitre the Indore border in preparation for the evening's raid. It was rough, high desert. The air was thin, and in the elbows of the creeks and streams there were hot white boulders. We saw few people, save for some poor villagers. And so when we encountered the mysterious tower *brimming* with soldiers, we dismounted swiftly, in amazement and alarm, and hid behind a nearby hill.

But though we watched for half a *ghari*[1], the sentries' heads never flinched, blinked, turned, or spoke to one another, but stared relentlessly off at the surrounding hills.

It was not until 'Abd al-Wali passed me the glass, the illusion was dispelled. For by its grace, I could make out now that the soldiers' heads were carved from stone, and rising and striking the dust from our *kurtas*, we went down the mountain to the ground on which the tower stood.

But as we approached, I received another shock, for the heads were not the work of art—or magic. No. They were the *heads of men*, severed at the neck and implanted in the masonry in parallel rings. I had heard of such "pillars of victory" before, but had never seen one, this being my first campaign, and circling the tower in the auspicious manner[2], I inspected the heads more carefully. They were Rajputs[3] one and all, and were filmed with a fine grey grit. It was this that had given them the illusion of stone.

I studied one: the head of a boy no older than myself with a moustache like black down. His cracked and swollen lips were puckered as in a kiss and his eyes closed as though he were dreaming.

Above him, set into the crest of the tower, its architect proclaimed:

Jafir Bahadur Ghazi,
Ruler of the Universe,
Shadow of God on Earth,
Chief of the Circumcised,

---

1. Translator's Note: a *ghari* equals twenty-four minutes
2. *pradakshina*: circumambulating clockwise
3. *Rajput*: the dominant warrior caste of Rajasthan

Cherisher of the Poor,
Light of this World,
Lord of the Islands,
Raised this Pillar
To commemorate
His Victory over
The Infidel Wretch
And Son of Misfortune
Mul,
King of Indore.

Clearly, my brother Jafir had been here.

Chapter 16

The memoir had such a gruesome gravitation, I had to pull myself away. Though, even then, the hideous pillar continued to disquiet my imagination. The scene of the action, Rajasthan, was in the Indian northwest, not far from two archeological digs I had worked across the Pakistani border. The question was, what did the book have to do with my Lady? Rajasthan was 6,000 miles from Dorset.

I ordered up dinner, but Vidya didn't touch her seafood salad. "Look, I can order something else . . ."

"It's brilliant. It's just . . . I don't think I'll ever be hungry again."

I studied her. God, she was lovely. Her face had the sheen of beaten gold, a hint of the Timurid or Hun in the cheekbones, and a dramatic Indian nose that flared like a sail and led her face like the prow of a ship. It had a daring yet delicately thin and hawk-like line, almost Egyptian in its profile.

Now she produced a battered pack of *Silk Cuts*. I lit one for her and she sat for a while, smoking, saying nothing, staring off at Turnham Green, letting the smoke drift from her lips to her flared nostrils. It was something I believe is called "French inhaling."

"Where'd you learn that?"

"What? Oh," she said, dashing out the butt. "A stupid trick. At convent school."

"You're *Catholic*?"

She shook her head. "It was the best school in Nairobi." She looked apologetic. "I don't smoke—anymore. I just threw these in my bag."

I laughed. "You mean, they belong to some *cop*?"

She smiled wanly.

"Let me ask you something."

"You may ask," she said, stabbing another cigarette between her lips in a way that did not promise an answer.

"When did you find Jai?"

"Midnight," she said without hesitation, pluming the smoke past my ear.

"So you weren't at the 'after' like you told the police?"

She looked surprised. "You don't really think I go out drinking alone until four o'bloody clock in the morning." She gave me a look that said if I did, I was an idiot. "I was there for a moment round *hof* eleven."

"But why do that?" I said. "Lie, I mean?"

I waited. No answer was forthcoming. Finally, I asked, "Are you sure of the time you got back home?"

"The clock in the hall was striking twelve."

"And . . . ?"

Again, I waited for some explanation about why she'd lied, or what had happened next, but she offered none and finally—it was like pulling teeth—I asked, "And what were you doing between midnight and the time you called?"

She paused, then stubbed out the half-smoked fag. "I'm afraid I *cahn't* tell you."

I found this retort incomprehensible, considering how critical her answer was. Was I expected to take her innocence on faith, without even a clear and convincing explanation? I thought for some moments. "Can you give me a *hint*?"

She held my gaze steadily, then looked away. "Whilst in Mumbai, we stopped at a shop for antiquities. The shopkeeper was an old mate of Jai's. There was the usual palaver and the sipping of *chai*. And that's when Jai brought out the book."

"Book?"

"The one you sent him." She looked me in the eyes. "The *enchaunted* one."

I looked into hers. "You mean, *enchanting*, don't you?"

She sat back, looking half-amused. "My dear man, I am not some villager whose first language is Gujarati. I am well aware of the different meanings connoted by its past and present participles."

"And how would a book become enchanted?"

"How? By *chaunting* over it, I presume."

I felt a sudden strange *frisson*. She reminded me of an urban archeological dig. At street level stood a modern building with elevator banks and computerized lighting, but if you went to the cellar and dug in the foundation, you came across nameless ritual objects, the buried bones of sacrificed sows, stone phalluses and other bizarre, primordial things.

"And what did the dealer say?"

"He looked it over carefully. He even prized out a jewel and examined it beneath a lens. In the end, he pronounced it quite authentic."

"Authentically enchanted?"

She didn't smile. "The authentic memoirs of an Indian prince."

"I have the translation. Jai e-mailed it to me last night."

"You've read it?"

"Just a bit."

"Ah, do," she requested. "And now, if you'll excuse me."

"Tonight," I pronounced, "we cross the border to Indore."

Ghazil raised his eyes; concern deepening his brow. "Our orders," he said, "are to proceed due south." He

turned and squinted off at the horizon. "Even your brother went no further than this."

"I know," I said. "I saw his mark." And I described to him then the pillar of victory.

"Ah, ha!" Ghazil said with a sudden bark, as though recalling something marvellous. "I haven't seen one of those in years!"

"It's a barbaric custom that was almost lost. Happily, it is being revived by our family."

Ghazil savoured my insolence. Then he intoned, "Such things serve a purpose."

"Yes," I said, "to nauseate." For the smell of the heads wouldn't leave me alone.

"So you think it is wise? Raiding Indore, I mean?"

I turned in its direction. Star sapphires, pigeon-blood rubies, emeralds of the finest water, amethysts, carbuncles, garnets and gold were all mined from her rich, dry waste, so that if one had possessed that enchanted collyrium, which allows one to view the treasures of the earth, instead of a desert—tan and severe—you would have seen streams of Indian silver and frozen underground rivers of gold flowing through a glittering jewel-studded garden! Indore was, as the poet said, "a hell full of good things."

On the one hand, I couldn't blame Shri Ghazil. As my vizier, it was his office to question whatever I did, so that thought would be brought to our least endeavours. Still, it annoyed me. Just once I would have loved to hear him respond, "Yes, a wonderful idea!" But Ghazil is not like that and never will be.

And anyway, the true goal behind our entry to Indore was, I knew, neither jewels nor intelligence. Nor was it ivory, silks, silver, gold nor moonfaced maidens of a marriageable age to adorn my father's court and harem. Its purpose was even more pure and primeval: to cover ourselves with blood and glory, so we could ride like the wind, feel the night in our hair, test our mettle, flesh our swords and enact our youth upon the plains of Hindustan the way Ghazil had enacted his upon the sands of Aragon. The problem with Ghazil was that he was always attempting to find rational reasons to support the instinctual.

The nature of a hawk is to soar through the ether. You may say, if you wish, that it is gathering intelligence on the disposition of the pigeon population—but its wings, lost in the joy of their soaring, know no such thoughts or bounds.

Chapter 17

Say what you will about death, it's empowering. Tragedy, like some great, black Germanic banner, unfurls eagle wings in the sky of your life, obliterating, for a time at least, the dust-gray rags of everyday existence.

This, at least, is how I felt upon waking: as if, while I'd slept, the world had been dipped in a liquid significance. It was a feeling I hadn't had since the night that we'd recovered my Lady. Then I realized it was more than just Jai's death that had touched me; it was *love.* For Vidya.

I got up, showered, dressed and went down to the lobby. I wanted to read what the newspapers had to say about the murder, but after buying several, as I was turning to go . . .

"Morning," Houlihan said right behind me. "Widow awake?"

"Let the poor girl sleep. She's done in. What's your *problem*, Lieutenant?"

"S'not me with the problem. It's her. See, nobody remembers her at the 'after', except for a minute or two around eleven when she come in to use the phone. No one remembers her after that. And *that* ain't possible. Or are you telling me this *babe*, dressed in a gold *robe*, wearing a *dot* between her eyes, sat *four* friggin' hours *alone* at a table and *nobody* approached her? *Nobody* tried to pick her up? If ya think that, fella, you're not fully aware of the effects of testosterone and are a lost soul in a strange world."

I sighed. "What does it matter *when* she got home? She didn't *do* it."

"Odds say she did. Murder takes place at the victim's residence between midnight and six a.m.? S*pouse* did it—usually. While the *second* most likely person is the one who phoned it in." He grinned.

I rolled my eyes.

"Time of death's been established 'tween eleven and three. She got a *reasonable* alibi for those hours, we'd like to hear it. So as we can cross her off our list, get on with our investigation. Then again, we'd like to hear yours: 'Asleep alone in my hotel room' don't really cut it.

"Anyway it is now, she had plenty a time to go home, do the dirty, lose the weapon and after cleaning up and calming down, decide she didn't want to spend the rest of her life staring out a window in the British equivalence of Kerhonkson, New Yawk or Shawangunk or some other godforsaken upstate facility. Don't blame her; wouldn't wanna neither."

"Listen," I said, "if she were going to kill her husband, why would she do it like that? With a six-hour hole that she can't account for?"

He thought for a moment. "Maybe it was *your* idea."

"Me?" I said. "And what was *my* motive?"

"Girl like her, some guys want so bad they go a little crazy. I mean, hell, I'm sure you thought about it—what it'd be like. And I don't mean just between the sheets, though I can't say that would hurt too much, eh?

"With a woman like that, the world treats you different. Guys look you over twice, and all the chicks wanna know what you got in your pocket 'cause you must be hot, be with a babe like her. Walk in a joint? Hey, you're guaranteed a table. *Maître d*'s *love* dolls like her: gives a place *tone*. Then again, she's loaded. You aware of this?" He sighed, as if the fact depressed him. "Yeah. Thought maybe she'd knocked him off for his *shekels,* but it's *her* has got the dough."

"How much could she possibly have?"

He looked at me. "Sorry. I can't divulge that information."

"Lieutenant," I said, with as much composure as I could muster, "why don't you go back to Coney Island? Leave this thing to Scotland Yard."

"Can't. I got another three weeks . . ."

I turned on my heel.

"Hey," he said, stopping me with his fingers—a thumb and a pointer that closed on my shoulder like a vise. "Be *nice.*"

"*You* be nice," I said, removing his hand and starting off again.

"Donne," he shouted after me, "you sleeping with her?" The concierge and several of the hotel's guests paused in midbusiness to await my reply.

"Lieutenant, if I were, you'd be the last to know."

"Well, if you are," he said, "or planning on it, sleepin' with her, I mean, lemme give ya word a warning."

"No, thanks."

He gave it, anyway, to my back. "Sleep lightly."

Chapter 18

Vidya was awake and had ordered breakfast: coffee with heated milk, rolls and sweet papayas. Despite it all, it was a lovely morning and I didn't wish to spoil it by uttering Houlihan's unholy name. The sunlight, pushing past the blowing curtains, was hot on our faces, and where it touched the crystal glasses, little brilliant rainbows fell. We ate, talked, and sipped for hours, cried about Jai and laughed over nothing, immersed in that joy that comes to new lovers—a joy made all the more precious by our awareness we were on an island in the stream of time and would soon have to face the bloody mess all around us. Yet despite the past and our threatened future, in those moments, taking breakfast with Vidya, drinking in the wine of her presence, I felt happy— truly happy—for the second time in my life.

Now, as she rummaged for something in her wallet, I noticed a photo of a younger, plumper Vidya Prasad standing by a lake backdropped by snow-capped mountains. She was dressed in a wool suit quietly tailored to her curves, her shoulders shawled by one of those intricate, brilliantly printed Hermès silk scarves. "Which one's Everest?"

"None—as they happen to be the Swiss Alps." She paused. "This photo was taken at Montreux—on Lake Genève."

"And what were you doing in Switzerland at the time?"

"Posing for this picture."

"Before and after the picture was shot."

"Attending university."

"Really," I said, jumping upon this crumb of information. "What school was that?"

"I was studying," she said, "political science." She waited a beat. "I had this dream—fantasy, really—I could do some good for my country, Kenya."

"And . . . ?"

"My efforts were met with incredible resistance."

"What kind of resistance?"

"Oh. Racialism. Extortion. All manner of red tape."

"Such as?"

"Such as HIV-positive air force colonels who demanded I bonk them before they would grant me a certificate of occupancy for a one-room native school."

"You sound bitter."

"Yes? Well, I'm not." And with a quick kiss to both my cheeks, she disappeared to shower and dress.

I spent another several minutes drinking in the love I felt for her. It felt divine. Then I opened up the papers and my happiness departed. For in one was a story by a celebrated "Irish" New York writer, whose hard-boiled, somewhat schmaltzy style conveyed what he called "the human side of the headlines." Today's was entitled:

CLUELESS

The Professor   In the Study   With the Knife

He was Jai Prasad, one of England's top scholars. She was Vidya, his young, royal, and beautiful new wife. They should have been sublimely happy, and perhaps they were, until into the picture slipped Xander Donne, an American anthropologist and ex-student of Prasad's. "Donne was the son Jai never had," said Assistant Dean Claude J. Remus, "and like some sons, he was a disappointment. Jai had been grooming him to continue his work, but recently there had been, by all accounts, a serious rift between them."

Several witnesses noted a palpable tension between adopted son and surrogate dad when on July 28, Donne attended a wedding dinner at the professor's London home.

The following evening the professor was murdered. In his study. Not with a candlestick. Or even a knife. Hardened police investigators are appalled by the wild attack, which appears to have been made with a sword or machete. Several of the good doctor's fingers were found beneath the sofa.

Whodunit? Who knows? Such crimes have become a staple of life in this and other cities. New Scotland Yard is not without leads, however.

The body was allegedly discovered by the royal widow and reported to police by the prodigal son, who just happened to be visiting the dead man's home at 6:07 in the morning!

One of the more distinguished guests at the professor's wedding dinner the night before confides, "We were all looking forward to meeting the bride. She's royal, you know. And, I will say, she fits the role. Still, there was something odd going on. She seemed to be taking such an interest in Donne. And he, in her. It was . . . bizarre. Of course, the marriage wasn't a love match, you understand, but arranged."

When O when will we ever learn, folks, that nothing but love joins two people together?

As of last night, senior police investigators were openly speculating that the young stepmum and surrogate son did the old man in. Why? "Try lust," a source in the department says. According to police, both wife and ex-student, who eluded all attempts by the Big Guy to reach them, have denied involvement in the slaying. They have, nonetheless, retained a criminal attorney and are cooperating with the investigation "reluctantly," says a source. In fact, it's feared they may have fled.

Where to? Mrs. Prasad's lawyer declined to comment.

And, as of now, police haven't a clue.

I was stunned, then appalled, then absolutely livid. It was amazing how, without offering up *one shred of hard evidence*, the columnist had managed to convict us of murder—using even our lawyer as proof of our guilt.

Yet more disturbing was the realization that this story was only the preface to our arrest—a chumming of the waters of public opinion, so to speak, so that when the collar was made it would be greeted with the appropriate applause.

I know the smell of shit coming at me. And I wasn't waiting till it hit the fan. I phoned the front desk and announced we were checking out. For I was *damned* if I'd let them arrest us for murder! Even if we were granted bail, tried and eventually proven innocent, we'd begin by spending a couple of weeks in some human sewer like Brixton prison. Plus I had something called "work" to do. As for Jai's funeral, Vidya had been informed that they wouldn't be releasing the body until they'd concluded a battery of tests.

And so I decided we'd head for Dorset, intent on putting several shires and as many borders as I could between ourselves and the salivating metropolitan police. Oh, we could still be arrested. But why make it easy? Our local constabulary was notoriously territorial—and resentful toward New Scotland Yard. In the meantime, I intended to use every law enforcement, legal, academic, diplomatic and civil contact I could think of to get Houlihan & Co. to back off—or, at least, to think twice.

Vidya's reaction was to listen to my plan, then nod in agreement. There were no arguments, questions, or panicky looks. Coming from a third-world country gave her few illusions, I think, about the benefits of police custody.

She packed us both, and while she did, I dipped back in the "enchanted" book . . . .

I ordered auspices be taken and, as they were favourable, I went to my tent and worshipped my weapons. I bowed to my sword, *Tears of the Widow*, asking her protection and that she never be wetted by innocent blood.

When I was done, I watched the priests perform the ritual offerings of fruit, water, leaves and ghee, even as they invoked the Mother's Thousand Names[1]:

> She places Her children on the thrones of kingdoms,
> both earthly and spiritual;
> Power of royal abundance;
> Queen of this body;
> Ruler of the four divisions of the army;
> O, Giver of empires!
> Abode of Truth.
> You who never break Your word!

By the time they were chanting name 835, She Who Exists in Remote and Lonely Places, we were mounted and prepared to go, our horses dancing in anticipation.

Dusk had fallen. It was that moment when the sun has set but its light has not yet fled the air, and the sky still brims with an opalescent splendour. Adding its rays was the jewel of the moon.

We followed a track, breathing through the ends of our turbans so as not to inhale the thick brown cloud in which we lived, moved and had our being. Dust! It was as much a presence as the sun or the omnivoyant eye of God.

At the Chambal, we paused for our horses to drink. Its waters in the windless twilight were slabs and sheets of

---

1. The *Shrī Lalitā Sahāsranāma*

beaten silver, flawlessly fitted into the shore, as though cut and shaped by master craftsmen. Then the hooves of our horses shattered the illusion—or rather, they turned the silver molten—as we splashed across the river border into that "hell full of good things."[2]

Vidya entered from behind and laid cool fingers on my neck. "Ah," she said when she saw what I was reading.

We were out of London in half an hour. Vidya had the keys to Jai's Mercedes, which was parked outside the mews. I directed her to A4. She drove, I thought, with surprising panache, out-feinting and outgunning several London cabbies. Watching her drive, I realized again that I knew very little about this young woman with whom I was riding off into the sunset— other than that I was in love with her, I mean. Then again, I did know this: she was royal. Not that I was overly impressed by her title, as India had once supported more than three hundred *amirs*, *nizams* and *rājas* in several hundred princely states—some no larger than a failing fort, a dusty village or two and a stretch of eye-burning sea.

Nor did Vidya's kingdom exist any longer. Whatever its former historical status, it would have been subsumed by the nation at independence—years before Vidya was even born. Later, when the princely houses were stripped of their privileges, her family had departed, leaving the ancestral lands and *mandirs* in the care of a couple of beturbaned wastrels who had watched them molder back into jungle.

This, at least, is what Jai had told me of a visit home Vidya had made when she was young. And though the older peasants had *pranāmed* and hailed her father—*mahārāja ki*

---

2. Translator's Note: it is difficult to fix the exact location of the action. This cannot be the same Indore as the later princely state, since modern Indore is east of Rajasthan and was founded in 1731.

jay!—there was nothing left but sun and dust, nowhere to even sleep, and the royal family had left soon after, never to return.

Outside London, we stopped for tea and I gorged myself on scones and triple clotted cream. We must have spent an hour plus in the tea shop before once again pushing off. I had some idea it would be better for us if we didn't travel in the daylight.

Now *I* drove and I drove fast, noting the towns along the way. *Beer Hacket. Hanging Langford. Droop. Glanvilles Wooton. Bishop's Caundle.* With any luck, we'd be home by ten thirty.

Then just beyond Salisbury, on a dark and empty stretch of road, we ran out of gas. The Mercedes sputtered, then coasted to a stop as I wrested it onto the soft shoulder. It's true we hadn't stopped for petrol, but the gauge still indicated half a tank.

It was dark, though the sunset lingered in the west. My cell phone was out of range. A dim scape of fields and woodland stretched in all directions. Every few minutes, a car or truck would blind us with its lights, hurtling by so furiously that the idea of flagging it down or even sleeping in the car so close to the road seemed crazy. I thought of hiking into Salisbury, but the gas stations were long closed by now. And what about Vidya? I wasn't going to leave her alone on the roadside.

Most painful, though, was what our predicament seemed to say about me. *Stupid. Incompetent.*

"Right," Vidya said crisply. "Nothing for it then but to kip down." And she pulled from her suitcase a bundle of shawls, took her purse and jewels, then headed off the highway into the field.

"Vidya," I yelled after her. "Hey, *Vidya!*"

The ground didn't make such a bad bed after all. Its hardness was more than made up for by Vidya's tender presence and the soaring spire of Salisbury Cathedral. The church hovered above the tree line in the night like a mother ship or jeweled apparition. I wondered how many other lovers had lain in this field, staring at its revelation.

Beer, Hacket! Light the Bishop's caundle. They're hanging Langford! And while you're at it do something, please, about Glanville's wooton. Look at it droop!

"What are you muttering?" Vidya laughed.

"Oh, nothing . . . . Funny. I never saw you as into camping."

"Are you sure you know what type I *am*? Actually, I *have* spent time in the bush."

"The first night as a boy I slept outside, I saw a shooting star. And you know what shocked me, thrilled me, really? How completely *silent* it was."

Vidya said nothing; her eyes were closed.

I lay back and stared at the stars and at the waning moon clearing the trees. In its light, I studied Vidya. My eyes craved her. Her lines, like some sexual, magical architecture, drew me. My gaze kept returning to the plane of her face and to the exotic Tartar uplift of her cheeks. She wasn't a small girl: she had a luscious female heft about her, yet I found myself once again astonished by the fineness of her throat and shoulders. Lying there, looking at her was like drinking light—that bright elixir for which my soul had long been panting and athirst. And if that sounds like a line from an Irish drinking song, so be it; it's the way I felt.

Thus, I was surprised to find her open-eyed and watching me.

"Who were you with before Jai?" I asked.

"None of your damn business, is it?"

I put my hand between her legs. "Is *this* my business?"

She looked at me, but said nothing.

~ 122 ~

"You didn't answer."

"*Hanh!*"

Her cunt was bare, shaved hairless—something I found wanton and exciting. I probed until I split the flesh, divulging a cleft slicker than silk. I wormed in my middle finger up to the knuckle. At the invasion, Vidya opened her eyes and stared at me. Her clitoris was engorged, and I began to stroke it front to rear, as my first true love had taught me. I expected some coyness on her part but she impaled herself. I teased one breast. Its dark nipple was appealing, and I toyed with it until it became hard. I continued to finger her, stroking her clit and pinching her nipple—rather cruelly, if the truth were known, for she seemed to like it.

Vidya was tumescent now, her body involuntarily relaxing and clenching, her nostrils flared, her back arching. I scraped my nails up along her belly, eliciting the very lowest of moans. I purposely didn't kiss her, only diddled and frigged her, imagining her the spoils of war—a princess bound and forced to submit to my every whim and pleasure.

What a delight it was, what bliss! I swear, the sexual charge of that one encounter outweighed half the pain that I'd endured!

And all the while I watched her, the image of rapture. She was my polyglot, globe-trotting *Deshi* baby with a ring in her nose and a stiff British accent, a soft African undulation to her hips, skin the color of an octoroon and the cheekbones of a Tartar.

"Now it's time to come," I said and rammed my finger in her, hard. She began to pant—it sounded like snoring. Then her breathing stopped. Her eyes widened and she bared her teeth as though she was about to scream. I clapped a hand on her mouth and watched and felt her climax beneath me.

For a moment, she hung there, poised, and then, just as suddenly, she melted, released. The ragged tide of her breath resumed and she lay unmoving, except for her heaving breasts.

After some time, she touched me and I felt her feel the hardness of my erection. But I was more than sated by her satisfaction and I removed her hand, kissed her mouth, plumped the shawl beneath my head and, snuggling into her, fell fast asleep.

I awoke to a serious ringing in my ears, to the odor of gun smoke and something heavy pressing my legs. I sat up uncertain at first where I was, much less what was happening. Vidya was partly risen on her side. At the end of her arm, a puff of white smoke was slowly dispersing, and it was then I saw the diminutive pistol half-hidden in her hand. For a moment, I thought, I was dreaming! Then that it was aimed at me!

". . . the hell?" I scooted my legs out from under whatever was on them. It was, I saw now, the body of a man! Vidya, her arm still extended, reached out with her other and, gripping the body's head by its forelock, lifted it. The bearded face, its eyes like ciphers, had a small, nearly bloodless wound below the left eye. Vidya opened her fist and let the head drop.

"What . . ."

"He had a knife." Which was when I observed in the grass beside me the clip-pointed blade of a large Bowie knife. "He was bending down to cut your throat with it."

"You shot him?" I asked her. "Just like that?"

"You'd have preferred I'd waited until he'd killed you?"

Vidya said she'd been awakened by the crunch of breaking glass. A truck was parked behind our Mercedes. Someone had smashed one of our car's windows, unlocking its doors. Under the dome light, she watched a form moving about inside. As we had brought our valuables with us, she'd been willing, she said, to let the intruder take what he wished and go. But when he got out, instead of departing, he'd switched on a flashlight, playing its beam along the edge of the shoulder until it lit the swath of broken grass where we'd entered the meadow. Then, she said, he'd returned to his truck. And when he got out again, he had the flashlight in one hand and the long, dangerous knife in the other.

Only then, she said, had she drawn the pistol from her purse, watching, with a growing alarm, as the man entered the meadow, using his torch to follow our track. When he was so close it seemed that he might step on me, she'd shouted, "Stop! Now! Drop the knife. Or I'll fire!"

But if surprised, he didn't show it, but only leered, she said, shining the flashlight's beam in her eyes. Maybe he didn't see the gun. For without another word, he'd readjusted his grip on the Bowie's handle, and then "like a butcher getting down to his business," began bending over my sleeping form . . .

"Check his pockets," Vidya said. "Who is he?" I knelt down, surprised to find a pair of handcuffs on his belt. I opened his billfold, looking for a badge. There was none. Nor do cops carry Bowie knives. Vidya took from his hand the still-burning flashlight and we read the name on his driver's license: Henry Carlson Lewis Jones. Age 53. With an address in Surrey. "Know him?" I asked.

"No."

I started to replace it when Vidya said, "Wipe off your prints." She did the same with hers on the pistol, then let it fall beside the corpse. After that, she gathered our things, and started back to the roadway.

She moved with a certain purpose—a very different woman than the shell-shocked widow I'd encountered only nights ago. She opened the truck's tailgate and rummaging through the assortment of junk within, withdrew two pairs of work gloves, plus a four-foot length of rubber hose. She gave me a pair and put on the other. "Now bring the truck up alongside the Mercedes." I did. She handed me the hose.

"Now siphon some petrol from his tank to ours." I was doing that, too, when the crack of a gunshot made me flinch. I could just make out Vidya in the field by the body. What the hell was she doing? Shooting him *again*?

Moments later, she returned. "Right," she said, and taking the hose, threw it back in the truck. "Now drive," she urged. "And I'll follow."

Once more, I did as I was told. The only thing to do was to leave the scene and continue on, saying nothing. To have called the police would have been suicidal.

When our report of a killing we hadn't committed had brought upon us such suspicion and grief, to report another, two days later, that we *had* committed (even if in self-defense) would not only immeasurably add to our woes, but would multiply them exponentially. For the government of Britain does not recognize the right of its citizenry to bear arms. And while cutting down greatly on the number of shootings, the penalties for asserting that right are severe. Possession of a handgun carries a mandatory five-year prison sentence. Firing a semiautomatic pistol in public can, theoretically, get you ten.

In other words, what Vidya (and I) were doing was both patently criminal and perfectly right. Clearly, our only sane and sensible option was to cover up our connection to the killing. Every other road—even full vindication of our having acted in justifiable self-defense—could well lead us to half a decade in jail. Or should I write, *gaol*?

I drove slowly, keeping my eye on the lights of the lorry. After nine or ten miles, its engine sputtered, running out of gas. A turnoff appeared, and, alerted by the pick-up's blinker, I paused at the fork, as Vidya drove some yards down a wooded lane, parking the truck there.

A minute later, she got in the front passenger's door.

"How are you doing?"

"Tolerable, under the circumstances."

"Why, may I ask, did we just do that?" I motioned with my head toward the reparked lorry.

"Because if we'd left the truck back there, there's a good chance when the police found it, they'd find the body. In a day or two, its odor will be rank. I'm just trying to be prudent and careful, that's all."

I thought prudent and careful were odd words to use given she'd just shot a man in the face.

I resumed driving. "Where'd you get the gun?"

"It was in Jai's safe, along with my treasures. I swept them all up and into my bag."

"And leaving it behind? Tell me again why we did that?"

"Because, without the gun, it's murder. Justifiable, maybe, but murder all the same. With the gun, suicide's at least a possibility."

"A suicide," I asked, "who shot himself *twice*?"

She turned on me, angrily. "That's not what you heard!" She closed her eyes and took several deep breaths. "I realized as I left, the scene wouldn't play."

"Why's that?"

"FDR."

"FDR?"

"Firearm discharge residue. So I put the gun in his hand, and fired a shot across the meadow. They won't find the slug. And I caught the ejected shell. But his hand is now tainted. Without that, even with the gun, they'd have known he couldn't be the shooter."

I understood. In the States, we called it GSR, gunshot residue. "Can I ask you something?"

"Don't *ask* if you can ask it. Just *ask*," she said irritably. She started scrabbling through her pocketbook, then stopped and looked around. "I thought I left a plastic change purse here. On the dash. It had some cigarettes in it."

"How do you know this stuff? About . . . GSR? And murder investigations?"

"I know firearms," she said, setting down the bag, and placing her hands in her lap, apparently resigned to doing without one. "I was taught to shoot when I was a girl. As for the other, it's common knowledge. Don't you read mysteries?"

"You mean murder mysteries? No. I read field reports, research papers."

"Well, bully for you!"

I laughed. I deserved it.

"It's vital the body isn't found for some time. The gun's pointed backward, his thumb on the trigger. But even then"— she extended her arm toward the windshield—"it can't be more than eighteen to twenty inches."

"He was a big man. Say, twenty-four."

"And I shot him from at least four feet away. The residue around the wound won't match the shorter distance."

"Unless," I said, "the evidence is degraded by a week in the sun. And by whatever critters find him."

"Yes," she sighed, "or, at least, that is the plan."

Part IV

ALBION

*In one corner
of the infinite and indivisible
Supreme Consciousness,
there is a mirage-like appearance.
This we call the world.*

The Yoga Vasishtha

Chapter 19

While I drove, Vidya nodded off, her head bouncing lightly on my shoulder. The gray dawn was suffused with a fine pelting rain that smelled of Scotland and the sea. If it were raining in America like this, no one would have been about. But here, in the English countryside, old ladies in macs and wellies went about their marketing unfazed, riding their bicycles through puddles down the country highway.

I thought of the rain falling on the face of Henry Carlson Lewis Jones, and wondered if it would wash away the evidence. Then I remembered he was face down. His killing, coming so close upon Jai's, was chilling. What bothered me most was the thought that he hadn't been a mortal threat at all, that despite the knife (and his forced entry of our vehicle) he was just some old fool sticking his nose where it didn't belong. I mean, how could Vidya be so certain of the man's intent? He couldn't have been more than a silhouette. Or maybe she hadn't been certain at all, but was only pretending. Maybe, like me, she was scared shitless, and had overreacted, killing a phantom.

But if his death was chilling, leaving him felt even colder. He was likely someone's father, husband or son, whose presence would be missed. Then again, the prospect of years in a British prison was absolutely freezing. And though with luck and a great solicitor we might get off with eighteen months plus time already served, even eighteen months was not an option. There was nothing for it now but to accept what had happened, let it be and carry on.

When I parked, Vidya woke. "There?"

"Almost. But first, I need to talk to someone. Do you want to sleep? I won't be long."

She looked through the bug-smeared windshield at the hospital's faded brick façade. "No." She stretched. "I'll come with you."

We went inside. In her long skirt, Vidya seemed to be floating almost footless, down the hall, her hips swaying to some African beat. I admired her spirit. Her husband was dead, we had a homicide charge hanging over our heads, we'd killed a man and covered it up—yet despite it all, she seemed composed and, you might have thought, unburdened.

I brought her first to the hospital canteen, where we chewed stale biscuits and sipped mugs of milky tea. We held hands, for the sweetest intimacy had developed between us.

Not that I knew much more about her, for she was close-mouthed to an extraordinary degree. Don't get me wrong. I *liked* this about her: that she didn't continually chatter like some, turning every hangnail or broken heel into a psycho-drama. On the other hand, this made it difficult to find out much about her.

After breakfast, we headed for Strugnell's office. I wanted to tell him firsthand what had happened and see what sort of advice he could give. On the way, we passed a familiar door.

"Do you want to see something . . . *amazing*?" I said, and I turned the handle on impulse, letting the door swing open wide.

My Lady was lying on an aluminum gurney, looking—I don't know any other word to use—horrific. After the autopsy, they had not sewn her back up. An incision ran from her throat to groin.

But my shock was nothing compared to Vidya's. It took her a moment, I think, to comprehend what she was seeing. Then, when she did, she jerked as though scalded. "What *is* this?" she demanded.

"It's . . . the body of . . . Albemarle. The girl whose grave the book was in."

"But you said you were showing me something *amazing!*" Vidya glared at me with a fury I had not seen till now, and for a moment I thought she might go for my eyes; then her features reefed and she began to weep, rocking gently in the classical way that women have mourned the dead forever.

Whatever possessed me to do what I had, given all she'd just been through? "I'm sorry. I'm so sorry, Vidya," I said, taking her back out into the hall. There, she continued to weep, though no one paid us any mind. People cry in hospitals all the time, I suppose.

"I killed a man last night," she said. "I've never killed a man before."

"I know," I said. "And we'll have to live with it. And you know what? We can—and will."

I drew her close and held her until her tears had ceased. She sniffed and rubbed her eyes, smearing her cheeks and fingers with *kohl*. Accepting a tissue, she blew her nose—*honk!*— a comical noise that only endeared her to me the more, then excused herself and headed for the WC. I watched until she disappeared into the bathroom, then went back inside.

Christ alive, what the hell had I been thinking? For the creature before me was a patent horror, an eviscerated witch. She looked positively insectival, like those larval skins cicada nymphs, after years underground, bequeath to trees and fences. For this was the impression I had of my Lady. She was no longer there. Whatever presence I had sensed was gone, leaving behind this torn and empty shell.

Just then, the coroner came in. He blinked behind his rimless glasses and offered me an embarrassed smile that said he'd seen our little drama. "You're back!"

"Wooland . . . tell me, what's wrong with this picture? This really is obscene, the way she's been left. I mean, she may be just a 'specimen' now, but once upon a time, she *was* a living human being."

"Didn't mean to upset you . . . or your friend. Don't believe I know her . . . do I?"

"No."

He waited for more, but I wasn't in the mood.

I wanted to cover my Lady's remains. I found a piece of plastic sheeting.

"As the coroner, you have access to the police database, do you not?"

"I do, I . . ."

"I need you to look up a name for me. Henry Carlson Lewis Jones. White male, 52. Address in Surrey."

"It's a bit irregular."

"Yeah, well, so are you." It came out wrong. Here I was asking the man for a favor while insulting him.

He looked hurt. "C'mon," I said. "A joke. It's been a rough few days."

He nodded and started to go, when there was a god-awful noise and a sudden stench. The coroner was huddled over the sink. He came up teary-eyed, wiping his lips with the back of his hand.

"Bit of a bug, I'm afraid." He ran the water. "Donne, I'll give you a call a bit later. Right now, I really need to go home."

Chapter 20

What had we hoped to find in Dorset? Peace, sanctuary, acceptance, freedom? Would any one of these have been so much to ask?

The report of Jai's murder had made that morning's *Daily Mirror*, and the phone was already ringing as we came in the cottage door. Apart from reporters requesting interviews, most of the calls were from colleagues and acquaintances, ringing to express their sympathy and concern. Still, the subtext of most, if not all, was clear: I'd been besotted by a foreign enchantress. For my own sake and for my career's: *dump her, ditch her, head for the hills!*

Even more disappointing were my contacts at the Dorset Constabulary. After bragging for months about their influence and power, they claimed to have little leverage with New Scotland Yard—and they certainly couldn't be seen meddling in an ongoing murder investigation!

One of the more supportive calls was from my department head at Exeter. Expressing his shock and horror at Jai's murder, he wanted me, "Al," to know the college stood behind me all the way. What a "tip-top job" I'd been doing lately! What with my Lady and the commission. *Total faith, feather in their cap, chin up, pip, pip.*

With Houlihan, we'd called his bluff, at least. Obviously, he had no hard evidence against us; all he could offer was intimidation and, this time, it had failed. Not that I thought we were out of the woods, but the fact that the CID wasn't waiting to arrest us upon our arrival was a clear indication they didn't yet have a case. Now, if we could just keep our heads down, they *had* to come up with better suspects than Vidya and I.

Until then, I decided, I was going to try to live and work as before. I'd be *damned* if I'd let my life be turned upside down by a crime I hadn't even committed. The one caveat was that I was afraid of leaving Vidya alone. For Jai's attacker was still unknown, and I had the recurring, uneasy feeling the intended target was Vidya, not Jai.

"Don't worry, darling. I'll be fine. I know you have things to do." She had showered and was seated at the kitchen table, wrapped in a white terrycloth robe, her wet black hair shining as though oiled.

"What will you do?"

"Unpack. Get settled. I love Dorset."

"Oh? Been here before?"

"Not really."

I found her answer extremely annoying. What did that mean? Either you had been to Dorset or not. There really wasn't some *third* option, was there?

Maybe she sensed my mood, for she looked up again and said, "I'm a frightful nuisance, aren't I, darling?"

"Hardly."

"Oh, I am." She gestured at *The Dorset Echo*, folded open to another sensational account of the crime. She gazed out the window. "Perhaps I should go."

"*Go?*" I cried. "We just arrived. Go *where*?"

After some consideration, she swung her gaze back to mine. "Is it the servants' day off?"

"Uh . . ." I lied. "That was yesterday. They'll be in by noon."

Taking my hand, she slipped something on my wrist. It was a torc, forged of reddish gold with terminals bearing Celtic-looking heads.

"What's this?"

"Just a little gift. For your kindness. And devotion."

"My, God," I said. "It looks real!"

"Oh, I'm sure it is. Lakshmi Auntie said it had been in the family for generations."

"But Vidya," I protested, "do you know what this is worth?"

"Nonsense. It is a trinket only." And with a quick kiss to both my cheeks, she disappeared into the bathroom.

On my way to the college, I stopped in the village to have the Mercedes's window replaced, the gas gauge fixed, and the car cleaned inside and out. Henry Carlson Lewis Jones's fingerprints were surely all throughout it. I also took the clothes we'd worn and dumped them. The bullet's impact had surely sprayed us with his DNA. Finally, I stopped at Ruby O'Connell's. Ruby had cooked and cleaned for me on occasion and I asked her now if I might hire her as housekeeper. She allowed I might, provided I took on Willie, her husband, "as the gardener, sir."

Willie waved back from his seat by the telly where, at ten forty-five on a Tuesday morning he was sucking down a bottle of brown Badger Ale.

"Don't have to pay 'im much," she winked. "But I wouldn't trust 'im on his own, I wouldn't."

"You have a shotgun, Willie?"

He nodded.

"Bring it."

"Got something else," he said, and responding to his whistle, a wolfhound appeared, the size of a small war pony.

I nodded. I felt good not leaving Vidya alone.

My inbox held a six-inch stack of anthropological reports pertaining to "Holders Woman," as my Lady of the Bog was now officially known. I withdrew them with anticipation. Jones's and Jai's deaths still sat like great undigested lumps in my stomach, rising, at intervals, into my craw. So, it would be a relief to attend to tragedies other than my own.

The lab analysis of my Lady's stomach indicated it was nearly empty, save for a thin gruel of grain and wild herbs. There were traces of ergot—a psychotropic growing naturally on rye—which meant that my Lady might have been high and hallucinating. The amount was small and the report didn't state the clinical dosage, so she might just as well have been stone-cold sober. It was one of those facts open to diametrically opposed interpretations, of which there seemed to be so many.

Her intestines contained eggs of *Trichuris* and *Ascaris*—parasitic worms that had probably caused her some gastric discomfort—and the roots of her hair harbored nits, though no adult lice were found. Other than that, there was "a total absence of necrophiliac fauna on the skin." In other words, my Lady had no flies on her, from which one could almost certainly deduce that she was buried immediately upon her murder.

One of the more interesting studies analyzed the pollen in her nasal cavities, lungs and hair. These tiny spores, borne on the wind, are practically indestructible and can paint a detailed picture of the climate, flora and precipitation for years and seasons long since gone. The data confirmed my wingéd surmise that my Lady had been buried in mid- to late-July. Spores of land clearance weeds and a noticeable absence of pine and oak indicated a landscape extensively farmed. Further, by correlating the pollen record with conditions reflected in the rings of ancient pines, the palynologists had arrived at a death year of 1327. This was in broad agreement with the language of both the book and the runes. Everything, so far, was lining up nicely—until we came to the radiocarbon dating.

Here, the findings were wildly at odds. Though my Lady's body yielded dates of 1290, 1260 and 1222 ACE (± about 120 years), the wooden stakes and surrounding peat dated to the seventeenth century!

I sought out a copy of the runic tracings. One line of the inscription was carved upon each stake. However, on the reverse side of the third stake were four more runes: ᛈ and a group of three others: ᛜᛩᛟ or *D-O-M*.

I discovered Rumple in a temporary office down the hall.

He stiffly and kindly offered his condolences and—remembering my final conversation with Jai—I graciously accepted them. As I still had not found a historical reference, I asked: "Could it be that her name wasn't Albemarle? That those runes say something else?"

"Unlikely. In binding runes, the name was all important. It *had* to be included. '*Ic beshrew*,' 'I curse,' had no effect. '*Ic beshrew*, Donne.' Ah, now *that's* a rune of power."

"I found several more. A sort of capital P."

"*Wunjo*. Stands for joy, bliss. In Spencer, it adorns the flag of fairyland . . . associations with the grail. But used alone, as it is here, it's said to induce madness."

"Madness? In whom? In Albemarle?"

"Oh, I think not. Albemarle was dead. Or about to be. Did you find three others?"

I nodded. "*D-O-M*. "

"A second *o* was likely dropped."

"'*Doom*?'"

He nodded. "The doom of madness, of *wunjo*. On whomever breaks the holy runes."

"Breaks the runes . . . ?"

"Well . . . removes the stakes."

I smiled grimly and soldiered on. "The stakes are a different age than the body. Could it be from anomalies in the C-14?"

"Unlikely. The fluctuation for that period was factored in. There's still a three-hundred-year difference."

This was baffling. For if both sets of dates were true, then Holders Woman had died around thirteen hundred. Three hundred years later, she'd been buried and staked. That didn't make sense.

"I noticed," I said, "that her blood is B negative. That's uncommon here and, as I recall, is often found in gypsies. Since she has a pierced nose, I was wondering if perhaps she could be a gypsy girl, killed, you know, for telling fortunes."

Rumple chuckled. "You surprise me, Donne. I'd have thought you more conversant with *basic* European history."

I smiled.

"Gypsies—or *Roma*, as they prefer to be called—do not appear in Western Europe until the mid-*fifteenth* century. So she can't be what you call a 'gypsy,' now can she?" He sniffed. "Another odd thing: the body was found in conjunction with a number of artifacts."

"You mean the treasure?"

"No, no. *These* artifacts were found in strata *above* the body. Two hundred and seventy-seven coins, to be precise, dating from 1306 all the way up to 1937."

"What kind of coins?" I asked, both excited and dismayed—for to do this job properly *you had to know everything*: bones, coins, blood, gypsies.

"The oldest is a groat from the reign of Edward I. Most everything else is farthings, pennies. One testoon. A gold unite from Charles I. Oh, yes, some shillings from the late nineteenth century. What does all this suggest to you?"

"It suggests," I replied, "a devotional cult attracting monetary offerings, dating from the time of her burial onward, by people who were poor. Probably the peasantry offering up their ha'pennies in return for some blessing—except for the unite, which makes me think the lady of the house must have learned of the cult and made an offering of her own."

There was a pause. Then Rumple admitted drily, "Yes. It suggested much the same to me."

I saw her now, bundled in sable, flinging the bullion into the bog. The coin arcs in the wintry starlight—gold returning to its source. But who is she making her offering *to*? Who does she think is down there to claim it? What has moved her to sacrifice such a sizeable piece of wealth? Is her daughter hemorrhaging to death in childbirth? Or her beloved son wasting away, the victim of a troll wife's enmity that only a more powerful sorceress can dispel?

"And if coins were deposited as late as the 1930s, the tradition that inspired it may still be known. It could be recorded somewhere," I said, with some excitement, "or someone who knows it may still be *alive!*"

What I didn't share with Rumple was my hope that the book would throw some light upon these mysteries. Instead, I handed him the original codex, without happening to mention Jai's English translation.

I left him poring over the rare manuscript, astonished, while I went back to my own office and printed out another chapter of Sikandar's story.

Soon after crossing the river border, Sikandar's war party had encountered Rajputs. In a pitched exchange, the enemy was routed—though only when the dust had settled did Sikandar learn what he had won:

"... not pearls or emeralds, gold or silks, but something far more precious and delicious. Their knights were escorting an enclosed palanquin in which were, apparently, ladies of the harem."

Chapter 21

There are four things, Ghazil says, before which the wise are not bold: fire, kings, saints—and *women!*

Remembering this, I advanced with a mien of the utmost restraint. For imagine the terror in the breasts of these ladies as strange, armed men approached their carriage!

I parted the palanquin's curtains. Its compartment was black against the blindingly bright sunlit morning and so, with a bow, I invited its occupants out.

I don't know what I expected next: the arched instep of a delicate foot, or the swan's neck curve of a brown and many-braceleted arm? So I was caught completely by surprise when a shrieking Rajput, wielding a *katar*[1], leapt at me from the darkened box—only to find himself, well before landing, impaled on 'Abd al-Wali's sword. For a moment he hung there, eyes bugging, looking down in stupefaction, as if he couldn't imagine how such a long, sharp knife had found its way into his soft, fat belly. Then with a jerk, 'Abd al-Wali withdrew the blade and, raising it up, brought it down with a *clang* that was heard in Kabul! My would-be assassin dropped in the dust and through the cleft in his skull, I watched his brains decant: a surprisingly delicate, blood-flecked gray. I looked away, discomfited. For I'll admit, I was not used to such sights.

---

1. *katar*: A type of knife with a handle perpendicular to the blade, allowing it to be gripped in a fist and punched.

Instantly, however, came something that was. A furious presence invaded the air: some demon summoned by this sacrifice of blood and, under the vengeful spirit's spell, my men threatened to run their prisoners through.

There was an uncertain second, as half-a-dozen upraised sabres trembled in the morning light.

Then 'Abd al-Wali laughed, and taking up the dead man's shawl, drew his sabre through it. He smirked in his handsome, reckless way, then discarded the bloody rag, like an offering. Perhaps the spirit accepted it and withdrew, for instantly the tension lessened. Grumbling, my men lowered their weapons. Flies were already feasting on the dead.

It was then a young woman, dressed in mourning, slipped from the darkened box. Abasing herself, she pressed her face into the dust and grasped my calves with hands of such soft, prehensile strength it sent shivers up my loins. "My Lord," she declared, "we surrender at your feet."

The *pandits* will ask, what else could she do? She was surrounded, after all; her protectors vanquished. But I tell you now, rare is the one who surrenders with grace. For *sharanam*, the word she used, means not just "to surrender to" but also "to take refuge in"—less like a king surrendering his army than a soul surrendering to God.

For the longest time she lay like this in perfect supplication. Then, rising to her knees, she sat back on her haunches and, breaking a thread from the fringe of her sari, solemnly joined it about my wrist. It was a *rakhi*, the traditional thread of protection that on the full moon day of the month of *Srāvana* sisters bind around the wrists of their brothers, asking for their benediction.

Was I moved by this act, at once so bold, inspired, and submissive?

~ 143 ~

Yes; for though to her I was the furthest thing from a brother, and *Srāvana* was more than five moons hence, she conferred the gift upon me now with the perfect faith of a girl, as if she truly did believe in the protective power of this frail act and strand.

More moving still was the sight of her face. The *pallav* of her sari had slipped, and in keeping with her state of mourning, her thick, black hair was undressed and free, though its dark disorder only made her seem a hundred times more lovely—like the face of Mother Kali Herself. And like Kali's, there was madness in it, even if hers was circumstantial: the effect, I assumed, of her fear of rape. Nor was her fear a groundless one. For another man, unenlightened by Ghazil, might have treated his enemy's captive wife in a considerably bolder way.

"Who are you, Lady?" I asked, not unkindly.

"First, O Lord, you must promise your protection."

Some note in her voice, imperial, demanding, gave me a moment's hesitation. And anyway, favours too easily won are not savoured. "*I* must do nothing," I informed her firmly. "It is *you* who are *my* captive."

Lifting her head, she looked me in the eye—as wellbred women are taught never to do. Her nose and brow were streaked with dust from her obeisance; her eyes, an unearthly blue, were shocking in her golden face—though in their depths I saw no fear any longer, only an ardent intelligence and will.

Her willfulness intrigued me. "Arise now, lady, and say who you are."

But despite my command and the presence beside her of the freshly killed soldier, she clasped my legs and once again pressed her cheek to my knees, bathing my feet in the falls of her hair. "First, O Lord, you must grant us your protection."

It was maddening, really, but what could I do? A prince's first duty is to protect the meek and all who take refuge in him. Yet, I might have been able to refuse her still had I not looked down upon her upturned face. It was the essence of petition. Her eyes were poised upon the cliff of my answer, and the jagged tracks of two gold tears shone on her cheeks like holy rivers in the sun; while something about her upper lip made me want to *nibble* it! And so, moved by these many lofty considerations, I spoke those words that were to cost me so much later: "Very well. You shall have it."

"Swear it! On the highest Lord!" She said this with such ferocity of feeling it surprised us both, I think, for instantly she lowered her eyes and, abasing herself once more, placed her forehead on my toes.

"I swear it," I said, "on He who made me. Now arise," I commanded, "and say who you are."

But there were sounds, once again, from the palanquin. 'Abd al-Wali gripped his sword as we watched the carriage shiver and shake, then spit a child.

The boy looked about with kohl-smeared eyes at the flyblown corpse and the tableau of warriors. He was one of those children who, whether out of enthusiasm or anxiety, seem to *yell* whatever he says, for he turned to the girl at my feet and wailed, "MOMMY, WHO ARE ALL THESE STUPID SOLDIERS?"

My men laughed loudly. There was the sound of a dozen sheathing weapons, like an iron sigh. Even the wounded sprawled on the ground seemed to draw a breath of comfort.

I bowed. "Your son is right. Allow me to introduce myself . . ."

But the Lady replied, "O Lion of the Throne of Chosroes, there is no need. Your fame precedes you."

Her answer pleased me, and I smiled benignly now at the young widow dressed in white (the Franks, I am told, dress their widows in *black!*) and reaching out, drew her to her feet.

"Who are you, Lady?" I asked once again, more curious than ever now.

She covered her head and lowered her eyes. "I am Mayura, Rani of Indore."

I was dumbfounded. "You are . . . the *Queen?*"

She bowed her head in affirmation.

"But . . . your Lord . . . ?" It was a foolish question. Raja Mul was dead. I had, most likely, seen his head—and I quickly amended its direction, saying, ". . . that is . . . how is it you didn't follow him into the flames?" For this was their barbaric rite: the widow burned on her husband's pyre.

"The King commanded otherwise."

"Before he died?"

"The *new* King."

"Ah, and he is . . . ?"

"Here," she said, drawing her boy to her bosom. She gazed on him lovingly. "He begged me, '*Amma*, please don't leave me.' And I obeyed. For without me . . ." she playfully covered his ears, and said in a voice so low I wondered if I'd heard her rightly, ". . . they will slay him."

A distant apprehension gripped me, like that faint unease that flusters the heart at the first hint of distant thunder, and it took me a moment to locate its source. For what did I care about the fate of this child? Then, with a sort of inner percussion, I realized I must, as he and the Queen were now under my protection. I considered this. "And who is 'they?'"

The Queen raised her eyes to the sunburnt hills, as though she saw the future approaching like a monster. In that moment, everything seemed to stop: time, the river, the flies drinking blood from the wounds of the soldiers. "Our enemies," she said in answer to my question.

And the world began to run again.

It was the word "enemies" that did it, I think, breaking the spell under which I had fallen. For it was only then that the implications of my promise, so heedlessly given, made themselves plain, accompanied by a prickling sensation of heat that had nothing to do with the April sun. I remembered Ghazil's injunction to never promise anything in haste; too late! For I had just done an astonishing thing. I had just pledged the arm of my protection to the King and Queen of the Kingdom of Indore—our country's oldest and bitterest foe!

Chapter 22

I closed the book with a feeling of amazement mixed with one of deep unease. The precipitousness of Sikandar's promise of protection was not unlike my own to Vidya. And the role, it seemed, was as new to him, as it was to me. With Jai alive, I had always been the protectee.

And then there was the Queen's dead husband, and Vidya's bracelet which adorned my wrist. And a host of other odd parallels, too.

Or isn't *every* good book like this, spiked with remarkable ties and alignments to one's own life and loves and times?

Yet I also felt the rising hope that I had come at last upon my Lady's identity—though how an Indian queen might end up in a Dorset bog . . . Still, Mayura's age, status, hair and eyes were the same as my Lady of the Bog's. Then again, they were the same as Vidya's—and thousands of other women, too. Plus, if my Lady *was* Queen Mayura, why did the runes call her "Albemarle?"

Willie was in the garden, leaning on his spade, gazing with a countryman's pleasure at a white horse in the distance racing across the downs. Odin, his young wolfhound, drum-rolled his tail at my approach. Willie nodded. "Quite the rider."

Only then did I realize the figure on the distant horse was Vidya. Why did this—or anything else about her—surprise me?

Inside the cottage, Mrs. O'Connell was fixing lunch. It was odd; nice; jolly, really. Suddenly the house was full of beasts and people. It was only then, I think, I realized just how all alone I'd been.

The buzzer rang and I opened the door—on two bobbies. One of them wore an apologetic expression while the other one looked grim.

"*Die*, sir," the first one said. He was a bright young chap with an earnest expression.

"Good day to you, too. And what can I do for you?"

"Sir," he said in his formal way, "we have come into possession of some photographs of the Holders treasure taken the very night it was stolen."

Oddly, I felt some slight relief. At least, they weren't here about Jai's death—or Henry Jones's murder.

"You have them," I said, "because I took them, and gave them to the coroner to pass on to you. I thought it might further your investigation."

"Yes, sir. Did. Helped mightily. Have a squint, sir." He held up a photograph I'd taken in the basement. "Now this book, sir, one in the picture? We understand it's in your possession."

"No longer. I gave it to Dr. Rumple this morning."

This confused him. "But *was* in your possession—for some time, we understand."

"Only a few hours. For the last nine or ten weeks it's been in London, in the custody of a scholar there."

"Sir, the question is, was it or was it not in your possession after the treasure was purloined?"

Purloined? Whom do these fellows read? Edgar Allan Poe? "Well, of course, it was. I removed it from the hoard only moments after this picture was snapped. It's the one thing that wasn't taken."

"Yes, sir. And do you see my point?"

"No," I said, "as I don't believe you made one."

"My point, sir, is the treasure was stolen. To be frank with you, to this date we have no knowledge of by whom. However, *after* this date—the day it was pinched—*you* were in possession of a piece of it."

Ill-spoken as it was, I did not like the implication. I wanted to tell them this had already been sorted out by Jai and the Yard's antiquities squad. Then I realized their investigation was local. And, as in most bureaucracies, one hand doesn't know the other. "It was in my possession," I explained with some care, "because I removed it for examination. I was investigating a murder for the CID, and I thought it might help identify the victim."

"Understandable, sir. Quite understandable. And since you were removing a piece of evidence—and, I might add, property of the Crown—you, no doubt, signed for it, along with the time you took it out."

"No," I said quickly. "I just borrowed it. For the evening. It was late. There was no one to sign it out *from*."

"Ah, yes, sir. We're all a bit like that at times. Like to skirt official procedure. But you must have told *someone* you took it. We understand the coroner was with you at the time. Tell *him*, sir?"

All this was said very nicely and civilly, but I was damn sure they had already spoken with the coroner. "No, I didn't," I admitted. "I saw no need. I was just bringing it upstairs for examination."

"And is that what you did, sir? Take it upstairs."

"I, uh, honestly don't remember now." I was getting rattled. "I think, I meant to go upstairs—but instead, it was late, I was tired, and went home."

"With the book?"

"Yes."

"Anyone see you?"

"Not that I know of. It was one in the morning."

"And when was the next time the book was seen?"

"Well, the next day, I sent it off to Dr. Prasad. I also told Professor Rumple I had it."

"I see. Now, this Dr. Prasad, could you give us his number, sir?"

"I could, but it wouldn't do you much good, I'm afraid."

"Oh? And why's that, sir?"

"He's . . . dead."

"*Dead*, sir?"

"Yes, he was murdered."

"Oh, dearie me. That's right terrible, sir."

"Yes, he was a good friend."

"And have they anyone in custody, sir?"

"Not yet."

He looked confused. "But if he died, sir, after you'd sent him the book, how did you get it back?"

"I was . . . uh, in London at the time."

"At the time of his *death*, sir?"

"Yes. I reported the body."

"Did you now?" he said, deadpan. "And you did all this, *after* the treasure was stolen."

"Well, of course."

"There, now. See our problem?"

"Problem? No," I said, "I didn't see your point before. And I don't see your problem now."

"Problem, sir, is the treasure's pinched and then a piece of it shows up in *your* possession."

"If you're implying that *I* stole the treasure . . ."

"We're just saying, sir, if you had signed the book out or said something to someone, then we *might* have a record of when it was taken. But the coroner believes the book was *with* the treasure when the two of you left the basement."

"Well, of course, he does. He didn't see me take it."

"Yes, sir." I was losing their attention. "Mind if we look around?"

"I most certainly do."

"And why's that, sir? Something to hide?"

"To search my home, you'll need a warrant."

"Sergeant." The second cop, whom I'd almost forgotten, was pointing at my wrist.

"Interesting bracelet that," the first bobby said. He lifted my hand. "May I ask where you got this?"

"It was a gift."

"From whom?"

"That name isn't relevant here."

"Oh, but I think it is. May I?" He slipped it off me and held it up against the photo of the treasure. "Feel it's only fair that I give you a caution, sir."

"Caution received."

"The person's name, sir."

"Look. Can't we leave her out of this? She's a guest."

"We don't get it from you, sir, we'll just have to get it from her, now won't we?"

There was nothing for it. "All right. Prasad."

"Prasad, is it?" He paused, as I watched the penny drop. "Not like the chappie who was murdered?"

"His widow."

"Is *here*? With *you*?" The way he said it made it sound like the most incriminating thing in the world.

"I told you. I'm a friend of the family."

"And where is Mrs. Prasad now?"

"Not in." (I was technically correct.) Though no sooner had I uttered this falsehood than Vidya appeared, escorted by Odin. She was splashed with mud from head to boot, above which she wore jodhpurs and was tapping a black leather crop on her thigh.

There was a moment while the coppers drank her in. "Sorry, ma'am, but I guess we were expecting someone . . . *older*." We all knew what he meant. "Yours, ma'am?"

"*Was*. What of it?" She was giving the bobbies only half her attention; with the other, she was absently stroking Odin and flipping through the mail.

"May we ask where you got it, Miss?"

"A wedding gift from my Lakshmi Auntie."

"Can this be verified?"

"Ring her up."

"Her number, miss?"

"Oh, I don't know it, offhand. But I'm certain you can suss it out. She's Rājmata of Udaipur."

"Raj *what?*" the bobby queried.

"Queen Mother," I translated, "of Udaipur. India."

"Though I warn you now, the lines are atrocious. It could take you *days* to be getting through."

We seemed to have reached another natural impasse. As in London, it was our word against the cops' suspicions. At the moment, our denials still carried the day. Actually, I think it was Vidya's royal presence—and Odin's large, protective one.

The silent one whispered something, prompting his colleague to say, "We'd like to borrow the torc, sir. For analysis."

"You'll have to ask Mrs. Prasad."

"Oh, *take* it," Vidya said dismissively, as though dealing with a couple of insolent servants. "Leave a receipt with Mrs. O'Connell." And flinging the leather whip on a table, she and her monster ascended the stairs.

Chapter 23

When the police were gone, I did the only sane thing I could think of under the circumstances: I made myself a cup of tea. Then I sat in the garden and drank it.

There's a saying in the East: "Of the fifty-six strategies, *flight* is the best." Briefly, I considered Mombasa, then Mumbai. But being fugitives would have meant the end of life as we knew it, and the end of my career, too. Then again, defending ourselves against a charge of murder—or two—surely would have the same effect. The bobbies had clearly been putting me on. I don't know why I hadn't copped to it sooner. Jai's murder was page two news, making their queries (*"Dead, sir?"* *"Oh, dearie me, sir . . ."*) not merely coy, but sinister.

Well, they could inquire all they wanted. I hadn't killed Jai and I hadn't filched their filthy treasure and they'd have one hell of a time proving I had. So who did?

My cell phone rang. The roughhewn voice was all too familiar. "Been doing some legwork. Prasad, he's got enemies? Nodda bit. Guy's bu-*loved*. No one's got one bad word to say. Shtoopin' his students or somebody's daughter, and the dad or the boyfriend takes it poorly? Nuh-unh. How 'bout his job? Well, yeah, is a coupla anthologists don't like he shoulda been made head a department, 'pointed above 'em—but these guys ain't gonna *kill* him for it. Even though they're *Dons*. You know, like Corleone?" He chuckled at his joke. "See where I'm goin'?"

"No."

"Comes down to this—you and the wifey there's our only real suspects."

I was silent a moment, then hung up, dismayed.

Wooland looked no better than when I'd last seen him. Furred black patches, missed while shaving, lurked beneath his jaws, and a long canvas bag, once a smart promotional gift, drooped in his fist. He wore a shapeless wool pullover and a pair of threadbare carpet slippers—as though he'd sauntered into the summer evening unaware he wasn't shod.

He began with an apology. "At the hospital the other morning, I had no idea your friend had just been killed. Why I didn't mention it then. I'm so very sorry."

"Quite all right, Wooland." And I imagined him having spent the weekend alone in his stuffy office, bent over his computer.

"Anyway, you asked for some data. On Henry Carlson Lewis Jones. So here: there's been a series of utterly horrendous double sexual murders in Surrey. Couples with car trouble stalled on the roadway are approached by someone who cuts the chap's throat and abducts the girl. She's raped, then stabbed to death, slowly."

"What do you mean, *slowly*."

"Multiple stab wounds, none to vital organs. It's . . . torture. She dies eventually of . . . uh . . . *exsanguination*."

"And . . . ?"

"Henry Carlson Lewis Jones is the CID's chief suspect. He's been questioned by them twice but they've gotten nowhere."

So Vidya had in fact read him perfectly for the sadistic predator he was. And, in doing so and shooting him dead, had saved our lives. And, no doubt, others'. I wanted to say, "Well, that's the end of your double sexual homicides in Surrey." But instead I said, "Thanks, Wooland. I owe you one."

Vidya was seated in an armchair, leafing through a women's magazine.

"What are you reading?"

"*Stew*-pid," she said, and flung it down. "It's all about boob jobs. As if big bazooms were the secret of happiness."

I lowered my gaze twelve inches or so. "Aren't they?"

She blushed. It was charming.

"What is it then? The secret of happiness."

She smiled a Mona Lisa smile. "*Santosha.*"

"*Contentment?*"

She nodded. "Accepting whatever happens to befall you. As a gift—from God."

I fixed her with my eyes. "Even your husband's murder?"

She fixed mine back. "Even your own."

I gave her answer the two beats it deserved, then told her what Strugnell had said about Henry Carlson Lewis Jones, omitting only the woman's torture.

"Thank you. There's always that doubt, you know, scratching like a dog at the back door of one's mind."

"Why did you take the gun?" I asked. "A semiautomatic? You know the penalties for that type of thing."

"I could say I was scared. Or had a premonition." She thought for a moment. "But neither is true. Sometimes I'm just . . . *bad.*"

She looked at me challengingly, almost as if to test how I'd respond.

I laughed. "Well, I'm glad. Because if you hadn't been bad . . . we'd both be good and dead."

The question that now arose was this: had Henry Jones killed Jai Prasad? If he had, then with Vidya's shot, frontier justice had been done. And we could all breathe a little easier, too. It certainly fit with my intuition that Vidya had been the ultimate target. Look at the timing. The buzzer had rung minutes after her return. Jones had watched her enter the mews, then followed. If he'd meant to kill Jai, he'd had all night to do it in. Why wait till his wife came home?

Then there was the blade. A website maintained that a Bowie of that style and size was capable of chopping through two-by-fours! So it could have killed Jai.

On the other hand, there was no proof at all Henry Jones was the culprit. Or that his stalking us in the starlit field was anything but an unrelated attempted crime of opportunity. Nor, having missed once, that he'd trailed us from London. We hadn't been followed. I was certain of that. Nor could he have known we would stall out in Salisbury. Nor was his MO entering flats.

In which case then, there was someone still at large who hadn't yet gotten what he—or she—really wanted.

I went round the house and checked our defenses. Willie's twelve-gauge was broken open on a table in the front hall, loaded. I'd shown it to Vidya. An unsheathed machete leaned in a corner. I hefted it and cut the air. This was more my style. Then there was Odin.

After dinner, over trifle and coffee, I told Vidya what Houlihan had said—about us being the only two suspects.

"I'm not sure how smart we were—to get *involved* like this." She sighed. "I'm afraid it makes us look guilty at worst—heartless at best."

"Well, it's too late now. And anyway, Jai was more than your husband. He was my dearest of friends."

"You loved him. I know. Still there's no decent reason why *you* should have your entire life . . ."

"Look," I interrupted her, "I'm seeing this through. To the end. And not just because I loved *Jai*—because I love *you*."

I'd said it. *There*. And with a force and suddenness that surprised us both.

She regarded me coolly. "Even if it means . . . ?"

"Going to hell and back? If I have to."

"But it's *me* they suspect. And these scandals have an awful way of besmirching everyone they touch."

"Yeah? Well, I don't give a fuck." I took her hand. "I don't care about that. I'm going to make certain that nobody hurts you. You have to solemnly promise you'll let me."

She nodded, slowly.

"Good," I said. "Now tell me this: where you were that night between twelve and three."

Obstinately, she shook her head. "You misunderstand. It's not that I'm unwilling . . . It's . . . I *cahn't*."

"Try."

"Read the book."

"The book?"

"Yes. The *enchaunted* one." She nodded, smiled, kissed me sweetly, then accompanied by Odin, ascended the stairs.

I sat there checkmated, stymied, stopped. I was in the midst of attempting to solve two murders, cover up a third and prevent a fourth. I didn't see how I could do this successfully without Vidya's full cooperation.

In fact, it wasn't enough *not* to be charged with Jai's and Jones's killings. Both cases had to be resolved and shut. If not, with Jai, a cloud of suspicion would hang above our heads forever. And if the cause of Jones's death weren't ruled "self-inflicted," who knew what future hell we'd face? An advance in forensics ten years hence (like fingerprints in 1900 or, more recently, DNA) might someday link us to Jones's killing through some form of evidence we didn't know exists.

But what could I do? I couldn't *beat* it out of her!

So, following Vidya's request, I got out the "enchanted" book and opened it to another chapter, one that—I sincerely hoped—would help solve the mystery of *both* my Ladies.

There are four types of persons, Ghazil always says, before whom the wise never go empty-handed: a god, a guru, a king—and a child. Since our youngest guest was two of these and his mother was a queen, I gave orders they be suitably fêted and fed. Carpets were spread, wood and water gathered, fires kindled and food prepared. You may question the wisdom of such a *durbar*[1] given our position, but wherever he is and whatever he's doing, a prince must always be a prince. Besides, my men were hungry and the wounded needed care.

I presented the Queen with an embroidered shawl made of a wool so soft it has usurped the name of its country, Cashmir, and is worn, I hear, by ladies of the harem as far away as the courts of France.

To the young king I gave a blade whose handle held a *ser*[2] of purest gold. I also awarded him one of our Afghans, with which he seemed to be enamoured: a splendid young bitch, thin as a splinter and shy and wild as a divine shadow. His gifts I chose with special care—a knife and a hound— to afford at least symbolic protection, though protection from whom or what I still couldn't say. Then 'Abd al-Wali drew a mouse from his pocket, making the boy (and the men, as well) gasp with alarm as he gulped it down—only

---

1. *durbar*: royal court
2. *ser*: a measure equal to about one kilo

to withdraw it, moments later, alive and wriggling from behind the child's ear!

For this admirable feat, he received from the boy a look of utmost adoration and from the Queen, a ruby of the most excellent water, weighing half a *misqal*[3]. No sooner had he received the gem, however, than it vanished, and we watched again with mounting discomfort as he searched for it frantically, only to discover it (at last!) beneath his turban. This final bit of flimflam was greeted with cheers, and while the men applauded, the Queen arose and entered the tent I'd erected for our use.

The moment I entered she turned to me, all pretence of social graces gone. She looked like a woman at the end of her tether who is resigned to prevail by sheer force of will. "I am . . . *beset*," she said, glancing warily about her, like a person encircled by ravenous beasts.

"Beset? By whom?"

"By whom are we not? To the north, the Uzbeks raid our villages, while to the east, we are threatened by your brother's men. To the west, even now, the Rana of Mewar is raising an army with which he hopes to seize my throne. I have begged him to put aside these unworthy ambitions, but . . ." She paused.

". . . those are the least of my worries, really. The greatest threat is from within." She looked about her, as though the beasts were closing in. "Every time I eat, I fear my bread is laced with poison. Every time my son is out of sight, even for a moment, I panic, wondering if I will see him again, or if I won't be called, 'O Queen, come quickly, a terrible accident has befallen . . .'" She looked away, biting her lips, refusing to finish the inauspicious sentence. I looked out the tent at the little king, gingerly stroking the head of his dog as 'Abd al-Wali entertained him.

---

3. *misqal:* a measure equal to approximately ten carats

"People see a woman and a boy on the throne and are tempted to dream dreams they shouldn't."

"And why merely dream them?"

"Because they are *cowards*," she said with a venomous contempt. "They know what they plan to do is a sin and so they extemporize, torn. They're like a pack of dogs that know they mustn't filch a *chapāti*[4]. If kept at bay with a stick, they'll behave. But turn your back on them for even half a moment and they will rush inside and snatch your supper. Then, as the saying goes, 'The dog sits in the cook's place.'"

"Today," she confessed, "I don't know where we were going. We were supposedly visiting the shrine of a Saint, but," she conceded, "*this* is not the way. The jackal your companion killed was, I fear, more our jailer than protector. So I prayed to the Goddess to come to our rescue. And the next moment . . . *you* appeared."

There is something delightful in being viewed as an instrument of divine intervention, even as I marvelled at the ever-expanding ramifications of my vow. Not only did the Queen require protection from my brother, Jafir, from the Uzbeks, and from the impetuous Rana of Mewar, but apparently from her own ministers, too.

Regarding my brother, I said to her, "Know it will be difficult. To restrain Jafir is like trying to dam the sea. Reason means little to him, nor do others' desires. He follows only his own sweet will."

"Then what can I offer," she asked, "to persuade you? Allegiance? Tribute? I'll give you more than you and your men can bear."

Alone with Mayura in the desert tent, motes of dust swarming the sunlight, I looked again at her fulsome lips,

---

4. *chapāti*: a flat, unleavened bread

heavenly eyes, and the vivid silken cords of her throat—and I knew it wasn't gold I wanted.

She knew it, too, for with an almost imperceptible flutter, she offered herself to me. I cannot describe exactly how she did this, except to say she lifted and exposed her throat, tossing back her wild jet hair, and made a sound that is, indubitably, the syllable of surrender.

I covered her. She gasped, then gave herself without withholding one scintilla of her being. My tongue unlocked the vault of her throat: it was filled with nectar, and in her body's clinging weight and heat, I could feel the truth and fullness of her submission.

I thought I might take her then and there and moved to rip away her bodice, but she stopped my hand, saying, "Nay. For now, take this." And she opened her fist.

I thought at first it was a chunk of ice brought down from the Himalayas. In the heat, it was a welcome prize. Then it caught the light and ice became fire! Only then did I see it was a crystal or, more precisely, the largest and most astonishing diamond I have ever had the wonder to behold. "It's . . . *enormous*. It must be worth . . ."

"Half the daily expenditures of the world . . ."

I tried to envision such a sum. Take all the gold, coin and kind that changes hands in the course of a day, halve it, and you had the approximate value of the object in her hand.

She tendered it. I have handled gems; even so, I was shocked by its weight and water.

"This seals my surrender." Again, she took the dust of my feet. "Be true to me," she said as we parted. "And I swear to God I will be true to you."

Though our vow was one of lovers, it wasn't love of which she spoke.

Chapter 24

There comes a point while reading a book when it naturally absorbs you: you merge with it like ink in a blotter. You forget you are reading and begin to live and breathe the tale. Only later, looking up at the dismal subway relentlessly hurtling itself toward Brooklyn, do you realize that, for the past ten minutes, you haven't been on a train at all but in a rooming house in wartime London, or, in my case, soul kissing a Rajasthani queen.

This moment of absorption, like the precise instant of falling asleep, cannot be apprehended, as its very nature is a forgetting. So, too, for me, this merging happened. I slipped into Sikandar's world, losing consciousness—for a time at least—of whom and what and where I was as I wandered the roads and breathed the bloody and ebullient air of fourteenth-century Rājputāna.

In the tale, we were returning to camp, cantering over the high desert plain, filled with both excitement and apprehension. We passed an ancient hilltop fort, deserted save for a pair of kites riding the thermals high overhead. Then, with the waning day, our war party reached the river border, where we stopped at a little village to water both our horses and ourselves.

And as I dismounted, there came that time that always does when, subtly sated by the tale, you sigh and raise your eyes from its pages. But, oddly, when I did just that, all I saw was the tan desert plain stretching off in all directions.

At first, I was amused (if somewhat surprised), though as seconds passed and the illusion persisted, my amusement morphed into astonishment, then dread, and finally into that disorienting panic you feel when you *know* that you're dreaming and command yourself to wake, but the spell of sleep will not release.

I looked about. There were men and horses all around me, grayed with dust from head to toe. I could smell their funk, feel the heat of the tropical sun on my back and the cool river water between my toes.

Then to my wonder, my panic dispersed and I was flooded by a delicious sensation of youth: an emotional glow and physical well-being I hadn't felt in years. Tired as I was, I could run a mile if I had to, and to feel that strength and possess it in its fullness was sublime. God, I'd forgotten what it felt like to be nineteen!

Again, I looked about. Everything was the way it was in the book, only more *specific*. My companion's tunic was split at the shoulder; another man's face bore a strawberry stain. And the dust! We were covered in it, as though we'd rolled in a vat of flour!

A toothless old gent wearing a loincloth approached me now and touched my feet. He begged me to follow, leading me to a scrap of carpet beneath the shade of a banyan tree. At my approach, the villagers folded their hands in respectful greeting. My shadow shot a trembling plume in the air. And it was only then the penny dropped and I realized that I *was* Sikandar! It was *his* youth and vigor that flowed in my veins.

Yet more intoxicating than the strength of his body was the nobility of his soul. It existed beside my less innocent nature without either seemingly affecting the other—the way fire and water in a painted landscape lie side by side, yet never dry or wet each other.

The entire village was gathered round, gawking. The women wore saris without *cholis,* exactly the way that Vidya had described; the men's loins were wrapped in diaper-like rags. They gave off an odor of dried sweat and bitter lemon. A naked brown toddler staggered forward and, reaching out, touched the glittering hilt of my sword. Sikandar (and I) lifted him up and the child broke into high-pitched laughter. Then his little brown digit twitched and shivered, and he peed in my/Sikandar's face as everyone else burst out laughing.

I was appalled. But my alter ego joined right in as if the event were the very epitome of hilarity, the incarnation of mirth. And, alongside my dismay, I could feel his amusement—fresh and foolish, frank and free.

For instead of dropping the child in the dirt, he, in whose body I was apparently residing, threw the still-micturating urchin into the air so that the child shrieked with wild abandon and his golden stream arced in the sun, anointing us all. Sikandar (whom I was beginning to fear was a fool, noble heart or no) regarded this drenching as a ritual bath, equivalent to a dip in the River Ganges. To his way of thinking, the god in the child, delighted by our victory, was bestowing his blessings by pouring this rare oblation on our head! And I saw that for one who thinks in this manner, it's very easy to be happy.

I waited for someone to throw us a towel, but towels, apparently, were not yet invented or, none at least, were forthcoming (though I will admit if I hadn't known what the vile liquid was, I'd have found its cooling effects rather pleasing).

Then again, Sikandar's loving acceptance of the boy was politically astute, for it won the villagers' trust. Within minutes, we were brought bowls of rice and buffalo milk, sugared and spiced with pistachios, cardamom and raisins. Maybe it was my youthful appetite, but it tasted heavenly: like rich rice pudding, only better. After eating, we listened to the villagers' petitions. Those who were ill, Sikandar had examined by his physician who prescribed herbs, compresses, baths and massage. In several cases, I recognized the patient's symptoms and wanted to scream, "No, that girl needs penicillin!" but it was, of course, the year thirteen-something.

After the infirmary came the court of judgment. My royal Siamese twin had a standard inside him, a wheel of law, and he referred everything back to this measure—though for a fellow who claimed to be a gentleman and a scholar, his sense of justice was swift and tough. There was no inquiry into the felon's background. (Was he a substance abuser? Did he come from a broken home?) There was no chance to plea bargain, either. For a man who had raped a girl, Sikandar ordered emasculation and the sign of a vulva burned in his brow.

There were no lawyers, no appeals. No sooner was sentence passed, then the rapist was taken behind a thin wattle wall and a few minutes later, we heard a quick *thwhack* and a vicious sizzle, followed by a doglike yowl. Then 'Abd al-Wali strode forth grinning, wiping his sword. The last I saw of the unfortunate felon, he was seated on a blanket, his wound coated with tar, the brand still smoking on his forehead.

Yet, tough as Sikandar was, he was merciful. Several delinquents prostrated themselves and I could feel the weight of their contrition move him. One, whom he might justly have killed, he had whipped. Another was fined; the third, a hungry boy who had stolen a melon, was let go along with the sternest of warnings, a small silver coin, a basket of fruit, and the solemn assurance that if Sikandar ever heard of him stealing again, even a single corn of barley, he would return and personally feed his person to the water tigers, limb by limb.

Then, after our horses were fed (not hay, but strange, congealed balls of grain), Sikandar was weighed against bags of wheat, rice, mangos and barley, and rolls of silk and cotton cloth—a fraction of the booty carried out of Indore—which was then distributed to all. He cracked open a barrel of toddy and gave the children milk sweets and halvah. With a single gem, he established a fund to feed the poor, "with special consideration given to widows, orphans and to those smitten by the fist of calamity."

Finally, he ordered the planting of shade- and fruit-producing trees and the digging of wells and tanks for bathing, promising the villagers he would send an official to "dispense justice, regulate merchants, recruit artisans, collect taxes, provide alms for holy mendicants and reward loyal servants of the Shah."

In return for his bounty, the villagers fed us, praised us, opened their huts and hovels to us, offered us their daughters' hands in marriage and renamed their village Sikandarpur.

As we departed, the children ran after our horses for as far as their little legs would go. The men, already half-blind on toddy, smiled toothless grins, and the ladies beamed behind their new saris, except for a few young girls who were openly weeping and pulling their hair as, in the space of a couple of hours, they had fallen madly and hopelessly in love with 'Abd al-Wali Mirza.

Soon we came to the infamous pillar. In the cinnamon sunset, the monument looked less horrific than fey, like something astonishing seen in a dream: a house made of human faces. Its odors were masked by night-blooming jasmine mixed with the smoke of the tribals' dung fires. Still, a thin, fecal poison invested the air, and the moon tinged the heads with an unearthly splendor.

It would have been wiser—we decided, too late—to have passed by in daylight or have detoured around it altogether, for our men were superstitious, and the sight of the heads awoke in them terrors. We rode by in silence, averting our faces so as not to invite the Evil Eye. Once we had passed, Sikandar commanded the tower be razed, the heads returned to the widows of Indore, and the plaque dispatched to his father's palace.

Chapter 25

It was Ghazil who greeted us on our return. I don't know what I expected the distinguished counselor to be: his expression was even more pinched than I'd imagined.

Sikandar bent down before him and respectfully took the dust of his feet.

"No more of that," Ghazil protested. "You are clearly your own master now." He paused. "Though I will continue to advise you, if you so desire."

We watched from out of the desert dusk the caravan approaching. Humped on the horses' backs were the bent cylinders of silken *soumaks*, gold bars and silver plate, fist-sized bags of various gems, parcels of ambergris and aloes wrapped in purple paper. There were Alexandria candles, raisin wine and beakers of rosewater commingled with musk; even Shami apples, soap cakes and lemon loaves.

"What splendid plunder!" the old man crowed.

Sikandar corrected him. "Tribute," he said, and reaching in his *kurta*, he withdrew the diamond and flipped it with a feigned indifference.

Ghazil caught and beheld it for a time in silence. "This must be worth . . ." But he never finished, lost as he was in the immensity of his calculations. After a moment, he said, "And you received this from . . . ?"

"The Queen. Of Indore."

"In return for . . . ?"

". . . our protection."

"I see," Ghazil said, with somewhat less glee.

"Ghazil," Sikandar said, "I win a great victory and you act like it's some mean defeat. May I remind you that I conquered Indore in a morning, without the loss of a single man? Its Queen has pledged us her allegiance and has paid us great tribute. The jewels of her crown scraped the dust of my feet. Why, in the name of the Ever-Merciful, are you scowling?"

"Because not everyone will see it this way."

"And what other way is there to see it, pray?"

Ghazil sighed. "You unilaterally abrogated a dozen treaties and, without consultation, formed an alliance with an enemy queen. If viewed in this way, your actions could almost be regarded as . . . treason."

"*Treason?*" Sikandar asked, disbelieving.

"And another thing," Ghazil went on. "Your participation in certain native rites does not go unnoticed. Some claim you are an apostate."

"Why? Because I worship with my men?"

"Because you pray with them to others than the One."

"And what do *you* believe?"

Me?" Ghazil laughed. "I have no opinion, *theologically* speaking. But you should know that, in doing so, you give comfort to your enemies."

"I am more concerned with the comfort I give my men." Sikandar shook his head, and plucking from a passing horse a mango, ripped back its skin when Ghazil reached out and seized it, rudely.

"Listen well, Sikandarji. If you do not first inspect with greater care the morsel on your tongue—or gaze more deeply into the nature of the sediment that seems to cloud your drinking water—these very details, beneath your dignity to observe could, in the blink of an eye, remove you from this world, and all your grand designs along with it. Our *enemy* gave this mango to you."

"Our *former* enemy. Present *ally*." Sikandar snatched the mango back and bit into it. Oh, it was delicious.

"Now," Ghazil continued, "if we were to analyze the Queen Mayura's actions—all sentiment aside, from a purely strategic point of view—how might we describe them?"

Sikandar, I could tell, did not like the direction in which the conversation was heading. Nor did I. Though I, for one, had no say in the matter. I was beginning to grasp my unique position: I was Sikandar's *mute* and *inactive* Siamese twin. I shared his mind and body, his memory, senses and his thoughts. I could taste the fruit, revel in his jubilation, and feel his desire, fear and pain, but I could not speak, act, or intercede.

Sikandar sighed. "*Bheda*."

"*Bheda*. Yes. Divide and conquer. Pick one of the princes and align with him. Let the two brothers fight it out between themselves and, when both have exhausted their forces, walk in."

"Except it didn't happen that way! I doubt at first she even knew who I was!"

"Sikandar ibn Musa Khilji al-Hind! Do not play the fool with me. Do you really think that Queen Mayura doesn't know the makeup of your house? Do you think her astrologers didn't cast your fortune the day you were born and haven't been poring over it since, probing it for weaknesses?"

And though this observation was meant to give Sikandar pause, it gave instead a lovely consolation. Sikandar imagined Mayura saying his name and studying his character long before they'd ever met, and he found in this a curious comfort.

"Next."

"*Upekshā*. And *sāman*."

"Ah. 'Overlooking' and 'conciliation.' You attack her country, but she doesn't seem to notice. A minor infraction not worthy of mention. And with *sāman*, she charms the beast in you with words of praise and sweet appeasement, the way a snake charmer charms his deadly slave. Did she claim your appearance was divine intervention? You're blushing. Ah, I see she did. Next!"

"*Dānā.*"

"Gift giving. Good. And not just any gift, but the mother of diamonds. Of course, if our kingdom falls to hers, she will get it back. And more. So while it's a gift to you, to her, it's more . . . an investment. Fifth?"

Sikandar didn't answer. Even I found Ghazil's belittling tone difficult to bear.

"I am waiting."

"*Māyā.*"

"Deception. And how did Mayura utilize *māyā*?"

Sikandar sighed. "She sent three guides. We must assume they are spies."

"Of course, they are. Did she send an ambassador, too, with his staff?"

We looked at Ghazil. "She is sending one. Yes."

"Of course, she is. And they will all be spies, too. Perhaps the entire encounter was designed from the outset to insert her agents into our court. Did this occur to you?"

"'Abd al-Wali was leading us."

"*Jī.* 'Abd al-Wali. Whose mother is a Rajput princess."

Sikandar was outraged. "Are you accusing 'Abd al-Wali . . . ?"

"I am stating his lineage. And finally . . ."

"*Indrajāla.*"

"Ah. *Indra's net.* Those eyes, are they really that beguiling? Or is it her lips? Whatever it is, it must be absolutely mesmerizing to make you walk into her lair . . ."

"I walked out of it, too," Sikandar protested, "with the biggest gem in Hindustan . . ."

"That, you did," Ghazil conceded. He held the diamond up. "It *is* magnificent, I will admit. And bound to bring you untold grief."

Once again, we were mystified. "Why grief? It will bring us peace and great prosperity. After all, I have struck an alliance."

"Yes. With our enemy and the enemy of our allies, and by so doing have thrown the balance of power into chaos! What will our allies do, now *their* enemy has become *our* friend?

"And let me remind you of something else. Your brother publicly vowed to conquer Indore. He will not be pleased with what you've done. For having allied with *her*, you must now oppose *him*. What's that?" Ghazil asked, suddenly, pointing to our arm.

"Nothing. A *rakhi*."

"That *she* gave you?" A marvelous smile broke forth on Ghazil's lips. "*Now,* I see. You are *smitten*. This is not a political alliance. This is . . . a *seduction*! And by one long practiced in the art."

"She is hardly a temptress. She's the mother of a young boy. Both her life and that of the child are in danger."

"And do you know why? It is said she is unearthly. That is why they wish to dethrone her."

"*Unearthly*?" we both asked.

"Some say she is an *apsaras*, a nymph; others, a *yakshi*[1], *rākshasi*[2] or *vetali*[3]—but all agree, she is not of this world."

"She is a widow," Sikandar protested, "a royal widow with a small child."

"If so, she is a self-made one. For Rāja Mul did not die in battle, as you may suppose. It is said he ran, and she was so shamed and enraged by his cowardice that she picked up a saber and slew him herself. They also whisper she is

---

1. *yakshi*: a female fertility genie
2. *rākshasi*: a demoness
3. *vetali*: a vampire

~ 173 ~

corrupt and enjoys revels with *aghori-tantrikas*[4] in cremation grounds."

"*Pish*," Sikandar said. "Gossip. I'm sure they tell similar tales about us." Anyway, whether Mayura was a demoness, a murderess or a libertine was not the issue: "I have given my word. Now I must keep it."

"Why?"

"Because at the basis of all, there must be good faith, Ghazil. There *must*. If the word of a prince means nothing, then nothing else has any meaning—neither contracts nor vows."

"Do you recall that dispute you had me settle in Dhun between that tailor and that merchant? Each month, they would agree on a fair price for the tailor's labor; when the work was done, the merchant would pay.

"One month the tailor's payment was short. He inquired why. The merchant said, 'Well, yes, you did sew that garment for me, but the lady who ordered it changed her mind.'

"The tailor replied, 'Exalted sir, this was not our understanding. Our agreement was that I would sew this cloth and you would pay me two rupees. The agreement was between you and me, not myself and the lady. I am sincerely sorry if you lost on your transaction, but whether you gain or whether you lose does not absolve your debt to me. For twenty years, I have not shared in your profits; why should I now begin to share in your loss?'"

Ghazil looked interested despite himself. "And what did the trader say?"

"What *could* he say? He was a greedy fool. I ordered him to pay the tailor the two rupees, plus two hundred more, and a hundred to the court for wasting everyone's time.

"But that's not the end. The very next month, the merchant went back to the tailor with new fabric. The tailor

---

4. *aghori-tantrikas*: Practitioners of tantra, particularly those unorthodox rites involving meat, wine, *ganja*, and sexual relations

examined it, then pushed it away, saying, 'Cannot you see this fabric is torn?'"

"'Torn? Are you blind? It has just come from the weaver!'"

"'The fabric I speak of is your word. Now that you have broken it, no amount of mending can repair it. For if your word meant nothing to you last month, why should it mean something tomorrow?'

"And so ended a twenty-year partnership—one highly beneficial to all."

"You are saying . . . ?"

". . . that the fabric won't be rent by me. I gave this queen my word of honor. I swore it on the Highest Power. How can I betray her?"

"Will you betray your Sultan, then? And your clan?"

"Ghazil," Sikandar pleaded, "I have sworn an oath! Before the gods!"

"The gods be damned!" Ghazil declared. "It's not the gods you have to worry about. It's Jafir. Do you know what he will do if he thinks you're a threat? He will impale you on a stake in the middle of his courtyard. There you will writhe and squirm for a week until death mercifully overtakes you. Is that what you want? A stake up your ass? My God," Ghazil thundered. "You've forgotten the very first lesson I taught you."

"Hardly; it was *matsa nyāya*: the Law of the Fish: 'Big fish swallow little.' The problem, Ghazil, is that I am not a *fish*. I am a *prince*. And I intend to act like one."

"Why?" Ghazil called after him. "So that you may congratulate yourself on your righteousness?"

Sikandar paused and said over his shoulder, "For no other reason than I feel wretched when I don't."

Sikandar (and I) made our way to the river. There, in the tepid pools, I glimpsed our reflection. We were wearing a red floral *kurta* with matching turban, and lovely pearl-and-ruby studs.

I tried to make sense of my condition, though even then, I could feel the heat of the sun-baked boulder and hear the cacophony of desert birds bedding down for the night.

What *was* this? Was it a book? A dream? A vision? It was filled with so much love and squalor, gems and death, poetry and cruelty—and parallels so unique to my life—I could only believe it was my own. Perhaps some primordial part of me yearned to experience the fullness of life, to hold real gold and priceless jewels, or maybe some ancient eye inside me needed to see red blood spill, pooling in the ochre dust, and the white of defleshed bone.

Our tent stunk to high heaven. The odors of horse and human manure competed with those of smoke and curry. There was no furniture to speak of, nothing but rugs and a folding table, no semblance even of privacy and quiet. Someone was singing in a nearby tent and a servant was snoring loudly in the corner.

The tent flap opened and 'Abd al-Wali entered, his arms around two gorgeous *houris*. Where he found them I can't imagine, though from the way they were dressed (or *un*dressed, really) and the wanton boldness of their gazes, they were clearly not your village virgins. "Hey, Kando!"

I hoped Sikandar chose the one on the left—a delicious, sloe-eyed slut in an embroidered vest and harem pants. For a moment, she seemed surprised to see him. Then she turned and pranced, daring us to follow, her anklets tinkling and her heavy breasts exuding a carnality that left me weak in the knees.

Thus I was dismayed to feel her presence creating no heat within my brother. "Oh, Great One," he said to 'Abd al-Wali, "you will have to be twice the man tonight."

'Abd al-Wali frowned. "Kando, come. Surely the King of Rajasthan deserves a little love."

Sikandar laughed, unhappily. "Be careful what you call me, brother. 'Many a tongue has cut many a throat.'"

"Kando," 'Abd al-Wali pleaded. "Look at her!"

But Sikandar wasn't interested. He was thinking of the Queen of Indore and remembering the heavenly realm of her eyes, except the Queen was thirty miles away. Instead, Sikandar shook his slave awake and asked him for a drink of water. The man returned with a sweating *kalash*. Christ, but it was poisonous: hot and reeking of saddle leather.

Then the slave unrolled a Persian rug. This was our bed. Was I missing something? The man was a prince. He owned a diamond the size of the Ritz, and this is where we were sleeping tonight? On a rug, on the sand, in a room with a fool and no furniture—a rug that was crawling with fleas and vermin?

Occasionally, the courtesans flickered in his mind as one of them giggled or moaned in a nearby tent, sounds soon lost in his longing for the Queen.

He replayed their encounter. Ghazil was right. If viewed in one light, the Queen's overtures could be seen as an attempt to undermine their kingdom, a covert campaign of political war. But what a harsh and wretched light to view things in! In its glare, every goddess was a demon. No, Sikandar did not believe this was her motive. He had felt the tension, seen her fear and grief. It was not manufactured.

As for Ghazil's conviction that he'd been seduced, that, too, was nonsense. Sikandar did not deny that Mayura was lovely, though when he recalled her, it wasn't her loveliness he remembered but her *fire*. He kept seeing the way she spoke of her enemies, her mouth spitting poison, her eyes hot, burning stars.

He remembered a time as a boy when he and Ghazil had come upon two dueling Mamelukes. When Sikandar had asked why the men were fighting, Ghazil had motioned to a woman nearby and said, "That girl has a hole between her legs. These men are killing each other over who will stick their thingamajig in it."

Sikandar and I both laughed at the memory: his introduction to "the birds and the bees."

Eventually, he said his prayers. Christ, but they went on forever! He thanked God for this and the Goddess for that, and at least thirteen other deities for his victory in Indore. He thanked the Earth for allowing him to walk upon Her and for giving rest to his weary head. He thanked the rivers for their water and then called down blessings upon his ancestors, father, people, and the Queen.

I tried to sleep, but it was useless. Instead, I kept picturing the Queen of Indore, helpless, on her knees before us. There are men for whom such sights, instead of inciting their chivalry, bring out their worst. Perhaps I am one. For as Sikandar fell asleep that night, I found myself imagining the many bold and wanton things that such a man as I might have done.

Chapter 26

I returned to Dorset in the dead of night—or more precisely, the dead of morning. The clock read 4:29 a.m. I had begun reading Sikandar's memoir at nine o'clock the previous evening. Seven and one half hours had passed.

I looked down at the book. It was open exactly to where I'd just been: with Sikandar asleep on the flea-bitten rug. Had I been reading—or dreaming? Or had something entirely *else* occurred?

I went upstairs. Despite the hour, Vidya was seated on our bedroom floor, cross-legged and bent at the waist so that her brow was pressing the carpet, her ringlets covering her face like a veil. It was difficult to say what she was doing. Meditating? Praying? Bowing? Sleeping? A stick of incense fumed before an idol of Ganesh. The elephant-headed god, noose in one hand, axe in another, a cobra girdling his voluminous belly, was dancing on a mouse, an illusion made all the more vivid and real by the fluttering light of a flickering candle.

Sensing my presence, Vidya lifted her head and drew back her long black hair. She looked at me slowly with soft, dark eyes.

"I know where you were the night Jai was murdered."

She said nothing.

"In the *book*."

She gazed at me intently, then bowed to her god.

"Why didn't you tell me?"

She uncurled her legs and stretched them to the side. "Would you have believed me?"

"No."

She made a very Indian gesture—a side to side rolling shake of her head that has any number of meanings, including: yea, nay, never in a million years and maybe.

"Now tell me, Vidya, what happened."

She paused for a moment. "I *did* go to the theater. And I *did* walk home. I got in at midnight. Just as I said."

"And Jai was dead?"

She shook her head. "He was seated in the study, covered by his shawl. He would do that—draw a shawl up over his head—when he wanted to sleep or . . . just retire. I was trying to decide whether to wake him or not when the buzzer rang. I queried the intercom; there was no reply."

"So you buzzed them in."

She shook her head, no. "Jai had warned me. He said it was how miscreants gain entrance. Still, I wondered if perhaps the intercom was again out of order and so I went downstairs to see who it was. Actually, I thought it might be you. The lift was engaged, so I took the stairs, but when I got to the lobby, no one was there.

"I realized then I had neglected to fetch the post. It was wedged in our mailbox and I struggled with it for quite some time, ripping it frightfully, I'm afraid. When I was finished, I rang for the lift. It came straight away.

"The door to our flat was open a bit, though I couldn't recall if that's how I'd left it. The moment I entered, I smelled something odd, almost like . . . *animals*. I thought it might be the gas at first, so I went to the kitchen. Then I returned to the study and Jai was . . ." Reliving the moment, she closed her eyes.

"You didn't phone the police. Why?"

"There was no . . . *urgency. You* saw him. There was blood . . . on . . . *everywhere!* . . . Then I noticed the book on the rug and picked it up. You see, I had this fantastic notion that someone had come out of the book and killed him."

"Come out of the *book*?" I asked, in disbelief.

"Correct. For Jai had told me it was *enchaunted.* He said it was infused with *maya shakti* at a time when people could still do such things. And that it would captivate whomever read it. So when I saw it, I picked it up. No sooner had I read a line or two than I was . . . *gone.*"

Believe me, I knew what she meant.

"But weren't you afraid the killer was still around?"

"Truly? No. I don't know why. And a moment later, I was . . . somewhere else."

"Where were you?"

For the longest time, she didn't answer. Then in a faraway voice she said, "In a tower. In a desert place. At night. The stars were unbelievably bright. And I could smell the smoke and bougainvillea . . ."

She paused. "When I returned, it was getting light. And I realized then I'd been entranced for hours. And that, you see, presented a *dy*lemma. Because I knew there was no bloody way in hell I could ever explain to anyone, including myself— or you—where the bloody fuck I'd been!"

Christ, we were *screwed.* For up until then, I had still hoped she might be able to explain herself in some defensible way. There was no chance the police—or a judge and jury, if it came to that—would ever believe she'd been trapped inside a literary tower.

"And who were *you*?" she asked me now.

"A prince. With his men . . ."

"Ah," she said in a voice that made my heart go gray. "You're the one she fears will betray her."

I looked at her then in the light from the window. It was hard to say who had spoken those words.

"Tell the Queen we won't betray her. Tell her . . . we . . . Sikandar loves her."

I turned to the window. It had long been dawn: the white nights of English summers last a bare handful of hours. I looked out at the graying downs, the rolling hills, the rising sun.

Chapter 27

I didn't go to bed that morning but sat out in the lightening garden, trying to make sense of what I'd seen and heard. Try as I might, I couldn't. In Houlihan's words, I was "a lost soul in a strange world," a world of love and a world of magic that nothing in my experience permitted me to understand. For, like the little Dutch boy who found a hole in a dike that, left unchecked, would unbolt the sea, so I seemed to have come across a tear in the very fabric of existence—a hole that led to God-knows-where!

That the book's strange effect was like nothing I'd encountered was beyond discussion. Whether it was "enchanted" or not, I really couldn't say.

I did know this: I couldn't speak of it to anyone but Vidya. To have even hinted to my colleagues I possessed a codex that was somehow "charmed" would have been career suicide. Grants, funding, affiliations, publication and access to sites and materials would have dried right up.

The only person who might have explained it to me was Jai, and Jai was in a place beyond all explanations.

Somehow, I'd crossed a border. And if *I* had crossed in one direction, who was to say that a Rajput warrior, as Vidya had surmised, could not have crossed it in the other and, leaping from the pages, slain Jai with his sabre before vanishing back from whence he'd come, where no earthly Houlihan would ever find him. It gave "lost in your reading" a whole new gloss.

It was then I had the strangest notion, like none I'd ever had before: what if my life were also a story and Xander Donne a character in another enchanted book? I flipped between the two: Xander and Sikandar, but neither was any more real than the other.

I work with hard data: materials, dirt. I have never been a metaphysician. So to even entertain this notion told me this: that I had changed. It was as though with each immersion in the tale, I returned to Dorset dyed a deeper shade of Sikandar. For I *did* feel different: younger, braver, as though Sikandar's mind and person were subtly, but progressively, informing my own.

Then I had the wildest idea yet: if I *were* a character in some magical story, then why not play my role in it with all the grace that I could muster, and enact it in such a rollicking manner that it kept the Reader—whoever *that* was—up and reading way past bedtime?

Silly as it was, the fantasy was liberating. I felt lighter and freer than I had in days. I speed-dialed Houlihan. I thought I'd try *sāman* on him, conciliation.

"Yeah?"

"You know, Mick, I'm actually a homicide detective just like you. Only the cases I work aren't just cold. They're *below zero*. So since we're in the same basic business, why not work this case together? You show us yours; we'll show you ours."

"No can do."

"And why's that?"

" 'Cause you and your honey there is about two cunt hairs away from being grabbed. I tell you a thing, you'll just use it to fix up your alibis."

"There's nothing to fix. We *didn't do it.*"

"Maybe *you*," Houlihan conceded. "General census is you're a pain to the butt, but probably not a murderer. And I ain't sayin' she did it all by her lonesome. Coulda had help.

But lemme tell ya. For your *education*. Your lady friend ain't who she say she is. Nuh-unh. Not by a long shot. Now, how ya like *them* apples?"

"What do you mean?"

"Let's just say it's more'n I can put inta words . . . . You wanna, I can draw you a picture."

At the stationhouse in Stour, Chief Superintendent Dahmer's assistant laid out before me half-a-dozen grainy photos appearing to document a party of wastrels exiting a silver Bentley. A bald, squat, neckless monster in the foreground was obviously the bodyguard, and from the sedan's creamy leather interior, an older gentleman was emerging. His eyes were so dark and pouched with dissipation that it looked like he was wearing mascara. Behind him, jewel in her nose, cigarette in a glittering fist, bending in a way that displayed the creamy ravine of her cleavage, was a lovely young woman: your basic moneyed, Asian beauty. The bodyguard, whose colorful tattoos burgeoned from his collar, was holding the car door open for her while clearly peering down her dress.

"Goes by the name Rukmini Patel," Dahmer said. "Indian girl, Kenyan national. She's a . . . how does one phrase it ? . . . royal concubine . . . a ruling-class tart."

"Who's the old man?" I asked.

"Ibrahim Saluk Habib, international arms dealer and all-round bunghole. She was his plaything for a while. Disappeared from his entourage six months back."

"And The Hulk?" I asked, eyeing the bodyguard.

"Bunzo Doi. He's *yakuza*."

I studied the girl. "And you think this is Vidya. This . . . plaything of the sheik. But you're not sure."

"Hey," Houlihan observed from London by speakerphone, "it's not exact, but you gotta admit, the resemblance is there."

I scrutinized the photos. She *did* look like Vidya.

"We can't find any record of her in Kenya or Switzerland, where she says she went to school, or anywhere else for that matter," Dahmer added. "That's why we think she may be Rukmini Patel."

"That's absurd!"

"Is it? Rumor is she absconded with a pot of Habib's jewels and money. Could be in hiding. Could be dead. Or could have married Jai Prasad."

I rolled my eyes. "You really think the whore of some Saudi prince is going to enter into an *arranged* marriage with a professor of *religious studies* who made, if he was lucky, *sixty* a year?"

"Hey!" Houlihan offered. "Maybe it was love!"

"Yeah. It was love. And then she *killed* him."

Cartoon characters bang their heads against inanimate objects in frustration; as I left the stationhouse, I wanted to do the same. The slurs against Vidya were never-ending. No sooner was one answered than, hydra-headed, two more appeared.

Opening the hatch, I rifled a valise in which Vidya had tossed some clothes to be dry-cleaned. Don't ask what I was looking for. Something—*anything*—that *proved* who she was.

A Ravissant shawl. Two custom-made *salwar kameezes* devoid of labels. And an assortment of "western" duds by Dolce & Gabbana, Pierre Balmain, Prada, Tse . . .

A Louis Vuitton valise yielded a string bag containing several fire opals, a folded wad of Cape Verde *escudos*, and a cheap mirror—in short, nothing that would prove or dis-prove Vidya's identity. Neglectfully crumpled in the bottom of the tote was a notice of deposit at Banque Sarasin & Cie, 4002 Basel, for a cool 97,000 Swiss francs . . . And, in an inner pocket, an expired Kenyan passport in the name of one—Glory be to God—*Rājakumārī Shrī Vidya Rao.*

I noticed our cottage two miles away: every light in every window was burning. I stepped on the gas as a police van passed in the opposite direction, and pulled into our drive to find Mrs. O'Connell rushing about in breathless turns. Every door was thrown open and Odin, locked up somewhere, was barking nonstop.

"Please, sir, thank God you're home. Plod's searched the place from tip to toe. Take me a fortnight to put it right. Took some things, did they? Yessir, they did, sir. Lookin' for evidence, says he. Evidence of what? says I. Never you mind, missus. Rippin' up cushions, beddin'. Even had Willie here diggin' up the garden . . ." Willie, who was leaning on his spade, nodded grimly.

I went inside. The house had indeed been searched: every drawer of every cabinet opened; every cushion, cup and rug looked under. I had a terrible sense of violation and the faintest inkling of how a woman must feel taken against her will.

"You said they took things? What?"

"Books, clothes." Ruby went on, "Found a sword, sir, didn't they?"

"Sword? *What* sword?"

Odin came in with Willie behind him. "Big thing, wern it? Had a sort of animal's head, sir, on the handle, like."

"Vidya!" I called. And when she didn't answer, I panicked: "Where *is* she?"

"Asked her to come down and answer some questions, didn't they, now?"

"When?"

"Oh. Hour . . . hour and a half ago. Couple of 'em stayed behind rootin' through the laundry. Left just minutes afore ye come."

I stalked outside, jumping back in the car. I was already heading down the drive for Stour when the grill of a van ballooned in my windshield. Both of us hit our brakes, stopping just short of the other's front bumper. The van's door opened and Vidya flung herself out, marching defiantly back through the gate.

I made a rude gesture, denoting the act of self-copulation, put the car in reverse, pressed the remote and closed the wrought-iron gate on his bumper.

The news wasn't good. Two CID men had questioned Vidya for the better part of an hour, hinting at immunity if she'd turn Queen's evidence. They'd found a sword, they claimed, behind the radiator in my study; Lumilite had revealed the presence of blood. They'd be testing it further to see if the blood was human, and if so, if it was Jai's.

I was baffled. I *had* no sword; nor was I in the habit of dropping things behind my radiator. I was just paranoid enough to wonder if the police hadn't planted it, though unless there was a conspiracy between the local blokes and Scotland Yard, they'd be hard pressed to find Jai's blood on it! And without that, mere possession of a sword didn't strike me as a crime.

But I was mistaken. Vidya said the police thought the sword was from the stolen treasure—although it seemed to me that, even if so, that would be impossible to prove.

But again, I was wrong; for according to Vidya, the police believed they could match the sword's distinctive hilt with a silhouette in the photos.

This sounded to me like wishful bullshit! Yet how *had* a bloodied sword found its way into our home?

The only two explanations I could think of were: either the Yard had set me up or . . . Vidya had . . . But I couldn't go there. It was too painful to even consider.

And so instead of continuing on this train of thought or returning to Sikandar's story, I clicked instead a desktop icon, invoked the Altered Reality mode and spent the next two hours driving my BattleMechs, Storm Crow and Summoner across the wastes of the star Bone-Norman, where I savagely ravaged and digitally destroyed with my pulse lasers and ultra autocannon, every fucking thing in sight!

Having used the game in this immature manner to vent my wrath and numb my brain, I further altered my reality by falling asleep.

Chapter 28

I took my tea in the garden the following morning. Even here were reminders of the CID's depredations: in their demented search, they had torn up two newly planted beds. I tried to convince myself how absurd the whole thing was: how the sword could not possibly be the murder weapon. The rented cottage was two hundred years old; who knew what other hidden treasures it might harbor?

While serving me breakfast, Mrs. O'Connell filled me in on the local gossip. "Coppers think *she* stole the treasure. That's why she got her the torc."

"But that's ridiculous! She wasn't even in the country at the time. The torc was a wedding gift: a fact that might have been established by now if the CID would do its job."

"Yer right as rain, y'ar, sir. And there's the problem. Seems the Indian Queen Mummer don't take unsolicited calls, least not from the likes of the chief superintendent. Just don't ring the old gurl up and ask her twenty questions. They been dealing with her viziers and whatnots, trying to get through. And you should hear what the lads are saying."

"What?" I asked. "That she killed her husband?"

"Eh? No, sir. Saying she's cunning, they are. A fern witch."

"What?"

" '*Fern*.' From another country. Other day, your lady was bringing in Avatar when one of Seeley's grooms says something to her, fresh. Well, she give 'em a look, now didn't she? That night? Bloke has a stroke. Twenty-nine. Never sick a day in his life. Can't move, can't speak. Three wee 'uns. They's saying she a-done it."

"That's absurd!"

"Wife accused her. Yesterday in Stour. Told her they knowed a bad fairy when they seed 'em and they didn't wish her kind around."

"She *said* that?" I asked, aggrieved. "To *Vidya?*"

"Woman gets home, prize heifer's dead. Poor thing's fell into its trough and drowned! You should never have disturbed that body in the bog, that's what they're sayin'."

And it struck me there was no need to read *Sikandar*. In county Dorset, the Middle Ages were *now*.

Mrs. O'Connell, having unburdened herself of an entire village's worth of gossip, started to go. "And you? What do you think of her, Ruby?"

She paused for a moment. "Treats me fair enough." She thought some more. "Odin adores her."

I went inside, feeling more disturbed than I'd have thought. The accusations against Vidya just kept coming.

Well, witch or fairy, Vidya wasn't. I knew local girls with elfin eyes and flesh whiter than the ninth wave of the sea. If you'd told me they were fey, I might have half-believed you. But there was nothing airy-fairy about Vidya.

So why then *hadn't* dear Lakshmi Auntie returned the chief superintendent's calls? Is that how the Queen Mum responded to an official inquiry about her beloved niece? Or had she not answered him because—like everyone else—*she'd never heard of Vidya Prasad*?

For in the time we'd been together—brief, albeit—no one had called for Vidya. *No one!* No brother, sister, mother or friend; no former employer or business associate; no ex-lover or ex-college roommate, had phoned or sent so much as a note—at least that I'd observed. And though her name and news of her husband's murder were in the press on four continents, no old nurse or former teacher, no near or distant kin had rung with their condolences or to inquire how she was. I mean, really! How was that possible?

It was almost as if Vidya Prasad had descended from heaven, bodily, last May, in order to wed Jai—or, perhaps, ascended from hell!

Vidya was in our bedroom, folding clothes on the bed.

"Heard you had some trouble in Stour."

"Oh. Hardly 'trouble.'"

"Heard some old biddy accused you of being some kind of a witch."

"Yes, that was a new one to me."

There was an awkward silence. "Look, Vidya," I said, trying to sound offhand, "the police can't find any record of you in Kenya. Or in Switzerland, for that matter. How come?"

She paused, then said in a voice I didn't recognize, "You know why. You've always known why. You just won't admit it."

"Admit it?"

She tossed more clothing on the bed. "Who I am. What I've done."

Her answer knifed me. I'd have said she was kidding, except the Lady Vidya wasn't much of a kidder, nor was there the least amusement in her eyes.

"I don't know what you're talking about. All I know is . . . I *love* you."

"You love *whom*?"

"You. Vidya . . ."

She smiled a smile I'd never seen on her before—arch, wicked, worldly wise, the leer of a dominatrix. "And what if

I'm not Vidya? What if I'm . . . that wicked fairy? What's her name?"

"Come on, Vidya. That's not funny."

"Isn't that what the villagers are saying?"

"What if they are?"

"Isn't that why you showed me 'my body?'"

"What? No!"

"Then again, maybe I'm . . . *Rukmini Patel*."

That name on her lips frosted my soul.

"And how do *you* know about Rukmini Patel?"

"Oh, I know everything, Xan. It's one of the perks of being me. I know what the bull in that field is thinking. And what the sunrise will look like from the top of Bulbarrow on the morning of the night you die. I'm 'Vidya,' remember? Knowledge itself."

Annoyed at being so easily played, I said, "Look, Vidya, if you're trying to upset me, keep it up."

"Upset *you? Damn* your eyes!" she said, overturning the basket so that the sweaters she'd folded spilled back on the floor. "Did you ever stop to think what it might be like for *me*? To come home and find my . . . ? To be suspected of his murder and questioned by Scotland Yard? And even you! *'What were you doing the night Jai was killed?'* What the deuce do you *think* I was doing? And how in the bloody hell do you think your inquiries make *me* feel?"

I realized, then, too, that though *I* was a suspect, Vidya had never once asked me where *I* had been.

There was a long, frozen silence; then Vidya turned and stared out the window, wrapping herself in her long, thin arms. After a while, she began to cry, pathetically, without a sound.

But I wasn't about to be put off. "How do you know about Rukmini Patel?"

"*Idiot!* I was questioned by the CID myself. Re*member*?"

"Then why can't they find any record of you? Of Vidya."

"In Kenya?" She snorted contemptuously and said in a brittle, mocking tone, "Did your *leftenant* offer *baksheesh*? If not, no information will be forthcoming, I assure you."

"And Switzerland? I don't believe they demand *baksheesh* there."

She shrugged and made a wearisome gesture, as though to indict again my American naiveté. "I traveled there on another girl's passport."

"How come?"

"There were problems leaving Kenya."

I waited for more.

"Mr. Daniel arap Moi, our fearless leader, had gone on one of his periodic rampages and closed the border to a long list of Asian families, mine amongst them."

"But isn't that dangerous? Assuming someone else's identity?"

"Irregular. Hardly *dangerous*. I doubt the Swiss would have had me *shot*."

I reached out to hold her, but she wouldn't be held. She pulled away.

"Please don't doubt me, Xan, ever again. For if you do . . ."

Chapter 29

When I awoke . . . I was in love with her. I know no other way to say it. I awoke to a feeling that outranked every other, to a presence and affection like some luminous essence poised beside me in the night, and for two or three of the sweetest seconds I have lived, I revelled in it, the exquisite throbbing pulse of love. And only then, and by degrees, did the night assert its black priority and did the pain of my predicament come upon me full well—and I turned and groaned at this clash of worlds, like stars colliding, the one without and one within.

For there was no time to sip the nectar of my new feeling. I got up at once and proceeded on my way, disturbed that sleep had claimed me without my knowing—but grateful, too, that in its house, I had seen what I had. I loved her. I would not betray her.

As for me, I went downstairs, though not before randomly opening "the book" to the passage above, though I closed it as quickly, before it could swallow and sweep me away. Despite my conversation with Vidya, I didn't feel badly. Maybe I'd begun to accept the thought that, like it or not (and like Sikandar), I was being challenged and changed: that my Lady, the book, Jai and Vidya were all intent on expanding my identity, altering my outlook and reforming my so-called "American naïveté." It was as though I had built a life for myself, an academic ivory tower, that didn't include love, magic or murder—except from afar—and now all three were beating down my door.

Online, I googled Henry Carlson Lewis Jones, but found nothing. His body, apparently, had not been discovered, and the longer it wasn't, the better for us.

I thought about Jai and his terrible death, and again, I came up empty-handed.

And so I turned to another murder and the question that was eating at the back of my brain: if my Lady's burial was medieval, why were the stakes and runes used to bind her cut circa 1675? That made no sense to me at all.

But, as I considered it, something else did. There it was again. *Linguistic drift. Huldres'* becomes *Holders. God be with you* becomes *goodbye.* Thus "Albemarle" was probably not her name at all—*but what her name had become after 350 years!* No wonder I couldn't find her in English history!

Encouraged by this fresh direction, I looked up "alb" and was returned this quote from *The White Goddess* by Robert Graves:

> **Britain derives its earliest name, Albion, from Albina ("the White Goddess")** [whose] **name accounts for the Germanic words . . . alb,** *elf, and* **alpdrucken,** *the nightmare or incubus . . . and is connected with the Greek words* **alphos,** *meaning 'dull-white leprosy' . . . and* **Alphito . . .** *whose more polite title was* **Marpessa,** *'the snatcher' . . . 'the White Lady of Death and Inspiration' . . .*

This was remarkable, as the nymph-like "*alb*" and the rapacious "*nightmare*" were the forms in which "Albemarle" had appeared to Strugnell . . . . In fact, Oberon, Shakespeare's King of the Fairies, was, I learned now, originally Alberich, the Old High German *alb,* "elf" and *-rîh-,* "ruler." Though *alb* also was associated with whiteness.

Then there was the name's final syllable, *marle,* whose silent *e* would have not been silent then. *Mara* was an ancient worldwide name for the goddess of death, while *mare* was well-attested-to in fourteenth-century England. As Tylor states in *Primitive Culture,* "The *mare* in nightmare means spirit, elf, or nymph; compare Anglo-Saxon *wudurmaere* (wood-mare) = echo."

Had my Lady's original title then been Alba Maere, meaning White (or Good) Spirit? Or was it perhaps Alba Mara, meaning the exact opposite: Fairy of Death?

"Believe in elves and fairies, Willie?"

"I'd na say yes, and na say no."

"Smart. Still, there's something about them I don't understand. I mean, are they bad or good?"

"They's elementals, sir, don't you know?"

I shook my head. "No. I don't. What do you mean?"

"Well . . . what be an element?"

"Oh, earth, fire, water . . ." I replied.

"Right. Now is water bad or is water good?" Willie answered himself. "Depends, don't it? If the water's in a cup of tay yer drinkin' or it's washin' yer clothes, it's good. It's not so good if yer drowin' in it, see my pint?"

I did.

Adding Willie to my list of local sources, I was checking my e-mail when the title of one of them stayed my hand. I clicked on its attachment: *Rukmini1.jpg.* There were also a *Rukmini2* and *3,* which, when opened as well, filled me with the keenest sense of despair.

In the first photo, a naked Vidya Prasad was seated astride some faceless fellow, her full, brown-tipped breasts thrust before her, head thrown back in a frieze of bliss. In the second pic, the boy was on top, and a woman's red-stockinged legs clamped round his waist. That the girl was Vidya was beyond discussion. The third and final JPEG was the second shot uncropped, revealing just beyond the couple, a woman's painted toes.

"Where did you get these?"

"Off the Net."

She was quiet for a moment. "I suppose I could claim it isn't me."

"You could. Thing is, it *is* you." I waited. "Care to comment?"

She took a breath through flared nostrils, closed her eyes and sat back on the couch. Then she replied, "Only that they were shot and posted without my permission."

"You mean, you didn't notice somebody was taking your picture while you were fucking?"

She flushed at the cruelly worded question. "I wasn't . . . *posing*. If that's what you think."

"You weren't making a porn flick? That's good to know, since it seems there *were* other people present."

She nodded. "It was a party."

"*Party*? I think the word is *orgy*, Vidya. Or is that what they call a party in Kenya?"

"It wasn't Kenya," she said, obstinately missing my point. "It was *Roma*."

"Ah, *la dolce vita*," I cracked, with an irony I didn't quite feel. "And how did this . . . 'exciting alternative lifestyle' . . . come about? I thought you were in Kenya, educating poor African children."

"This was afterward, when I went to Berne for university. I fell in with a group of kids . . . not *bad*, just *wild* and into all the things kids are into . . ."

"Don't tell me. 'Sex. Drugs. And rock 'n' roll . . .' Or was it hip-hop?"

"Then I met Ivan."

"I thought his name was Ibrahim."

"Before Ibby. He said he was a Russian Prince . . . "

"But turned out to be just another hustler from Croatia."

She smiled wanly. "Not Croatia. But by then he had introduced me to Ibby and his gang."

"Who were . . . ?"

"The oddest crew, I thought at first. Later, though, I really came to adore them."

"Yes," I said, "I can see from the photos."

Vidya laughed with a sort of weary self-derision, then described to me how Ibrahim Saluk Habib—twenty-two years her senior—had courted and won her. "You must understand this: Indian families are extremely protective. I was brought up wrapped in a silk cocoon. At nineteen, I wasn't permitted to go to a *restaurant* alone. It wasn't until I went to Berne that I began to experience . . . *other* things."

"Like?"

"Wine. European culture. *Men.* At first, it was a lark. A grand adventure. Ibby was smitten—with my title as much as by me, I think. We travelled all over: the Aegean, Monte Carlo, Amsterdam, Bali. There were private jets and spas and *masses* of servants and a constant stream of gifts: jewelry, cars, food and drink, entertainment and fine clothes. It was intoxicating. One day I'd be shopping in Nassau; the next, flying off to Telluride to ski. A fortnight later, we'd be in Maui, having a luau."

Now it fell into place: the clothes, the *serious* jewels, the ardor and sophistication of our erotic encounters, the cigarettes and French inhaling, her international queenly style, hosting skills and hard, high polish. "But how did he afford it? Didn't you wonder?"

"Ibby? Rich as Croesus. His business made astonishing sums. And he didn't fancy paying taxes. That was another reason we were always on the go."

"That, and to stay ahead of the police."

"*Police*? Hardly! Ibby was a most respectable soul. Your own vice president, Mr. Bidenji, had us to lunch in Delaware. Another time, the president of Columbia . . ."

". . . University? Oh, you mean, Pictures?"

". . . the country, held a fête in Ibby's honor. Ibby wasn't some common criminal."

"Just an *un*common one."

"Really, I don't know why you're saying that," she said, petulantly.

"Vidya, the guy's an arms dealer. A black marketeer! Didn't you know that?"

"Arms dealer?" She didn't seem disturbed. "I suppose he might have sold some arms. He bought and sold a lot of things. Anyway, your own country happens to be the biggest producer of guns and *mis-syles* in the world. Why do you produce them if you don't want them sold?

"And as for smuggling, you're more foolish than I imagined if you believe it entirely wicked. How do you think those of us living in underdeveloped countries acquire goods? If there were no smugglers, no one would have a color telly, VCR, perfume, soap, lipstick, CDs or even a bottle of mineral water! It's fine for *you* to lecture us on the evils of black marketeering when you can go to 'the mall,' as you call it, and buy a dozen of anything you choose!"

"All right."

She was quiet for a moment. "Later, I had an experience . . . that . . . made me see how *few-tile* incessantly feeding one's appetites were. And . . . ultimately unfulfilling. So, I left."

"With a chunk of Ibby's cash."

She looked irate. "Without a *sou!* I *did* take the jewels given as gifts, and my clothing—but they were mine, after all."

"Yeah. You'd earned them."

She let that pass.

Still, I pressed her. "And . . . ?"

". . . I flew to Delhi and spent two months in Udaipur with my Lakshmi Auntie. I was there when she got a call from Jai's family, who were seeking a suitable bride. I was twenty-seven, an old maid by their standards. They'd convinced themselves, I think, I would marry Ibby and when I didn't they were shocked. They desperately wanted me to marry and by then I was not so deeply opposed. Anyway, I found Jai *gallant* and, more than that, *humane*. He was everything I believed a husband should be." She paused. "Until I met you."

"It's not the pictures, Vidya. I'm not a prude. And you certainly have a right to your past. It's that you *lied to me*. You're not even Vidya! You're Rukmini Patel!"

"I most certainly am not. Patel is the name I used to get out of Kenya. And I used it in Switzerland because I didn't want it known I was there. Later, I found it useful. But when I left Ibby, Rukmini stayed behind."

I shook my head. "Why didn't you ever tell me all this?"

She paused for a moment. "Perhaps for the same reasons you never told me about that waitress in Boston you shagged in the loo while your date sat with Jai, eating clam chowder."

"There's a difference."

"Is there?"

"None of my ex-lovers might have murdered your husband."

"And you think *Ibby* did? That's rich. If you'd ever met Ibby Habib, you'd know just how absurd that is."

"What about his bodyguard? Big burly guy without a neck."

She shook her head. "He's capable of it, surely. But Bunzo does nothing on his own. And why on earth would Ibby hurt Jai?"

"Jealousy?"

"Flattering, but I hardly think so. Ibby had a string of women. There were a dozen young beauties in line behind me."

"So you don't think some character from this chapter of your life might have offed Jai."

"No, I don't. And if so, I can't imagine who or why."

"So that leaves us with some dirty pictures."

"Yes. And your knowledge of my *pahst*, which isn't as impeccable as you may have imagined."

I considered this. "Did Jai know?"

"Oh, yes. He called me his 'crimson woman.' He said he'd sown wild oats himself, but it was so long ago, they'd all been eaten!"

"So who sent me those pictures?"

"I *cahn't* say. But I'm glad they did."

"You are? *Why*?" I asked, truly mystified.

"Because," she said, after a moment's consideration, "it's a terrible thing to be loved for whom you're not."

Chapter 30

That evening the local paper announced a body found in a Wiltshire field by members of the Wiltshire Wings, a bird-watching club, had been identified as Henry Lewis Jones. As it was barely three days since the night of his killing, I worried about the condition of the corpse.

I went online but found nothing more. Other than the body's identity, the police weren't talking. Entering the search term "Wiltshire Wings" however, returned another story, also dated today, announcing the sighting of a rare "Indian White-backed Vulture" by members of the Wiltshire Wings "feeding in a Wiltshire field."

It took me a moment to put the stories together, and to realize on what the bird had been feeding. At once, my hopes danced and flared. Then I thought, what was becoming of me, that such a grisly event could make me feel so happy?

I called and asked Strugnell if he could find out more.

"Not easily. They keep that stuff under lock and key. I'd have to have a bloody good reason. Anyway, I have my own problems. Palace wants to know when I'll rule on the treasure. Even though it's lost! And I can't—can I?—'til I know who your bleedin' Lady Albemarle is! And why the hell they buried her with it."

"Look, it's clearly 'Treasure Trove.' Whoever she is, she was sacrificed, and the treasure was buried as a sacrifice along with her. You don't make the gods an offering intending to take it back."

"Can you prove that?"

"No. But I will."

"Who can?"

"Why don't you ask Rumple?"

"Typical academic. Moves at the speed of shite. I need answers, Donne, and I need them now."

"Christ," I said, "you sound like my father."

"Well, least you had one. Mine ran off when I was two."

"And your Mum?"

"Ah! Died when I was young."

"Oh, I'm sorry, Wooland."

"Topped herself."

Something thick and ill in his voice made me pause. He grunted. "Watching the telly, Lilly and me, when I noticed something out the corner of me eye."

"What was it?"

"Mum. She'd set herself alight and was coming through the kitchen—not a word out of her, mind you."

"Set herself *on fire?*"

"Doused herself with kerosene and struck a match."

"While you were watching *TV?*"

He named the show.

"Jesus, Wooland, what did you *do?*"

"First . . . didn't know what it was, did I? There were just these . . . flames. Then, through them, I recognized Mum."

"Good God, man! What was she doing?"

"Burning. She passed behind us and went out to the porch."

". . . was she . . . *screaming?*"

"Not a word out of her," he said almost proudly. "Not a peep. Outside she just sort of . . . folded. I remember trying to get near her and getting . . . *fried.*"

"What did you do?"

"What *could* I do? I was only nine. Watched her. Burn. Patches of pink showing up through the char, and her hair—Mum had the most beautiful, curly red hair—flaring then powdering black 'til she was bald."

"You watched her . . . *die?*"

"Oh, no. She lingered for a week and actually died of some infection." He said this with the barest minimum of emotion, as if he were describing a pile of burning autumn leaves.

"Jesus, Wooland," I said, aghast.

"Way I see it, Mum was in a load of pain. Only way out was to end it all."

"Still, there are lots of ways to end it all, don't you think?"

"She was a good Mum," he said loyally.

I bit my tongue.

"May I make a suggestion? With all the nightmares you've been having, it might be a wise to see a shrink."

"Why should I when I've got you?"

"Because I'm an *anthropologist,* Wooland."

"Oh, I don't need a shrink. Just a good jaw now and then. *There!*" he said, apparently knocking back a beer. He smacked his lips. "See?" he said, belching lightly. "Feeling better already."

I asked that Willie keep an eye on Vidya, then walked across the downs. It wasn't my conversation with Strugnell, but the one with Vidya that disturbed me. And it wasn't the pictures. I didn't give a rat's ass about the pictures. She, like us all, was entitled to her past. No, it was the feeling I was being played, and in ways I didn't understand. And for a moment then, that shadowy tongue that had licked my heart before licked my heart again.

For I couldn't seem to get my arms around Vidya, in any way but one. Every time I did, she morphed into something new.

Social hostess. Shell-shocked widow. Sexual temptress. Life saver. Faculty wife or gangster's girl? Swinger or gun-slinger? Social worker or cover-upper? Dear companion or codefendant?

Or, maybe, I thought, she's just a complex, beautiful, fascinating woman, and as paradoxical as are we all. Yeah, that sounded closer to the truth.

I passed the stone circle. A field of gorse and heather descended to a cattle path that wended its way past the wishing pond. It glittered in the grayish light. Lost in thought, when I looked up again, my Lady's grave was visible in the distance.

But her grave had been transformed: both desecrated and consecrated. "Nighthawks" with metal detectors had scoured the land for thirty, forty yards around, drilling scores of probe holes into the sod even while, on the edges of the cutting, there were a dozen memorial bouquets—including what looked like a hand-written prayer.

I turned from the grave to the bog in which it lay. In the rainy evening it was a melancholy station, a maze of streams and waving grasses brightened by loosestrife and overhung by silver willows. As I imbibed its desolation, a primal panic rose inside me. And I understood viscerally, then, why bogs were so long regarded as doorways to the underworld and the ideal sites for sacrifices—and how easily one could become disoriented here and, subsequently, lost or drowned.

So when a little old man came doddering down the track, I will admit I felt relieved.

He was, it turned out, the "grandfer" of Sam, the lad who'd first unburied my Lady. Rail thin and spry enough in a creaky sort of way, he clenched between his strong, stained molars the bitten stem of an unlit pipe. When I referred to his grandson's find, he nodded: "Say Queen Abby's buried here."

"Queen Abby?"

"*Good* fairy, don't you know? Used to bring her sickly wee 'uns. And barren wives would spend the nights where you're a-settin'—sometimes even barren cows!"

"Who was she?"

"Agh!" He scratched his head with the stem of his pipe. "Fairy Queen. Lived in the pond down by the stones, 'til some saint or other made 'er shift. Me grammy said ye'd see 'er of a night on a pale horse, leading souls of those who would die on the morrow. That's how she ken Rector Kingman was a goner. She'd zeed his ghost the night afore he died riding a pure white mare with Abby!"

Sensing he had my full attention, he went on: "Well, bein' a 'ooman, even if a *fairy* one, but didn't she fall in love? In order to wed, she took the form of a human queen. But her lad was betrothed to one Jessica Meeks who, despite her name, was anything but. Declaring she would not be cuckolded by any heathenish fey, she learned from her lover boy where he was a-meetin' Abby. Then when Abby did appear, the girl's Da and brothers caught her in a net.

"Well, didn't they have the fight of their lives, as Abby took on one hundred shapes: tiger, camel, pizen sarpent, she-bear and giant coney! Holy water was sprinkled on her. It smoked and hissed and burned her flesh like tanner's acid until at last, scarched and exhausted, she came back home to her original form: that of a beautiful, black-haired 'ooman in whose dark heart the light of Christ never has entered once—nor *will!*" He paused for dramatic effect and breath.

"Now, bein' immortal, she could na be slain and so she was buried, staked to the bog with golden pins. Bound like that, she's prey to fiends who ravish her cruelly night after night. And so, 'tis said, if you walk the downs when the moon is nil, you can sometimes hear her moan with pleasure, even as she weeps in loneliness and shame."

Trying to hide my fascination, I said, "And her name, you say, was Good Queen Abby?"

He fitted the unlit pipe in his teeth. "Good Queen Abby, yis t'was."

"And did people ever make her offerings?"

"Na me. But me Grammy did."

"Really! And how did she do that?"

"How?" He glared at me like I was daft. "Tossed 'em in the bog. Even offered up her watch, Grammy did. Barkin' mad, volks said she is. It's when we thought Da ha' been killed in the war."

"What war?"

"Why, the *Great* One. Later, we heard he was guest of the kaiser, and the Boches eventually *did* let him go. So you zee," he winked, "maybe old Abby done the trick."

I thanked him warmly for his reminiscences, and asked if he'd ever seen Abby himself.

"Abby. Pookas. Boneless Ned. And a black dog once, with eyes like barnin' coals!"

"Really?" I said. "And what did it do?"

"Well, he give me an evil, thievin' look, now didn't he?" Then he sucked on his pipe, jerked at his cap, and as if he'd thought better about speaking of such matters, marched straight off without another word.

I was almost certain now that the legend of Good Queen Abby held a distant memory of Lady Albemarle. Just as peat and sphagnum moss had formed around my Lady's body, so other myths had conflated her own until she had blurred in the minds of the folk with the Fairy Queen and primordial Mother. Everything was falling into place.

And moving to her grave, I noticed something I hadn't seen before. Around the margins of the hole, the peat was a different hue and texture. That is, it was peat laid down at a *different* time than the peat that was surrounding it.

I hurried home, looking for a quote I had kept for future reference, though it took me some minutes before I could find it:

> **While bodily incorruptibility was associated with sainthood in Russia, on the continent and England it was generally regarded as proof of vampirism. Such bodies, whether disinterred by accident or design, were often burnt or staked . . .**

There it was! Three hundred fifty years ago, by "accident or design," someone had unburied my Lady! And given the times—the Puritans were in power and witchcraft trials at an all-time high—her perfect, unspoiled, undead corpse was surely thought to be immortal, a vampire sleeping in the bog by day and rising to stalk the country by night. And so, that day she was first uncovered, no one had suggested preserving her in some museum. Instead, a blade of dread had stabbed the parish. Persuaded by the Puritan clergy and divines, they had removed her heart and reburied her, staking down her wandering spirit with wooden crooks and hand-carved curses—even as the common folk (the uninterrupted chain of artifacts showed) continued their offerings as they had for centuries.

For, when a cow was lost or a loved one dying, it wasn't to the chapel of the saint the simple folk turned—but to their Lady. There, in the dusk or dawn or midnight, with witnesses none but the wheeling stars, they made their sacred pacts and pleadings and offered up their secret prayers.

Still, there was one nagging question. If the runes were carved in the seventeenth century, why—*ingesusnam*—was their form and English so damned old?

But the answer to that was simple enough: the inscription was traditional, with Jesus only the last in a long list of gods in whose name it had been uttered, and Albemarle the latest in a long line of fiends. For in sacred formulas, archaic words and language endure, so that to this day good Christians pray, "Our Father, Who art in heaven, hallowed be Thy name . . ."

It was Strugnell calling. "Book you found? Wasn't part of the treasure. Lads unearthed it, wrapped in silk. Tossed it on the hoard."

"How very scientific of them. Have they never heard of *strata*?"

"Course not."

"Do they remember where they found it?"

"It was dark."

"And the silk. What happened to it?"

"Somehow got left behind, and the next night were a cold one. One of the lads threw it on his filly."

"And that's where it's been for the past three months. On a horse's ass."

Strugnell laughed.

I wasn't surprised. In archeology, such things happen all the time. The Bedouin boy who found the Dead Sea Scrolls spent the better part of the following winter burning them in his stove for warmth.

"And where's this cloth now?"

"Aren't I looking at it? Fine design. One end's got a sort of fringe."

"What're its dimensions?"

"Say . . . six by one."

"Feet?"

"Meters."

"Thank you." It was a sari.

So my Lady really could be Queen Mayura!

Eagerly, I reopened the "enchanted book"—hoping to confirm her identity once and for all. On the page to which I turned, however, we were fighting a wild, Afghani tribe . . . and as we watched them coming at us, some central nerve inside my body quivered with a sort of sickening joy— for being charged by five hundred ululating Uzbeks is, in truth, an indescribable feeling, and one you record in the depths of your bowels.

But God was with us. We turned their charge and in the end, we counted forty-seven enemy dead, including their chieftain, Aziz Beg Khan, plus twenty-nine prisoners, some of whom were maimed.

Approaching them, I gave them a choice: join us or die. Every one to a man opted for the former. In fact, some of them wept and kissed my hands, though I had few illusions. They would be loyal for as long as they shared our booty.

'Abd al-Wali, who was strutting about like a peacock who believes himself the reason for the autumn rains, led me to the spoils, including treasure from other raids. I inspected a golden crown inlaid with yellow topaz and coral. An inscription declared it the Rāja of Indore's, and I wondered how it had come into their hands. Was it seized in a raid? Or had my brother plucked it from the head of Mul (I did not believe he'd been slain by the Queen) and given it to their Khan? However obtained, returning it brought me great satisfaction.

I had the chieftain's hands removed and placed upon a golden plate, the crown secured between his fingers, and sent it thus to the Rani of Indore with this greeting:

> O Queen — The grace of He without Stain allowed me to retrieve this Precious Crown from One who is now a Traveller on the Highway to Annihilation. May you remember me always and read in this gift the Sign of my Brotherly Love and Protection.
>
> Prince Sikandar

Then I ordered that the chieftain's head be separated from his body, wrapped in straw and conveyed to Jafir with these words:

> O Brother — I send you the first fruits of this Harvest of Uzbeks who dared to flourish in our father's field. May you be pleased with this offering and read in it the Sign of my Loyalty and Brotherly Affection.
>
> Kando

I had other pieces of the Khan sent to other restive princes. Then the headless, armless, legless corpse was hung from a balcony, beneath which pooled a sty of blood in which the pups and piglets wallowed.

Finally, I had the heads of the enemy dead removed and piled in the town square. They looked like bearded human fruit. Regrettably, they would not stay up. Whenever a dog nibbled an ear, the whole pyramid collapsed and heads went rolling, careening about like cabbages. So, after some consideration, I ordered built a pillar of victory, for whose uses I was gaining a new regard. On it I had carved:

> On this spot, in the year A.H. 725, Prince Sikandar Khilji delivered Khadya from a band of mutinous Uzbeks, dispatching 47 of their Crooked Souls to the Hiding-place of Nothingness. Let this Pillar be a support to all who uphold Dharma and may these faces of Ruin appear as a Warning to those Ungrateful Servants who would become their own Masters.

Finished with these measures, I went to the Chambal and bathed the dust and blood from my body, watching it swirl away in the stream. I felt elated. Life was sweet. And it struck me now that everything my eyes took in was mine: men, women, horses, jewels.

My servant, Ram, laid out fresh garments; donning a lime-green floral robe and a silken turban, I went back to the town square where I had myself weighed against cotton, paddy, grain and fruit, milksweets, *ghee* and toddy, which were then distributed to the poor.

Declaring a holiday, I invited the town's nobles to a wine-feast in a merchant's garden, which I renamed *Vijay-abagh*—that is to say, Garden of Victory.

Dancing lulis and beguiling charmers whose caresses would have captivated the hearts of angels incited the assembly, while musicians sang that graceful ode:

> Sing, Minstrel,
> fill my cup,
> for the world has ordered itself
> As I desire.

And what was a song by the great Nizami without another tune by Khayyam?

Later, I patronized Nāmadev, the captain of my scouts. And to my loyal commander, 'Abd al-Wali, whose bravery was unmatched, I presented a golden robe of honour. I then gave orders that whosoever amongst my men might wish for exhilarating drinks and drugs be not debarred from using them.

That evening, the village women brought us roasted pigeon and the wine of the country: a rough white with a nose that we consumed in swinish quantities. Sitting there before the yellow fire in the chill desert night with gold in our pockets, squab in our mouths, wine and the smoke of *kif* in our blood and the grease of the sweet, white doves smeared and shining on our sunburnt faces, we revelled in the nectar of victory and youth, thinking it but an appetizer, a hint of things to come. And yet, alas, I tell you now, my life never tasted so sweet again!

Part V

JAFIR

The antidote is hidden in the poison.

—Rumi
The Diwan

Chapter 31

I awoke to two cops standing over my bed. Vidya, too, was hovering above me—though as our eyes met, she dropped down beside me and laid her head upon my chest.

"Now, now, miss, there'll be none of that," the bobby fussed. The CID man cleared his throat. "Alexander Donne. We arrest you for the murder of Jai Prasad. You have the right to remain silent. Anything you say may be taken down and used against you."

I looked up at the two of them, staring down so intently. I recalled the wine-feast in the pleasure garden, overseen by the pillar of heads.

In one world, I was the rising man; in another, a murderer—when, in fact, I was neither.

Maybe that's why I was the calmest one there. For being charged by the British police with murder is really nothing compared to being charged by a band of ululating Uzbeks!

Then something happened that savaged my calm: they handcuffed Vidya and led her away.

". . . *you* know the type: family of six, kids and all, wasted on an Easter Sunday; German *turista* gunned down in China-town by a 'Ghost Shadow'—worst shots in the fuckin' world! Or some tony professor, like your buddy, Prasad, cut to bits in his book-lined study . . . . Cases like that tend to stick in the public craw. Citizens demand action. Governor calls hizzoner; hizzoner, the commissioner; commissioner, the deputy commissioner of pleece—and next thing you know, some fuck's got a microscope and is lookin' up *my* rectum."

"Good to see you, Houlihan," I said.

"Likewise," he said, with something almost like affection. "N'other words, bunk, this thing ain't gonna quit—if that's, you know, the two of you was hoping."

On a table in the interrogation room they'd laid out the "murder weapon." It had a prop-like air, as if its sight was supposed to jog my memory.

Houlihan shifted his position and tone. He tweezed his pant crease between his thumb and pointer and hiked his cuff, exposing too-short socks and a hairy band of skin the color of inorganic poultry, before setting his pointed *Italiano* shoe on my chair. He leaned in closer, exhaling the odor of mint Life Savers.

"Look, we got possession of the murder weapon. We got motive, opportunity. Just trying to figure how it all went down. Help me, here. I'm sure there's a reason well-set-up guy like yourself . . . Hey, he insult you? Accuse you of coming on to the wife?

"Look, way I see it, you didn't *plan* it. *Nah.*" Houlihan shook his head in vigorous self-agreement. "You brought him the sword as a *wedding present . . .*"

"That's why you nicked it. Along with the treasure."

Houlihan ignored his partner's remark. ". . . 'Cept you got into an argument and it got outta hand and, *wham*, you whacked him one. Am I right?"

"Wrong. I told you. I didn't kill Jai. I don't even think it was Jai they were after. I think it was Vidya. And that they still are!"

"And who is 'they'?"

"I don't know for certain. But here are two names. One, Bunzo Doi—Ibby Habib's soldier." And I saw the *yakuza*'s enormous trapezius and tattooed tree-trunk neck. Vidya was naïve. You don't walk away from a man like Habib with trinkets worth a quarter of a million dollars.

"And the other?" Houlihan asked, unimpressed.

"Henry Carlson Lewis Jones."

That stopped the conversation. "And how you know him?"

"I have my sources."

"You know he's dead?"

"No. How'd he die?"

"Let's just say that's 'classified.'"

He looked at me. But I saw the information enter.

"Anyway, this sword isn't from the treasure," I continued. "Look at its condition! And if I had killed Jai, would I really be so stupid as to bring the murder weapon *home*?"

"'... weapon in question,'" the CID man read, "'... is a twelfth-century blade of Kura ... Kuruz ... Cora ...'"

I snatched at the page. "'*Khorasan* ...' It's in Iran."

He snatched it back. "... '*manufacture*, worth in today's antiquities market from ten to twenty thousand pounds ...'"

"Was that?" the lieutenant wondered.

"Twenty, thirty thou."

"For a *sword*?" Houlihan whistled through his teeth. "I can see why you weren't gonna chuck it in the river."

We all turned and looked at it again. Rainbows danced in its damascened steel. I reached out and hefted it—quick as a whip. "This knife probably severed hundreds of heads. They used to build them into towers, you know, or pile them up like so much cabbage in the market."

They looked at me tensely, clearly sorry they had brought it in. I cut at the air, once, to unnerve them further, then laid it back down. It was removed.

The questioning went on for several more hours. If I'd had any sense I'd have called my attorney and stayed mum—but I was beyond sense. Having dodged pikes, spears and arrows, I believed I could handle whatever Houlihan & Co. threw my way.

Why had I killed Jai? Wasn't Vidya involved? Hadn't I seen her at the party and been so smitten by her beauty that I'd resolved then and there to slaughter anyone who stood in my way?

"Oh, yeah. I like a girl, I just kill her guy. Why fool around with *dating*, eh, Hools?"

Then they switched crimes. How had I come into possession of the book?

"Because Jai's isn't the only murder under investigation. I was probing one myself before I was accused of this one."

"Trouble is you started probing with your dick."

I invoked *upekshā* and let it go.

Houlihan sighed, put his feet up on someone else's desk, leaned back in his chair and switched personas. Suddenly, it was the *philosophical* Houlihan. "You know the *law*, Donne?"

"Enough to know I haven't broken any."

"Cause what I discovered in the course of my *over*long and *under*paid public career is there's *two* sets of laws, the *writ* and the *un*writ. *Writ* is what they teach at law school. *Un*writ is a certain *predisposition* on a part of the judge slash jury to think in certain ways. One of the more *innaresting* of these little-known, *un*writ laws of *jersprudence* is what we call 'The Bimbo Walks Rule.' Ever hear of it?"

I hadn't.

"Rule says, in a felony conviction with more'n one defendant one a who's a babe? *Male* defendant'll have the book trown at 'em while the bimbo *walks*. Just the way it is. Maybe folks don't feature sending ladies lovely as Vidya Prasad up the river."

"What exactly are you trying to say?"

"Saying, this case goes to trial? You, my friend, are looking at L-wop."

" 'L-wop?' "

"Life—without parole."

"L-wop."

"While your partner, the beau*teeful* Vidya Prasad? Even if convicted, is gonna get five years, *max.* Trust me. Why? The bimbo *walks!*"

I turned away. I knew *bheda* when I heard it—"divide and conquer." I wasn't falling for it.

In my cell, some of my defiance departed. I'd eaten nothing all day but a relish sandwich and two mugs of oversweetened tea, and I wasn't depressed so much as *empty.*

I lay on the bunk and tried to rally, telling myself they didn't have a case. But they *did* have a case and not a bad one at that. Many poor sods have been hanged by the neck until dead on evidence more circumstantial.

On that cold thought, I fell asleep and had the most vivid dream. In it . . . **I was back at the palace, reviewing troops with my father, the Shah. Storm clouds were amassed in the west and a harsh wind buffeted the canopy under which we sat, making its timbers squeak and groan.**

Lightning flared and thunder crackled, startling white cranes into flight. That's when another sound sickened my heart, as if the bones of the very earth were breaking—a fractious roar that shook the desert floor. And the Tent of Heavenly Dignity folded.

Blessedly, I found myself unhurt. My father, however, lay pinned by a heavy spar, the toes of his slippers pointing at heaven. He murmured, then started to gurgle and gasp, as though drowning in some invisible sea.

Sami, his boy, threw himself on him, lavishing his pumpkin beard with kisses. Then the dome of heaven broke and fat drops of hot rain began to spot the desert floor. Scattered at first, they grew quickly closer until, within minutes, the drops converged into rippling, wind-whipped sheets of water that swept across the desert plain. And wherever these curtains of water touched down, spray boiled up in all directions.

An ecstasy seized the audience. They began to dance, revelling in the start of the monsoon season and praising aloud the Lord of Storms.

Thunder broke so close it hurt. The strange confluence of the people's joy, the pouring waters, and my father's crushed and sodden form united with my own bewilder-ment and shock to make me want to scream aloud. But though I did, no one heard me.

Even those who'd heard the tent collapse believed it was a peal of thunder—when in fact, I tell you now, it was the sound of an empire falling.

"Bada-*boom*, bada-*bing*!" Houlihan pronounced as he led me from my cell.

"Time?"

"Six thirty-five."

"A.M.? Jesus, Houlihan . . . Not more questions!"

"Nah. You're headed home."

"You mean . . . I'm being *extradited?*"

"Did I say that?" Houlihan tucked something in the pocket of my shirt, the way my grandfather used to slip me money. A policewoman brought a wire basket containing my wallet, change and keys.

"What's going on . . . ? Where's Vidya?"

Houlihan looked surprised. "You don't *know*?" He shifted uncomfortably. "Thought you'd put her up to it."

"Put *who* up to *what*?"

He took a breath. "Your girlfriend—Miz Prasad—one you been telling us coulda never done a thing like that?" He waited to make sure we were both thinking of the same person. "'Just confessed."

Chapter 32

By the time I got home it was still early morning, though given the day's unchanging gray light, it could have been any hour between dawn and dusk.

Other than the charge against Vidya, Houlihan had told me nothing. I called her solicitor, but learned little more. Vidya was claiming she and Jai had argued, and that at some point he had whacked her with the flat of the sword. Insulted, stung, she had wrested it from him and the next thing she knew Jai was dead on the floor. Panicked, she'd frozen for the next several hours, before thinking, at last, to call on me.

I wanted to see her, to hear from her own lips her confession, but being neither kin nor counsel, my requests for an interview were ignored.

Stranger still, even if she were a cold-blooded murderess who'd hacked her husband into a dozen bloody chunks, some part of me still loved her. Wasn't that bizarre?

I called Houlihan. But all he would say is: "She's claimin' self-defense. But the evidence shows she came at 'em while he was sitting and practically took off his head. *Nasty.*"

I hung up again and sat back down. Had it all been a lie? And, if so, to what end? Or had she thrown herself at me the night of Jai's murder like a drowning woman, hoping I would somehow save her? But how in the world was I to do that? And yet some part of me wanted to shield her from everything cold and cruel in this world, even as a wiser part said that I couldn't, nor should I even try.

Did Vidya have a temper? Sure. "Fiery" is how she'd once described it. But though she may have barked a bit, it was always short-lived. That she was capable of killing I knew full well. But I could not see her raising a sword or machete and butchering Jai—and *while he was sleeping.*

Unless she hadn't killed him for any good reason, some stubborn voice inside me said. Unless she killed him because she's *bad.*

And that grim little tongue of darkness and terror darted and licked my heart once again.

I badly wanted to shower and change, but an elderly woman, big boned and formidable-looking, was knocking at my door. Once upon a time, she must have been "handsome." Now, the rosebuds on her scarf were the only feminine traces left—the rest subsumed in that British matriarchal style that eschews as nonsense all softening refinements such as lipstick, jewelry or footgear other than "sensible shoes." My visitor's most distinctive features were a Grecian nose, flanked by a pair of feline eyes that were green, lit, and unreadable as a jaguar's.

"Marla White," she informed me briskly, holding out a large, nicotine-tinged hand. When I showed no signs of recognition, she said, "Marla White-*Strugnell.* And you are . . . *Donne.*" She made it sound less like my name than condition.

"How do you do? Funny, I was only recently speaking with your husband."

"Very. As my husband's dead. You were speaking with my son."

I must have looked as surprised as I felt, for she raised a brow.

". . . I . . . thought you were . . . *deceased!*"

She barked a laugh that managed to sound both decadent and proud. "Whatever gave you *that* idea?"

I started to say, then caught myself.

"Well, I suppose we should get down to it. I came here, you see, to ask that you stop interfering in Wooland's affairs."

"How so?"

"You've upset him terribly."

"I have? And did Wooland ask you to tell me this?"

"Of course not." Her mouth and chin were like a marionette's, with deep grooves and hidden hinges.

"Then what makes you think that, Mrs. Strugnell?"

"I prefer White. Because he was doing far better before all *this* began."

"All *this*?"

She started to answer, then stopped and studied me anew with an aversion that almost approached admiration, the way you appraise a wonderful monster. "You're a smooth one."

"I beg your pardon?"

"You can't gull *me*."

I could see him in her now: the same oversized frame and rampant energy. "Pardon me, Mrs. White, but your son must be . . . forty—and it will be *his* decision and *mine* to terminate our friendship, should we so decide."

She glared at me. Then her eyes rolled weirdly upward, her pupils grew, and for an instant that was almost one instant too long, some ferocious old intelligence looked out at me. I saw it see me—and I saw that it saw I saw.

Then like the spectacle lids of a snake, her pupils shrank, the presence vanished, and the horrible old Englishwoman reappeared.

"You're a very *disagreeable* young man!" she pronounced as if it were official. "Good day." And lifting her umbrella, she opened it with a threatening *thwock*, raised it like a banner, and marched off into the rain with that heads-up, eyes-straight, forward-leaning bearing with which the British once subdued the world.

The message light on my answering machine was blinking, and hoping they were calls from Vidya, I played them back. The first was from Rumple, announcing my suspension from the Royal Commission until my legal status was "resolved." Until that time, my access to commission files and materials was, he said, "rescinded."

The second was from my department head, who wanted to talk about my "affiliation with Exeter," though we both knew what he meant by that was my soon-to-be "*non*-affiliation" with Exeter.

And that, as far as I could see, was that: the beginning of the end of a once-promising career in the field of anthropology.

"Fuck 'em," I said, "if they can't take a joke." But the joke, quite clearly, wasn't on them.

That night I hit bottom and almost drowned. My long-held belief I would prevail against whatever life threw at me was trashed so completely by my depression and pain that I could taste on my tongue the sickening blackness I had tasted first at fifteen. The darkness came in drips—and waves. I writhed on the couch, unable to find a physical pose or mental posture that was bearable. A poisonous worm ate at my heart. Though its bite had never been so sharp, it was chillingly familiar, as though I'd carried this parasite around with me forever.

For the pain was *mine*. The shocks I'd endured—Jai's death, Vidya's confession, the collapse of my professional hopes and dreams—had only caused the wound to throb. But the wound and its pain had been there in me for as long as I could remember. All I'd done was manage it, like a man beneath an onerous burden, who continually shifts it from shoulder to shoulder and from hand to hand, yet never once, even by mistake, thinks to set it down.

It was then, on touching absolute bottom, that something inside of me let go. In the course of a week, I had lost it all. And if the fellowship went, so would my home, as the cottage came with it. Yet, even then, after all these subtractions, something remained intact and whole: and that surprising something was *me*. I felt like an author whose characters rise, rage, love, win, lose and die—and yet, throughout, remains, at heart, apart and unaffected. Student, anthropologist, American, prince, Indian, warrior, lover. All these were roles, costumes I wore. And suddenly I was naked—and free.

I had made two vows. The first: to protect Vidya. And nothing removed could stop me from that. Whatever I'd lost, I could still keep my word.

My second promise had been not to doubt her. And as I recalled it, I felt what Houlihan had stuffed into my pocket. It was two sheets of folded paper, the first, a badly copied fax of a page from the *East African Standard.*

RUKMINI PATEL AND SIDDHARTH GAWANDE

Dr Neelakantha and Shruti Patel of Kilifi have announced the marriage of their daughter Rukmini, 28, to Siddharth Gawande. Mr Gawande, an electrical engineer, recently graduated from Rensselaer Polytechnic in Troy, New York, USA.

Rukmini—"Bubbles" to her many friends—attended Mwakiwiwi Secondary School in Mgange and the Institut Monte Rosa, Montreux . . .

I drew a breath. I wished them well. And *that*, at least, I thought, is *that*. On the second page was a note from Vidya. "Dearest Xan. Read the end of Chapter 23."

I knew the reference could only be to *Sikandar*, and so I opened to that chapter's close and read: . . . **dove I'd lent her flew in my tent. I picked it up and nuzzled the feathery shell of its skull, thinking I savoured the scent of her hand. From its ankle, I stripped a band. The message read: "Despite what they say, know I am true to you."**

Relieved, I wanted to pour out my heart to her, to tell her I loved her, tell her I would protect her and keep her from harm. But such feelings would have hardly fit on such a tiny scrap of paper. And so I wrote, "And I to you," and attaching my words to one of her pigeons, stepped from the tent, and let it go. It arose on high, circling the camp to get its bearings, then flew away in the direction of Indore like a tiny, silent shooting star. I watched it, a silver speck against the white desert sky, until it had merged with the bruise-coloured clouds of the steadily approaching monsoon rains.

Chapter 33

My brother wasn't born depraved. On the night of his birth, no jackals howled, nor were inauspicious signs observed: the temple idols didn't weep bloody tears, nor did stringed instruments play unbidden.

On the surface, he was every inch a prince, with a marble coolness and rock hard beauty. He was tall and slim hipped like a panther, with a prognathous jaw that would have been ugly on someone else but on *him* gave a look of heroic determination. Yet sometimes, at his most unguarded, I beheld a ghost behind his eyes beyond all bounds of human reason and constraint. What could one say to such a thing? How could one appeal to it—except with violence . . . or love?

Yet, when he appeared in public, surrounded by a magnificent cavalcade of soldiers, he had a light about him, a glittering charisma—even though it was the light of hell. And toward those in whom he saw no threat, he could be protective, kind and tender, even, and had often been this way to me.

Yet, inside him was a growing horror. Just as a man in a burning building will claw and stamp his way to safety, stepping blindly even on the heads of children, so, too, he would do anything to get it out.

And I listened as Sikandar replayed in his mind a conversation with Ghazil:

". . . three of the posts . . . sawn almost through . . . meant to pitch over in the first heavy gale."

"But who . . . ?"

"You know as well as I. He must be cursing his luck. For by striking and missing, he has shown us his hand. We control the capital, the palace, the treasury and your late father's guard and army. But our greatest advantage is that we know what your brother is planning to do. Kill you."

Which is why we'd been contemplating the character of Jafir.

It was *lila gaddi*, a game of thrones, to win which my grandsire, Bayazid, had exiled two brothers and blinded his son, and my father had imprisoned his own dear mother.

Why should Jafir break with tradition? For it is said, "Ten poor men can sleep beneath a single blanket, but two kings cannot share the same kingdom."

"What are you doing?" Ghazil demanded.

"Thinking."

"Think much longer and you won't have a head to do it with."

I looked about us. Monsoon had renewed the desert. The hard gray pan had sprouted emerald hairs; cranes and flamingos flew about and the scraggly, stricken trees had flowered.

"Listen well. The Commanders of Five Thousand are even now plotting to take your head!" Ghazil raised a cup to Sikandar's lips. "Drink." (It was a measure of his trust in Ghazil that he did—for it tasted like poison.)

"If I have the *qutba* read in my name, there will be war."

"There is war already. Your brother killed your father. And he tried to kill you, too."

"I pray that isn't so."

"Damn your stubbornness!" Ghazil exploded. "If you don't care about yourself, think of *me*. How many hours do you think *I* will live once Jafir consolidates his power? And without a leader, our kingdom, which your father and grandfather cobbled together with threats and treaties and the blood of heroes, will break like bread into a hundred crumbs. Here," Ghazil said. "This just arrived."

It was a scroll from Jafir, done up in the usual manner: sprinkled with gold dust while the ink was wet. I read:

Unfeigned praise and pure thanksgivings are due to the sole object of worship, God. Our glorious father—star of heaven's arms, conqueror of Hind, adorner of the Kayani tiara, fitting heir to the throne of Chosroes, splendid nursling of the parterres of prophecy and saintship, cream of the Khilji dynasty, whose forehead bore the traces of bravery and ambition—all too soon hath quit his cage of clay and the bird of his soul escaped to roost in the cedars perfuming the garden of Paradise.

(May God illuminate his tomb!)

Since then, the young princeling, dearest brother, sweet Lord of Indore, father of the poor, slayer of Uzbeks, hero of Khadya, my loving *Kando*, hath without ground or reason engaged in disturbing the rose garden of love and brotherhood in which for long periods there has been no possibility of a breath of confusion. May the vernal flower of union and cordiality remain in bloom and by our solemn convocation, all efforts be made to strengthen the foundations of concord and cleanse the sullied fountain of our agreements . . .

"What does it say?"

"He wants to meet. And let me tell you now, he's furious!"

"He sends this, too," Ghazil remembered, drawing from his sleeve a Cashmiri shawl.

At the sight of it, my blood congealed. I put it to my lips and inhaled her sweet odour.

Sending me it was a grievous error. For if my brother had not provoked me in this way, I might, indeed, have given up the *gaddi* and fled to Basra or Kabul.

"Order the *qutba* read in my name. Have coins struck with my likeness on them. Send notes to our enemies, neighbours and friends proclaiming I have assumed the throne. Now, take me to it."

Well, all right! My own career may have been tanking, but Sikandar's wasn't. He was about to be King—an impressive promotion and position for a boy of nineteen years of age.

The palace was captivating. The carpets were Persian and of museum quality. Several rough-looking fellows holding scimitars fell into step before and behind us; courtiers and servants bowed. And feeling not unlike a king myself, I walked along within Sikandar.

Ghazil withdrew a large iron key and used it to unlock an immense wooden door. The throne of Hind was at the far end of a musty room in which pools of rainwater shone on the marble floor. The seat was sandalwood, inlaid with gems in the form of a peacock, a *mayura*. Sikandar approached it and dropped to his knees, speaking this prayer:

This crown comes to me of its own will.
I never wanted it.
But the Lord of Life had other plans.

Given that it finds me now,
Let me wear it in all righteousness.
Let me rule with selflessness and compassion, for
"In the happiness of his subjects
lies a king's happiness;
In the welfare of his people
lies his own.
A king's good is not
what pleases him,
But that which benefits his people."

Then he added:

All I ask is that you spare and keep her;
Don't let him harm her in any way.
For she, too, is my kingdom.

He bowed again, then assumed the throne. No sooner
had he done so:

. . . when all at once my heart began to ease, as though a
majesty was descending on me, a stately station, a princely
peace. A liquid bliss began to blossom in my veins and,
like a flower made of blood and honey, scent my heart with
a heavenly glee. I laughed with a joy I hadn't felt in weeks.
"What was in that drink you gave me?"
"Opium."
Then something most exquisite happened: a breeze arose
inside of us, a breath of peace and utter freshness—blank,
inarguable and true. It blew upon our consciousness the
way a child blows on a flickering candle, and in that instant,
seated on the throne of Chosroes, we nodded out.

Chapter 34

I came to upon my throne: an easy chair in my Dorset study. As I stood, I had again the clearest sense some part of Sikandar's kingship had also been conferred on me.

I lifted the machete now with a surprising, new confidence and ease, as if Sikandar's swordsmanship had also come along. I tell you, that book was . . . well, *enchanted*! I understood then, as clear as day, that Vidya Prasad had not killed Jai. She had confessed only in order to free me. And since she'd saved my life already, and granted my freedom, the next move was up to me.

I telephoned Strugnell. "What's happening with the Henry Jones investigation?"

"Stalled."

"Why?"

"They searched his house and found nothing linking him to any of the murders."

"Did they search his truck . . . or *car*," I added quickly. "I mean, whatever the hell he drives."

"Seems they can't find it."

"Why?"

"It's not at his home. Nor in any of the usual impound lots. At least not any in Wiltshire. Or Surrey."

"Have they tried Dorset? The county line is just a few miles away. Look, Wooland. This is your domain. Call them up and ask if they have his car. If so, notify Lieutenant Houlihan. Believe me, pal, you'll be a hero."

That was all I could think of at the moment. That and consulting *Sikandar Shah* to see how he had freed Mayura— if, indeed, he had. For Sikandar's story might perhaps suggest the way to set her free.

Jafir's castle sat four hundred feet above the valley floor upon a pedestal of living rock. Corpses on gibbets lined its approaches, like stations in some processional of horror. Some were skeletons; others, swollen human balloons with protruding tongues and great, blunt fingers resembling knockwurst and who, filled with putrefying gases, seemed ready to sail away on the next strong gale like floats in some hellish Macy's parade.

As we neared, the great studded gates drew back on silent hinges, like doors that open in a vision or a dream, closing behind us with a definite thud—the way gates slam shut in certain nightmares.

We crossed a moat filled with crocodiles sleeping in the sun and were guided up a long, spiral stairwell. The guide was required, as the stairs, I noted, forked in places: and while one tine led safely farther upward, the other ended in a leg-breaking pit at the bottom of which king cobras slid, or turned into a polished chute which, after a four-story slide and the last ride of one's life, deposited you in the moat below and the maw of some awakening beast.

Eventually, we stepped onto a gardened terrace high, high above the world. Looking down sucked the breath from your belly. I could see the whole country laid out below us.

Reclining in the shade of palms and mangos was Jafir . . . **seated in the *asana* of kingly ease. Lightly bearded, puffing a *hookah*, he wore in his turban a yellow gem, and a hooded hawk was perched beside him. It was he who exhaled the**

nimbus of royal fortune while I, the king, stinking of horses and drenched to the skin, approached like a beggar.

After the requisite gifts and formalities, they got down to business, Sikandar admitting he had "reached forth his hand" to take possession of royal territory. But, he assured Jafir, he had done so only to secure the crown and hold it for him, Jafir Shah, to whom he wished to hand it over now. As proof of this, Sikandar appeared before him today unarmed and unattended, his humble slave. And as he finished this declaration, Sikandar performed the "long-stick" *pranam*, extending himself on his belly fully so that his outstretched hands touched his brother's toes.

I don't know who was more surprised: Jafir or me. Then Sikandar arose to his knees and, taking his brother's hands, asked in return for one thing only: the Queen of Indore.

At this, Jafir burst out laughing. "You give me your kingdom? For a widowed whore?"

Sikandar admitted he was smitten. Besides, though giving up one kingdom, he was securing for himself another: for through marriage to her, he would rule the princely state of Indore.

At this, Jafir visibly relaxed. Perhaps the opium in his pipe was working. "Her throne was stolen. She only just escaped with her life. She begged for my help in regaining her kingdom. And . . . once redeemed . . ." He paused to give his words their weight, "she would help me . . . to unseat you."

Did Sikandar believe this? Was it *bheda*? I couldn't tell. For Sikandar was closely guarding his thoughts. And, thus far, Jafir had acted like a perfect gentleman, displaying none of the aberrant behavior for which I'd been prepared.

Jafir unhooded his falcon, Vajra. The hawk swiveled his head and, attracted by something, leapt from his perch, streaking skyward. Only then did I spy what he himself saw, a speck hurtling through the cloud-filled heavens. I watched as Vajra rose above it, then stooped and struck so hard and fast that speck and hawk appeared to fuse. Then, swooping low, he came racing home, the dove in his talons. He landed awkwardly, barely arresting momentum. He dipped his beak in the pigeon's breast. Its blood trickled out—which is when I saw its leg was banded.

Sikandar saw it, too, and stripped it in a stroke, palming the damn thing before Jafir noticed (even if the falcon did, hissing like some feathered serpent).

Sikandar made a sign with his thumb and pinky that signaled a biological urge, then arose and slipped behind a wooden lattice, making water in a golden bowl, even as he opened the message and read:

Lord Jafir —

In the name of God, the Benevolent and Ever-Merciful. 'Abd al-Wali, King of Hind, first son of Princess Chandi of Amber, sends you his greetings. Let it be known that he has seized the throne from your treacherous and faithless brother, and extolled the qutba in his own name. Knowing of this, you may deal with that Unfortunate One without fear of 'Abd al-Wali Shah's displeasure.

Our kingdom has no quarrel with Lord Jafir, provided he recognize its sovereign borders, extending for 93 kos at 48 degrees north-northwest from Gulkan to the southernmost

branch of the Chambal River, and from there due
East to the village of Mund . . . .

For a moment, Sikandar's soul almost failed, for no earthly
message, save of the Queen's demise, could have been less
welcome. 'Abd al-Wali had seized the throne! 'Abd al-Wali ibn
Qabil? He who had suckled at their nurse's other breast!

Then there were the implications, like distant echoes just
beginning to be heard. For if 'Abd al-Wali was Shah, then
Ghazil was dead, in prison, or in hiding, for the royal vizier
never would have supported the treacherous fool. It also
meant that if Jafir refused for any reason to let Sikandar go,
no army would ride to rescue and save him.

And how foolish of 'Abd al-Wali to think he might
appease Jafir by giving him one corner of the kingdom. As if
Jafir could be sated by anything but *all*!

Sikandar tucked away both note and his fear-shriveled
member. He knew he had to leave in haste, for it would be
only hours now before news of the coup reached Jafir. Yet
we still hadn't seen the Queen; didn't know if she was even
living!

"I beg you, again, O Jafir Shah: return me my slave."

Jafir was clearly pleased by our appeal. He lifted a finger
and the Rani appeared, borne on a litter.

But as she drew near, we both noticed something wrong
with her eyes. They were sewn shut.

"Jesus!" I screamed, though nobody heard. I looked on
Jafir as the psychopath he was, even though with the silken
pennants and the ramparts of the fort behind him, he looked
like the hero of a romantic fable, the exotic prince charming
every schoolgirl yearns to meet.

"Sikandar brings you greetings, my Queen. He's come to
reclaim you."

A light not originating in her eyes lit her face, like flaring candles behind her bones. "I would bow to you, my lord, but I fear in my blindness, I might bow to the wrong brother."

"It was unkind of you to seal her eyes," Sikandar said.

"Kinder than having them plucked by Vajra."

"Yes, but why do it?" Sikandar asked.

"For treachery against our clan."

"It's you who flaunt the signs of treachery!" the Queen declared.

"How can you discern what I flaunt or no, being quite unable to see?"

The conversation was going places I did not want it to go . . . . And I slapped the Queen, hard, across the mouth, and in the silence, said, "Allow me to take my unmannerly slave home."

"Yes, little brother; but, you must first take some food and rest."

"I would love nothing more. But if I don't reach Patpur by nightfall tomorrow, this fort will be assailed."

"Assailed?" Jafir repeated, in surprise. "By *whom*?"

"Shri Ghazil."

Jafir scowled. "You have placed a sharp weapon in the hands of a fool. And an old one at that."

"Old, he may be. Fool, he is not. And he would like nothing more than your head. Give him one reason to attack and he will."

"I will crush him! And drink wine from his skull!" And he gestured at a cup mounted in silver, made from the head of some unfortunate foe.

"You have six thousand troops. We . . . Ghazil has sixteen thousand. With patience, all of them will pass under your command. Or, if you choose, they will *oppose* you."

"Send a message."

"Any message I send triggers an attack. All that won't is my timely return—with the Queen. It was the one condition by which Ghazil permitted me to come."

"And you?"

I prayed to the Goddess of Words for inspiration.

"I not only trust but love you, brother. All of my life you have been the star I've followed. My one desire is to be your slave. It is why I have gifted you with the heirloom of our father's kingdom."

Whether Jafir believed me or not didn't matter. Like a *mantra* that counters the effects of snakebite—even if one does not know its meaning—this paean of praise consoled my brother's heart, for he fed on praise the way others feed on meat. He sat for a while in sullen deliberation. Then he said, "You must take food before you go."

"There is more than food that we require. We have a long hard road." Though the sun was shining, the western sky was a purple bruise, filled with mist and distant thunder. "I therefore beg you to restore my slave's sight."

Jafir assented. "Summon the tailor."

"*Tailor*?" I shrieked. It was outrageous. Then again, I asked myself, who did I think had sewn them shut?

Her sutures removed, the Queen fluttered her eyes.

"What do you see?"

". . . just a brightness."

"Your sight will return," Jafir reassured her. "For now, please wear this," and he bandaged her eyes with a yellow silk band. This act was performed with such kindness and grace, it was hard to believe that it was he who had blinded her in the first place. I felt a pulse of love for Jafir—one that had throbbed in me since our childhood—then stifled it, lest it hinder my plans.

"My guard will escort you."

~ 240 ~

And, waiting until my brother arose, I took the Rani's hand. "Where is your son?"

She looked unnerved. "I sent him to you."

I was impressed by Sikandar's performance. Despite the missing heir to Indore's throne, he had accomplished what he'd set out to do in a cool and nearly effortless manner. There'd been no swordplay, no derring-do. No genie or magic carpet had delivered them. He'd inserted himself into an invincible fort and removed the Queen from the grasp of a fiend. If he'd had to forfeit his kingdom to do it, so be it.

But congratulations were premature . . . . Five miles from the castle gates, they ran into what remained of Sikandar's loyalists: all ten of them.

"'Abd al-Wali," Ghazil spat, "has *manure* for brains. When the jailer refused to lock me up, they jailed him with us, but neglected to relieve him of his keys. We were out in half a *ghari.*"

As thousands of enemy soldiers were encroaching— those of Indore, 'Abd al-Wali's, and as soon as he learned of the coup, Jafir's—there was no safe place for us to run and we decided to divide: myself and the Queen taking ship from Cambay, while Ghazil and the Queen's young son headed north by horse.

Ghazil appeared to welcome this decision. I think he was itching to raise another prince. And he and the boy got along well. The child followed Ghazil about, swinging a stick and scowling like his mentor.

"I will raise him the way that I raised you."

"Sadly, I failed you."

"Not at all, Sikandarji. You lost your kingdom. You've kept your head!"

Then Ghazil solicited Mayura's forgiveness. "Those we knew as true have proved faithless. Those we thought were faithless . . . *Acch* . . . *!*"

Mayura drew Ghazil onto her lap. She bared one swollen, golden breast and pressed its tip between his lips, expressing it with her hand. I watched Ghazil gulp and swallow.

"You are now my son. And he is now your little brother. I beg you, O Great One, treat him as such, or you'll invite on you this mother's curse."

Then the Queen swept up her little boy, kissing him passionately again and again, weeping with an intensity that made us all ill at ease. I turned and took my leave of Ghazil. He looked quite stunned; the last teat between his lips was probably his mother's. Though as we departed, he called after me, crying, "Avoid marshes and defiles. Watch the light. Stay on the heights, Sikandar. Or, if you must, keep them to your right or rear. Remember, avoid battles by water, and when fighting on a hill, fight going *down* . . ."

Part VI

THE MOTHER

Be patient toward all that is unsolved in your heart
And try to love the questions themselves
like locked rooms or like books that are written in a
foreign tongue.

—**Rainer Maria Rilke**
Letters to a Young Poet

Chapter 35

There's an Indian saying, "the customs house and dawn." You take a covert route at night to evade customs, yet somehow find yourself before it at the break of day. Simply put, life confronts us with whatever we avoid.

It should not have been surprising, then, that our long flight from rank injustice ended with me seated before Houlihan in Stour confessing to Jai Prasad's murder. I had thought about it long and well, and had decided I would not let Lady Vidya take the fall. Enlightened by Sikandar's tale, I knew the only way to free her was to trade my kingdom for her, even if it consisted of no one but me. "She had nothing to do with it," I told Houlihan. "Nothing. In fact, she slept through the whole damn thing."

He waited. "It was just like you said. Jai and I argued. He brought up some things, ones I thought I'd gotten over long ago. I guess, I hadn't."

"What things?"

"Personal ones. About my character. And career."

"And you killed him."

"Not like that," I said annoyed. "The whole thing escalated. It got nastier and hotter. The sword was out, already unsheathed. We'd been looking at it earlier. Finally, I said something—about his wife, I think—and Jai launched himself at me out of his chair. I picked up the sword and he impaled himself. If you want to know the truth, he killed himself. He threw himself at me. And then, I guess, I went a little crazy. I don't really remember that."

Houlihan's face was without expression. You'd have thought after all these weeks of his begging, my confession would have made his day.

"How long you spend cleaning up?"

"Ten minutes. I couldn't get off the goddamn blood. It kept *smearing*. I took off my shirt. Then I slipped the sword inside my pants and down my leg."

"When you come back out, there were lotsa flies?"

"Yeah. Buzzing the body. I went out into the hall. The elevator was coming, so I took the stairs."

Long silence. Then Houlihan exhaled. "Always," he said, "with two perps? They point the finger at each other. Never seen a case before—*ever*—where they pointed the finger at themselves. So that in itself is unusual, right there.

"Then there's the flies. You say there were flies when you finished cleaning. And that bothers me, see, 'cause flies, they don't fly at night. You wouldna thought that, but it happens to be true. Flies can't see. Inna dark. You can sit with a fresh corpse all night long—I have—and, I swear, you won't see a goddamn fly till it starts gettin' light again. Then, in minutes, the place is swarmin'. Now that is just a natural fact. But since you're making this whole thing up, you wouldn't know that. So get the fuck outta here, Donne, before I charge your lying ass with something serious."

It's humiliating enough confessing to murder. More humiliating is not being believed. I drove home.

On my cellphone was a voicemail from Strugnell. "Right, you are. Truck was there. Total cockup. Jurisdictional thing. Only 10 miles from the body, but being it was another shire, no one thought of looking there. And yes, the CID was most appreciative. Embarrassed, but appreciative all the same. And oh, I hear you met Mother." He laughed, then added: "Sorry about that."

I shook my head. I didn't know anymore who or what to believe.

King Edward II had wavy hair, a straw-coloured beard and watery eyes. His appearance was proud, I would have said, save for several defects in his toilet: a boil on his throat besmeared with a poultice, a small tear widening in his hosiery. He was seated with **"his Sami,"** Sikandar writes, apparently referring to a male lover.

Mayura was presented as the "Queen of Hind" and Sikandar as "Shah of *Outremer*.¹" When questioned how they had reached his realm, they told him of their tribulations: of the loss of their kingdoms; of their exile, sea voyage, and sojourn in Alexandria; of the Venetians who had intended to sell them as slaves, etc. **And though neither of us spake the Anglish tongue, the English King did not either, and we conversed instead—myself in French and the Queen in Portuguese, rendered by a Spaniard.**

Then the Queen withdrew an emerald of a lustrous water, sized like a pigeon's egg, and placed it in his royal palm. *Dānā.*

The King nearly toppled off his chair, for he'd thought us "penniless," as his people call it. Happily accepting the gem, he returned our largesse by gifting us with a nearby manor, along with the income from its two hundred serfs. He further declared us Defenders of the Realm, so that by nightfall of our third day in Anglia, we were landlords and Anglish gentry, snugly ensconced in an old Roman villa.

---

1. *Outremer:* literally, *overseas*; a name for the Middle East

But though Sikandar and the Queen had reached safe haven, Sikandar's reaction come morning was of dismay. The villa, which had seemed so snug the night before, was all but falling down. The village so generously granted us was little more than several dozen thatched mud and wattle huts along a rutted track, inhabited by folk who looked on us with stark suspicion on rude, starved, frost-pinched faces.

For an unhealthy lot, our villeins were, suffering from all manner of woes: frenzies and fluxes, cardiacles, tooth-aches, cramps and rheumes, radegoundes and running scabies, boils and coughs and burning agues, griping in the guts and glands, the liver, lights and far reaches of the intestynes! And since their medicines were few and far beneath our own, my Lady brought about many wondrous healings through the application of herbs and tinctures.

For her pains, she was accused of indulging the folk. The gentry have a saying, "Bless a villein and he will smite you. Smite a villein[2] and he will bless you." And her con-spicuous kindnesses were looked upon ill. My Lady's reply was royal if undiplomatic: "They are *my* villeins whom I'll bless and smite as *I* do please."

In short, she ruled the manor like a mother and a queen. If a villein's child or calf were ill, she had prepared for it a special broth. Our third month there, she had two villeins hanged for killing a traveller, ending talk of her indulgent ways. On Thursdays, she worshipped the sheep, pigs, cows and horses with chanted prayers, waved lights and garlands in a way never seen before. And once a month she gave milksweets to the children. She was at once kind

---

2. Translator's Note: A villein was a person of a lower caste attached to a villa. However, due to the contempt in which their masters held them, the word has come to mean today any evil being, its former connec-tion to "villa" lost.

and demanding, hard to fool, generous, and fair. And she was young, imperious and beautiful, and wore robes that shone like the morning star. Was it any wonder then that our villeins loved her?

Our first year was bittersweet. On the one hand, we mourned our former lives and kingdoms, and the Queen often wept for her parted son, quizzing every traveller from the east for news of him, but there was none. Then again, we were so preoccupied with the demands of the manor—vegetable, animal, human, divine—so beguiled by the beauty of the passing seasons, so paralyzed by the winter cold, so entranced by the round of holy days and the stream of supplicants and distinguished guests who came to see her, for her name and fame spread far and wide, that our stolen kingdoms, bit by bit, receded from our minds. For we had found another kingdom which, while considerably smaller, colder and poorer, was just as earnest, real and true.

It was Bloodmonth—the season we sacrificed livestock—when the estranged English Queen landed in Ipswich at the head of a foreign army. At the news, King Edward and his minion fled to Wales, where at Christmastide, they were apprehended; his favourite killed barbarically, they say; and the King imprisoned and deposed.

For us it was an anxious turn. I counselled the Queen we quit this isle as the tides of power were swiftly shifting.

But my Lady would not hear of it, asking me what would become of our villeins.

"Our villeins are not my main concern. *Inishallah*, they'll endure—as villeins ever do, somehow, despite kings and wars, plagues and taxes. My concern is for my Lady."

But still she would not agree, claiming our position was not what I feared—and perhaps it wasn't. Until we unearthed the Saxon treasure.

A villein named Cedric uncovered it while ploughing the spring wheat: a magnificent hoard of gold and silver vessels, coins, plate, ewers and idols, in pieces numbering over a thousand! Though found on property deeded us by the former King, an odd and maddening Anglish law declared that any treasure buried with the intent to recover must go into the coffers of the Crown. The purpose of this strange decree was to frustrate those who would hide their wealth—only to "discover" it after the taxman goeth.

In order to decide its rightful owner, the crowner convened a "jury" of our peers who, upon its inspection, declared the trove a "heathen offring to Goddess Erth" containing many "horrid idoles bearing the masques of asirt'd feends"; in brief, a pagan sacrifice made with no intention of reclaiming and thus reverting to its finder, Cedric who, in turn, was owned by us.

This legal judgment was at once contested, for the Crown had no desire to forfeit so great a sum. The crowner was sacked and a new one appointed, even as a rumour spread through the shire that my Lady had manifest the treasure through a magikal pact with the Lady Diana, one of their most evil fiends. To complicate matters, the Bishop of Exeter claimed the treasure for his see—an assertion without one scintilla of merit. Nonetheless, he sued us for it. *Radix malorum est cupiditas.*[3]

---

3. *Radix malorum est cupiditas:* Greed is the root of evil.

Chapter 36

For the length of a day, a storm had raged: twelve hours of lashing rains had stripped the trees of their yellow leaves, pasting them on the flagstone walks like bending, melting Dali money—some surreal blend of bill and bullion.

I drove to Stour to forage dinner, examining wheels of three-year-old cheddar and crumbling bricks of Buxton blue, but in the end, I left without buying any. For I'd lost my appetite, and not just for food. There was nothing in this world I wanted—but Vidya Prasad back in my arms.

Returning home, I sat at the window. The rainy twilight was serenely beautiful; the platinum clouds were torn and the moon and stars were sailing through the tears. But, lovely as it was, I couldn't taste one bite of it; like some thwarted connection, its beauty was refused.

I slammed the table with my fist. Incited by Sikandar, I wanted to hang men, torch fields, loot villages. I wanted to descend on the jail where Vidya was, break her out and take her away. I wanted to see someone punished for Jai's death and my Lady's murder, and for all the pain that we'd endured.

And yet even as I railed, I knew the person I was most angry with was me. For I had failed *both* my Ladies. And the most disheartening part was that every day's failure meant another night that Vidya spent in jail.

Odin enacted my despair. He sat at the window, watching the road as if Vidya might come driving up it. Finally, after hours of patient waiting, he let out a yowl and collapsed in a jumble of bones at my feet, gazing up at me with large, reproachful eyes.

The ivory tower I had built was demolished, and in its stead, stood a pillar of victory, the ivory's hard, luxurious luster replaced by pitted, sun-bleached bone. Sartre said, famously, "Hell is other people." But I cry, unequivocally, "Hell is yourself!" I shook my head. I hated my destiny; I even hated the enchanted book, as both seemed bent on rubbing my nose in everything I'd spent my life avoiding. My mistake, I saw, had been letting out my love for Vidya and letting in her love for me. Doing that had compromised my defenses and now the locks of long-sealed doors were being turned by skeleton keys as if some ghostly janitor were bent on taking inventory of everything I'd locked away.

And I thought, then, what being a warrior means: you ride out from your castle, with all its comforts and defenses, to face the pain of feelings you've avoided all your life, against which you'd built your goddamn fortress in the first place!

Then it was midnight. Moonlight fell through the diamond panes and where it struck the kitchen tiles were eldritch signs and fatal symbols finger-painted in the dust: spirals, meanders and a ∨ that was at once a raptor's beak, a vulture's claw and woman's vulva. And in the dream (for that's what it was) I knew they spelled some crucial message, one—*alas!*—I could not decode.

Then the scene outside began to shift, like in those time-lapse films where melting clouds race the sky and rising vines entwine the trees—but here the film was spooling in *reverse*, and I watched in awe as years unpeeled, the stars unwheeled around the Pole, and seasons cycled back upon themselves from green to white to gold to green . . . And when it stopped, the wooden tower stood again atop Bulbarrow:

Item, that she worship the demon Glasya Labolas, a
great President, who commeth forth like a Dog and is
Captaine of all manslayers;

Item, that she adorth a Hed whom she calls
Gunesha, alias, Shax or Scox, a darke and high
Marquesse like unto Behemoth, with a hoarse and
subtill voice, and by this idolatry maketh riches to
flow, jewels appear unbidden, and buried treasure
reveal itself;

Item, that she worshipeth cows, snakes, curs and
cunning felines, and by this conjunction healeth many,
maketh rain to fall and drown the fields and trees
to flower out of season in contravention of the will
of God . . .

The list went on for several pages . . .

. . . that for these and other detestable enormities,
we pray the chattels, house and lands of the foreign
enchantress known as Mayura be seized by the
Crown, and that she and her hellish minions be
handed over to the Bishop of Exeter for the
application of ecclesiastical law.

This last phrase meant, according to our counsel, a
week or so of ravishment and torture followed by death
over a slow fire.

"My Lords, I am a lost and wayfaring queen come of late to
this fair isle. If I possessed the powers you ascribe to me, I
would have willed myself home long ago, accompanied by

my Prince, retainers and wealth. The fact I am here, with my life, lands and liberty in jeopardy, accused of being a sorceress and witch, is the most certain proof I have that I am not."

"You speak well, my Lady."

"It is the truth."

"Our Lord and Saviour Jesus Christ is the Truth."

"If so, then He dwells in my words."

There was a murmur from the gallery.

"How came you, my Lady, to these fair shores?"

"By the will of God—in the form of errant winds and shipwreck. Through the Bahr Al-Qulzum[1] to Alexandria. And beyond the Pillars of Hercules due north. Whereupon, your former Sovereign cast on us a look of mercy and granted us a vill, in the shadow of his royal umbrella."

Here some confusion ensued, as the "umbrella" was apparently unknown, and with it the concept of taking refuge underneath it.

"It is said that you bewitched the King."

"As he did us. With his love and kindness."

Throats were cleared as the former Monarch—once much loathed—was remembered fondly, now that his wife and son had deposed him.

"And did you not, with the use of knots, cause storms and gales to overtake the land?"

For the people were starving. Seven summers of constant rains had rotted even the seed in the field, and were followed by winters so cold and cruel that boats froze fast in Poole Harbour and wolves came down from their wooded barrows. It was only in the last two years that the ruinous floods and rains had abated—though the winters were still a far sight colder than many a villein's child could bear.

---

1. *Bahr Al-Qulzum:* The Red Sea

~ 253 ~

"I am not responsible for your country's clime. I am no more its cause than you yourself, Sir, are creator of the Great Hindu desert."

"His Excellency has condemned your healings as works accomplished through traffick with the dead. What say you, Lady?"

"I am perplexed. For how might the dead impart life and health, being those qualities they most sorely lack?"

A titter went through the audience.

"You are charged with worshipping heathen idols."

"Denied."

"You deny bowing down to an elephant of gold?"

"I deny worshipping it."

"Pray, what difference is there?"

"One of understanding. A wife may kiss her husband's likeness. She does not believe the likeness is her husband."

Open laughter spilled from the backbenches, drawing the Bishop's warning glare.

"Nonetheless, our Lord forbids the worship of graven images."

"The Lord engraved upon that cross?"

"He is the exception."

"And the bird above?"

"That is no bird, my Lady, but the Holy Spirit."

"That is no elephant, sir. But the spirit of God."

"And yet the Lord forbids you worship it."

"And where is this Lord you say forbids it?"

"Why, our Lord is everywhere!"

"Then He must dwell within my idol."

There was the buzz of conversation, as the Crowner and the Bishop conferred.

"Are you not guilty of denying Christ's authorship of this world, claiming it is born of the *Matres*?"

"Nay, I merely observed that mothers, as a rule, give birth to sons. Sons, rarely, if ever, give birth to their mothers."

"Lady, it is said you are much beloved by your people."

"If so, would it be a crime?"

"Loved, nay. But *adored* and *worshipped?*"

"I give them herbs and unguents. They are grateful, I think, to be rid of their pains."

"Do not they call you Alba Mère?"

"They call you many names, as well."

There was laughter.

"What means this title?"

"I am told, 'Good Mother.'"

"'Fairy Mother? Fairy *Witch?*'"

She conferred with her translator. "No."

"Are you not that one whom certain pagan prophesies foretell?"

She shook her head. "Pass on."

"And yet the people sing it in their songs."

"That may well be. For it's said, 'Whatever is too silly to say . . . may always be sung.'"

The Bishop pronounced:

> *She was fetys[2], prude[3] and dun of hewe,*
> *Na pale as snowe y-fallen newe.*
> *And through her smoke[4] as whyt as milk*
> *Her flesh was brun[5] and soft as silk.*
>
> *Modre makeless[6], Lady darke,*
> *Who n'er came to a fals heart!*
> *Amidst the tempters of the night[7]*
> *She has shewed us Paradise!*

---

2. *fetys*: neat, comely
3. *prude*: proud
4. *smoke*: smock
5. *brun*: brown
6. *modre makeless*: matchless mother
7. *tempters of the night*: the incubus and succubus

"What means this final line, my Lady?"

"I could not say. I did not write it. Anyway, it is fact well-known that minstrels are all lunatics, sick with love of drink or women. I see no reason then why I, a traveller, am accountable for the delusions of your country's poets."

Guffaws erupted from the gallery, followed by the Crowner's warning of eviction, even as the Bishop abandoned his spiritual examination in favour of the Crowner's material one.

"I have deemed the riches unearthed upon your lands to be 'Treasure Trove.' As such, they are to be handed to the Crown."

"And yet, in doing so, you overrule the verdict of your peers and the opinion of your predecessor."

"That well may be. Yet, such a judgment is mine to make. Therefore, I again command you: confer this treasure on the Sheriff of Dorchester for conveyance to the King."

"And I repeat that I will not so long as you threaten us with death." In the face of this refusal, the room went still.

"Then, my Lady, we will seize it."

"You will have to find it first. For it is reburied, and I alone know where." She waited to let this news sink in. "Still, I am not so naive as to think so petty an advantage will buy me justice—or my freedom. And so I offer this: I will give you seven parts out of eight of the treasure, and my life along with it. *But mine alone and no one else's.* In return, you will swear to do no harm to any other person, beast, crop, well, field, or habitation of Throopiddle Bryannt, so help you God."

For when Mayura had been seized, a number of our villeins had risen up to protect her, killing and injuring some of the King's soldiers—an act of rebellion that was normally punishable by extirpation of the village entire and its ground sewn with salt.

Appalled, I rose, but strong hands pressed me down.

"We have no need for your cunning offer, as we can compel you to give us what we seek. If you do not reveal where the treasure's hid, I will order you to Dorchester prison, not to be tortured, my Lady—not yet. Only to be shown the divers and varied implements employed to this end. Their mere sight, I am told, loosens many a bowel—and tongue!"

Mayura opened her mouth and displayed a crimson seed upon her own. "Should I crush this husk, my soul departs in the space of a minute. And there is no torment that you or the fiends of Hell may devise that I cannot withstand for sixty seconds."

There were cries from the audience. The Bishop rose. "Witch! Self-murder damns the soul."

"You care not a fig for my soul—nor, apparently, your own. For if you did, you would not damn it with the blood of an innocent queen, nor connive to thieve her wealth and land. And all in the name of *God!*" Her contempt blazed, hot and free, and then, as suddenly, it cooled.

The Bishop said: "We do this all for the love of God."

Mayura snorted: "Love is sacrifice. If not, it isn't love, but business. Where there's love, you give of your substance. And you don't count the cost. The shepherd loves his fatted lamb, but only for its meat and the silver it will bring him. Save us all from that kind of 'love.' My offer stands. Do you accept?"

"Our authority permits . . ."

"Very well . . ." and she oped her mouth as the gallery cried out and I and many others moved to stop her.

"Stay! We consult."

I tried to reach my Lady then, to get her to rescind, but was forcibly stopped—and when I finally caught her eye, she looked straight through me.

The parley went on for several minutes. The Bishop then said, "In the Church's mercy and compassion, it accepts your terms and swears to uphold them upon the blood of our Blessed Saviour."

"As I do, too. Upon my elephant."

"And now, having admitted your errors, I charge the guards . . ."

"Back!" Mayura warned.

The Crowner looked incredulous. "You break a vow only moments old?"

"We agreed that I would *give* my life—not that you would *take* it."

The Bishop and Crowner glared at Mayura. "What means this?"

"I choose my own death."

The Crowner and Bishop again exchanged looks. "We did not understand . . ."

Her scorn stopped them. "You sound like the villein's lad who went to Poole and was swindled of his corn. If you are so foolish as to agree to something you didn't understand, you would be best to keep it to yourself, lest your Master finds you wanting."

"Guards!"

"Tell them, stay! Or your King forfeits an enormous fortune, something which, for your own sake, would not be wise."

And so the final stalemate began over my Lady's right to die in a way of her own choosing, one that was only broken when my Lady conceded the right of the Crowner to witness her execution—and promised the Palace one half of the treasure, with a quarter made over to the See of Exeter and one-eighth part to the Crowner himself, for "his godly work of mediation."

All morning folk had gathered in the street outside, listening to reports of the trial. Now, as the Queen departed, some bowed or curtsied at her passage; others tried to touch her hair or kiss the silken hem of her sari.

"What poison sits upon thy tongue?"

Turning to me, she bit into it. Its crimson liquor stained her mouth. And I recognized the harmless betel.

Though my Lady carried herself with queenly dignity through the streets of Poole, once within our carriage, she clung to me like a drowning girl. She began to quake and pant and weep. Her flesh grew hot and she became delirious so that it was hard to understand her. Apparently, she was frightened of the fire—terrified of being burned. Then fear of drowning overtook her. Then fear of being entombed alive. And then she wept most bitterly that she would never see her son again, nor kiss his head, nor smell his hair.

At dusk, at the manor, she became as one possessed, declaring that all of Shiva's phantom army was gathered in the trees. She heard their talons grappling the branches and their wings fanning the overheated air, and she rent her garments and pulled her hair, proclaiming her clothes alight and burning.

At dawn, she became silent and slept without moving. When she awoke at midmorning, she was already half gone. Her eyes were empty, burned clean by an inner flame. She said nothing, but sat in the sun, telling her beads, drinking in the last noon of her existence as serfs, wise women, and nobles alike gathered at her feet.

Chapter 37

"Hey, bunk. Case against the little lady? Just took a very serious U-ie. Henry Lewis Carlson Jones? Forensic's been going through stuff in his truck. And they've found a number of personal items, souvenirs, belonging to three of his victims, plus to a fourth they didn't know was his. That's pretty damn conclusive. Now guess what? They dusted a change purse they found 'neath the seat and whose prints are on 'em? *Vidya Prasad's.*"

I said nothing. That was it. It was over. And having tied her directly to Jones's murder, they'd very soon be coming for me.

"So there you have it. It's a wrap. Case closed. They finish up the paperwork, they'll let her go."

I didn't follow. "Release Vidya? Why?"

"Why? Because if Jones there had possession of Miss Vidya's purse, he musta took it when he murdered Jai. Just like he did with his other victims. How else could he have gotten it? They didn't know each other. Phone, cell phone, e-mails, all that's been checked."

"And her confession?"

"Buncha crap. She did it just to get you out. Like you just tried to do for her. No. Case closed. And the CID is pleased as peaches. Eight murders solved. One inquest and it's all over. Not even a trial, seeing as Jones ate his own pistol."

Confused by the news, I began to argue: "But the truck, I heard, was ten miles away!"

"Yeah, so? Some citizen stole it. And drove it till it ran out of gas. Works for me."

"Oh." Stunned, I started to hang up, when Houlihan interjected, "Hey! Reason the Queen Mummer never answered our calls? She was dead or dying. Just talked to her what not and such, and he don't know Vidya personal like, but he did say that if she is who she claims, she's her only living female kin, and the royal title *devolves* on her. Another words, your little lady ain't a princess. She's Queen. Just thought you'd like to know, in case you wanna welcome her—*royally*, I mean." He laughed. "Hey, sorry for all the shit I gave ya. Just doin' my job. See ya round, Bunk."

I replaced the telephone in its cradle, then gave a cry of jubilee.

I rang the prison.

"Lass was released an hour ago."

"You sure? Where is she then?"

"Can't say, laddie, can I now? No longer in our jurisdiction. Perhaps they stopped for a shandy in Stour."

" 'They?' "

"Ah, didn't the carner give her a ride? Said he was headin' back her way."

I hung up, relieved. Strugnell was with her.

Funny, I hadn't thought Strugnell *knew* Vidya . . . But, of course, he'd seen her at the hospital that day.

Yet something was still bothering me. It was as though an image was slowly developing inside, like a Polaroid that I couldn't yet see.

I rang Strugnell's office and got his voicemail. I called his home; no answer there. Stour, where Vidya had been jailed, was twenty minutes away. So where were they? They should have been here half an hour ago.

Where could they possibly be? His Mum's? Desperate, I opened the village telephone directory, flipping through until I found her name.

White, Marla 22 Puck Lane.

Alba, Marla.

I felt a weird, galvanic shock, as if my nerves had spit electricity. Something skidded in my heart—followed by the memory of a newspaper clipping. *Streetcar Maniac Slashes Four!* Christ! It was the very first thing he had told me!

Then the Polaroid resolved, revealing another linguistic equation: *crowner = coroner*.

And I knew then I'd made an unforgivable mistake.

I was in the Land Rover, driving as hard and as fast as I dared, the machete and Odin on the seat beside me. I speed-dialed Houlihan, left a message, then veered hard off the county highway and down the disused, sodden track. Claws of blackthorn ripped at the Rover as its wheels threw up a thick, wet grit that its wipers only smeared the more, forcing me out the side window to see. *Too late!* I rear-ended Strugnell's mired Mini. There was a grinding crash as I slammed the embankment and spun downhill for forty yards.

For several moments, after the car stopped moving, I thought I might be sick. My ear ached. There was blood on the lintel. Odin, wailing, was wedged beneath the dash. The unnatural angle of his front left leg told me what he couldn't. But there was no time to tend the wounded. My door was jammed. I wriggled out the window.

What I saw next made me grab the machete. Strugnell stood by my Lady's grave, holding an enormous two-handed sword. I gave a shout and ran at Strugnell, losing a shoe to the mud on the way. I didn't see Vidya. I prayed he had left her somewhere unharmed. Then I saw the four upright stakes . . . and white knees protruding from the water of the muddy cutting.

With a cry, I passed him. This was my mistake. I should have taken his head when I had the advantage; instead, I dove in the flooded cutting, clawing at the muck. I felt Vidya's hair. I touched a shoulder. I yanked the stakes that were pinning her arms, but she was weighted down with an enormous boulder so that when I tried to lift her out of the hole, her crown barely broke the surface of the water.

"Wooland!" I panicked. "Help me. Please!" In answer, his broadsword nearly took off my fingers, burying itself beside them in the mud.

Someone else in me took over then. It was Sikandar who vaulted out of the cutting, raised the machete and charged at Strugnell with such a fine and focused fury that I saw the look of astonishment in Strugnell's eyes.

We stabbed, slashed, wheeled and parried. Yet even as we drove Strugnell back from the grave, I knew it was too late.

Strands of Vidya's hair floating on the water and a red-faced figure, wielding a pistol, panting down the muddy track are the two last things I remember seeing—just before I lost my head.

Chapter 38

... When I was born, my fists were empty. I leave this world trailing a caravan of sins. Last night I dreamt the severed heads of everyone I've ever wronged reproached me from an endless pillar: a village girl I kissed against her will, a merchant I cheated out of two *dinari* . . .

Sikandar filled his clothes with stones and stepped into the summer pool until the cold, silken stream had reached his chin. He remembered wading in the Chambal once, but it seemed like a dream from some other life. Another stride and the scarless pool would close overhead, bringing oblivion . . .

. . . when the warmest arms encircled me; and I felt my Lady's lips upon me. I turned and saw her then, her swanlike neck held effortlessly above the water. To call her beautiful would be untrue. Imagine the twilit hills, the wood, the failing light and rising moon become a face—a face that *loves* you!

She had bedecked herself in her wedding best, her gold and embroidered silk, though in truth, as is the custom of her tribe, she was dressed as much to marry Death, as me. And there, in the sight of God, the *djinn* and all our Fathers in heaven, we wed.

Then we were entangled in the ferns of the bank, where we wept another lake of tears and vowed to meet in Paradise, and kissed each other's eyes and hair until we filled the cup of that one night with all the love it might contain.

When the moon had freed the trees, I bound her to me for Eternity, and prayed that from her Paradise, she guide my life and keep her villeins.

Or did I dream?

For when I awoke upon the bank, both she and the summer stars had fled.

So it was at the appointed hour, my Lady gave the remaining eighth part of the treasure—and herself—as an offering. Astrologers had identified the propitious moment: near sunrise on Lammas morning. Before the priestesses left her there, they caught her blood in a bowl of gold to sprinkle on the folk, the fields and beasts, and harvested wafers of her breasts to plant with the seed corn in the spring.

O my Dear Ones, savour the exquisite taste of your life! Cuddle your young ones; relish the adorable warmth of their cheeks, the ticklish bliss of their little kisses. Eat a peach and marvel at its sweetness. Salute the sun; hail the Nightstar rising. Take pleasure on the breast of your beloved and comfort in the tender cave of her arms. Discard your ceaseless worries over *trifles!* For this world, which seems like a granite palace is, in truth, a caravansary, and you and I, Dear Reader, are travellers on the Highway to Annihilation. Only the Caravan Master knows for sure how long we shall remain; and when we go, our carts and camels—overburdened with a lifetime's treasure—do not go with us. The only coin we take into the Garden is the strength we shewed and the love we gave.

Chapter 39

In the summer of 1327 rains drowned the Wessex countryside. They ceased to fall on August first and, though late, the harvest was substantial, sustaining the folk and beasts through the winter.

In September, the deposed English king, Edward II, was executed at Berkeley Castle. Roger Mortimer, consort of the English Queen and the man most responsible, ultimately, for Mayura's execution, died three years later at the hands of the young king, Edward III.

In the East, Mohammed bin Tugluq assassinated his father and extended control over all of North India, where, according to Ibn Batuta's account: *"The sweats of shame and repentance had not yet dried on his brow when the rebel chieftain Giaffir* (sic) *Khilji was sent to Hell, along with all his ministers and servants."*

But this is ancient history.

Jai's death is ascribed to this day to the hand of Henry Carlson Lewis Jones, whose own death was ruled as "self-inflicted."

Strugnell was charged with Murder, Attempted Murder, Violence Against the Person and Theft and Handling—the last resulting from his pilfering of the treasure, which was found intact in the basement of his home (save for the two-handed sword already in police custody).

It was he who'd killed Jai. Believing me summoned by the fairy, Albemarle, whose spirit we'd freed, Strugnell had followed me to London and seen me on Jai's balcony with Vidya, whom in his delusion, he believed was my Lady rearisen from the bog. The following night, he entered their flat in order to kill Vidya, and coming upon Jai, shawled and sleeping, had cut him to pieces, convinced he'd slain the wicked witch. No wonder he was ill two days later when "Albemarle" appeared in the morgue at my side! (Or this, at least, is how I pieced the crime together.)

For Strugnell did not confess. While freely admitting to reburying "Albemarle," he denied all involvement in Jai's murder or even in the treasure's theft, protesting loudly to anyone who'd listen, "Don't you get it? She's Queen of the Fairy! She can do whatever the hell she wants!"

There was no trial. Remanded to a hospital for the criminally insane, Strugnell remains there to this day, though his mother, I'm told, makes the four-hour trip to visit him weekly.

As for me, I was hit by the flat of Strugnell's sword so hard, I was knocked unconscious. My physical recovery was impressive; my emotional one took time. I did draft a short white paper on my Lady, signed by the full Royal Commission, based upon which the newly appointed West Dorset coroner ruled the treasure a religious offering and, therefore, belonging to its finder, Sam—while Sam's family was more than delighted to donate the hoard to the British Museum in return for a still-undisclosed sum. The white paper further identified my Lady as the Rajasthani Queen Mayura, citing as evidence, among other sources, brief selections from the Indic book.

My biggest regret for all that occurred was my blindness to the maternal root of Strugnell's madness and the multiple tragedies it brought in its wake.

And blindness, it was. Marla White, twice suspected of sexual abuse of children in her care, had molested Wooland as a child—something I should have understood. For the name of the visitor climbing the stairs in Strugnell's first dream wasn't the evil fairy, Albemarle, but Marla Alba: Marla White. For the order of names displayed in a phone book— even one in a nightmare—is last name first.

Chapter 40

A year to the day we'd recovered my Lady, Houlihan appeared at the cottage door, throttling a bottle of Talisker scotch whiskey and sporting the gray beginnings of a beard.

"Looking good, Mick."

"Comes with retirement. Look at you!"

It was true I had upgraded my attire—though with no plumed turban, to be sure.

Odin barreled out and, rearing back, dropped his forepaws on Houlihan's shoulders. It was a satisfying sight: Houlihan going head to head with a creature as big and tough as he was. Then Odin spoiled it by licking his face.

"Odin, *down*! And go!"

Houlihan laughed and wiped his cheek. "Aw, he's limping."

"Only for your benefit. When he thinks no one's watching him, it's almost imperceptible. He's a strange dog. I sometimes think he blames himself for not being able to protect Vidya."

"Christ." Houlihan looked around. "Ya know what? I *love* this place. Forgot how *different* it was."

"You don't miss New York?"

"Kiddin'? People here? *Wait in lines!*"

"Queues."

"See?" he grinned, like I'd proved his point.

We went around the cottage to the garden in back where Willie was setting up tables and seating for seventy-five. Ruby brought out crystal glasses with a bucket of ice, and I cracked and poured the seventeen-year-old scotch, distilled on the Isle of Skye.

"To the Motherland!"

Houlihan sipped and ahhed in deep satisfaction. "Great stuff, this. Tastes like you're layin' face down in a bog. Oh. *Sorry.*" He shot me a glance. "Hey, how ya *feel*?"

"Better."

"Workin' hard?"

"Enough. I'm a lecturer at Exeter. In European prehistory. They're even acting like they might promote me, provided I get my doctorate."

"And?"

"I don't know. I like fieldwork. I've had enough of . . . *books.* For now."

"Hey! NYPD Widows' & Orphans' Fund? Thanks you for your very generous donation. Your thoughtful gift will go far in . . . easing the tragic loss of a breadwinner and beloved dad."

"You deserved it, Hools, for what you did. And anyway," I said, "one should give to the poor and to those smitten by the fist of misfortune."

"Gee, never heard it put that way. Nice. Lemme axe ya. How come you give the amount ya did? Not that anyone's complainin'." He squinted at a note. "Sixteen thousand two hundred twenty pounds."

"It's what I weigh. Times a hundred."

There was a long, searching silence. "Well, good. *Good.*"

We sipped the smoky malt and watched the last day of April greening the flanks of Bulbarrow Hill.

"Hey, how long you figure she was under that water?"

"Who? Oh, I don't know," I said. "A minute. No more."

"Not what Strugnell says. Said he had her staked down a good half hour afore you and me even came along."

"That's *impossible.*"

"Well, I know *that.*"

I changed the subject. "Mission successful?"

Houlihan set down his drink, drew on a pair of reading glasses and opened a small notebook.

"Found 'em. *Both!* One in Santa Clara, systems analyst; other, a trader outside Nairobi. And both of 'em say exact same thing, 'Yeah, they had a sister, Vidya.'"

"And . . . ?"

"*Et* by a hyena outside a Mombasa. When she was two. Even got a copy of the permission for cremation. So I showed this." He held up Vidya's passport photo. "Said she's a hottie, but they ain't never seen her."

Somehow, I wasn't completely surprised. "So who is it I'm marrying tomorrow?"

"Bunk," he said, removing his glasses and tucking them away. "Beats hell outta me. Sure is a honey, though." He rose to his feet as Vidya, escorted by a limping Odin, came out of the cottage, gracefully stepping through the garden, draped in a pale Kashmiri shawl.

Vidya neared. I stood up. "Darling, you remember Lieutenant Houlihan."

"Re*mem*ber him? The heroic *Houl*ihan? To whom we owe our very *lives*? *Lef*tenant, how *ah* you? Xan and I are *thrilled* you've come." Her smile was bewitching; her blue eyes, charms.

Houlihan took her hand, as Vidya warmly drew him to her, signing both his cheeks with lipstick red kisses.

"Unfortunately," I said, "Vidya's family can't make it."

Houlihan wondered if his daughter, Celeste, in England with him, might attend, just as Odin, for unknown reasons, began yelping, ecstatically chasing his tail.

Vidya threw back her head and laughed, then caught my eye—as she had at a dinner party not so long ago. Turning to the ex-lieutenant, she said, "But, of course, she's invited. Why, we would all be *enchaunted*, I'm sure."